Solo Sunderson

A novel

by

Nancy Baye

Published in Canada
Vancouver, British Columbia
ISBN 978-1-7779614-0-4

This is a work of fiction. Any resemblance to actual persons, living or dead, events or locales, is entirely coincidental.

This story takes place in a COVID-free world.

To my sisters.

With you, I'm never solo.

One

After the initial shock, Amanda realized she was plunging headfirst to the bottom of the city harbour, and knew she had a choice to make. The thought cut through disorientation, the encasing coldness, and a roaring in her ears. This was a sink or swim moment.

God, she was sick of those.

Sinking would mean no consequences for this screw up. Amanda had seen the box fly, slow motion, into the air, burnished bronze against wispy blue. That had been her bad, even though the damn sea otter started it all. Sinking would mean the end of the agonizing paperwork, the sleepless nights, the aimless wandering. Bonus points for never again having to clean the flat, wash dishes or do laundry.

The biggest perk would be the end of pain from losing her number one person.

The only downside was that she'd be abandoning O'Keeffe.

Only one downside? *Pathetic.*

Her momentum slowed and she righted herself, opening her eyes to a stinging sensation and a murky vista. Flecks of brown-green algae hung suspended in the water and a forest of bull kelp swayed. Her hands carved figure eights, anchoring her in place even as time telescoped. A second or a minute, she couldn't know. Her eyes adjusted but her contact lenses were probably long gone, swept away on a Pacific Rim current, landing somewhere around Alaska or maybe the Bering Sea.

It was quiet now, dare she say, peaceful.

Through the ballet of kelp, an ethereal figure appeared, and if Amanda had any breath left it would have been taken away by the sight. It was like looking at herself, only 20 years older. Ribbons of pale hair swayed as graceful arms—an otherworldly shade of green—danced to the soft tune of the water, calling her forward then pushing her away.

Come here.

Go back.

Talk about mixed messages!

But when something slithered around her ankle, panic clutched at her chest. A ghost was one thing, a snake something else entirely. Her soundless scream shot air bullets around her, draining the final bit from her lungs.

Get air!

She kicked wildly, propelled by survival instinct and a very strong pair of legs. Pulling through gusts of water, she thrust herself up towards the light—fully aware of the irony of the image. She broke the surface, shot a metre beyond it, and gasped for oxygen.

Four panicked faces stared down from the powerboat. Keira's auburn curls bounced in time with her flapping arms. "Are you a-right?" Toni held up the box, clutching it like a quarterback who'd seized the winning pass in the Superbowl. "Got it—I've got it!" The skipper bowed his head. "Very sorry

Miss Sunderson."

The fourth face, the one responsible for sending Amanda into the drink, was one that didn't belong in the scene—a sea otter. He cocked his head and squealed as if asking why the human was in its habitat, when the real question was why was he in theirs?

"You," Amanda growled, saltwater lapping at her mouth.

He slid his substantial weight over the stern and bellyflopped into the water, cascading another splash over Amanda's soaking head. "Gah!" she shrieked, treading water in jerky circles. Searching. When his head popped up three metres away, she narrowed a laser beam stare at him. "You've ruined this!"

Sensing impending danger, the sea animal's eyes widened into brown saucers. He jack-knifed under, churning a wake away from the boat.

"I'm coming for you, Asshole." Amanda took off in pursuit, employing the brisk head-up front crawl that she'd learned as a teenage lifeguard.

Shouts from the boat followed her—*Dunna chase the poor fella.*

Amanda—leave it.

Oh Christ, I ain't insured for this!

The warnings didn't faze her. She'd get him for what he'd done.

It had begun when the boat had sputtered to a stop, just shy of their destination. The skipper hoisted the motor to check for a tangle of kelp when the otter caught his eye. Amanda's best friends were quick to coo at the animal's cuteness, even as their shifting attentions, and body weights, set the boat a-rocking. When the sun broke through the morning clouds, dancing its beam across the harbour, Amanda took it as a sign that the time was right. She began the serious business of the day, when the marine weasel reappeared, lunging at the stern. Amanda jumped. Keira yelped. Toni shouted at the intruder, who thudded against the fibreglass, failing to get on the boat. A waft of dust rose around the three women. "Uh-oh," Toni said. "'Tis just a tich, not to worry," Keira said as her hand flew to her fringe, brushing away the fine dust that also settled on Amanda's shoulder. With that, Amanda slammed the box shut and gave into tears. The slippery devil's next lunge startled everyone, but landed him halfway onto the boat, making it sway like a rocking horse. The box quivered in Amanda's hand. Toni shouted, "Captain, deny him permission to board!" But onboard he was, skidding over the gunwale and thudding onto the sole, whiskers quivering in excitement as he began his investigation. The skipper rushed to help, but that redeployment of 200 pounds set the boat into another seizure, slamming the group against the stern. Amanda careened towards the raised outboard Evinrude. Seeking balance, her hand landed on the top of the motor. The momentum had loaded her full body weight onto it, collapsing it towards the water and taking her with it.

But wait, hang on, hold the phone. Amanda paused her predatory pursuit.

Toni had the box.

The realization flooded her with relief.

When the sleek head surfaced in the distance, swiveling around in search of his stalker, Amanda yelled, "Get lost and stay there!" Using a slow breaststroke, she headed back toward the boat, her breath slowing with each pull. The lighthouse rose above her, standing sentry on the craggy shore. The majestic rainforest of Lighthouse Park unfurled behind it as Cypress Mountain rose in the distance. Two kayakers glided past, one following the other, their strokes in perfect harmony. The sight stabbed at Amanda's heart. Overhead, seagulls cried.

She arrived at the gently rocking six-seater, the sound of the wake lapping against its hull. The skipper hooked a swim-ladder over the gunwale, nodding to the motor with a pale face. "Forgot to lock it in place. Very sorry, Miss." Amanda's hands grabbed the ladder and she hoisted herself onto it. She would not tip him at the end of the day, not a single Loonie.

Toni ordered the captain to grab a blanket. "Mands, how are you?"

Amanda reached the top of the ladder as a scrimmage of arms encircled her, pulling her onto the deck. "I'm quite upset!" She spoke through chattering teeth as she bent to uncoil the thick strand of bull kelp around her ankle, grateful that it wasn't a snake after all. Keira hugged the blanket around Amanda's shoulders, over the sodden dress that had doubled in length. Amanda felt her hair plastered against her skull. She had a thought, and her fingers flew to her earlobes, wrapping around the precious earrings that remained in place. She exhaled a sigh of relief and huddled into the warmth of the blanket.

Toni handed her the bronze box and Amanda clutched it, feeling its weight. She gazed over the harbour, letting her breath steady, before saying, "Mum always did love sea mammals."

Two

Screw up. That's what she was. One simple task to do, and she'd messed it up, turning what should have been a sacred event into a Three Stooges routine. The Beach House Restaurant, which now had a trail of wet footprints on its steps, had few customers in the afternoon lull. Amanda found the bathroom empty, a peaceful refuge, and relished her first minute alone in hours. Geometric tiles lined one wall, she rested her forehead against them, appreciating their coolness.

She hadn't wanted to scatter the ashes.

No, no, no.

Amanda had wanted to put them in a cemetery with a beautiful headstone, somewhere pastoral and peaceful. Somewhere she could visit anytime. But that was what *she* had wanted. Free-spirited Laura had loved the water, and made it clear that was where she wanted to spend eternity. Now she would.

Amanda exhaled, kicked off waterlogged shoes, then stripped off her wet dress, hoping that its 'Dry Clean Only' label was merely a suggestion. Someone could walk in on her, but she was beyond caring. With scratchy paper towels, she patted herself down, wondering when she got so thin. She opened a plastic bag, which held a fresh pair of underwear, courtesy of Keira. Apparently, when you've birthed a few kids, you need to carry around an extra pair, *just in case,* whatever that meant. She wrapped Toni's shawl around her, creating a sarong and decided that it looked fine. She wrung out the dress and squeezed it into the plastic bag.

The unforgiving mirror showed a geometric tile pattern stamped on her forehead, fringed by a tangle of blonde hair. Combing out the mess took forever, even though the hair had thinned over the past few months. There was nothing to be done about her usually blue eyes, now red and puffy. A few pinches on the cheeks brought a flush of colour to her face. She touched the small diamond and sapphire earrings looped through her lobes, took a deep breath, and exited.

An open kitchen lined one side of the restaurant. On the other side, floor to ceiling windows overlooked Kitsilano beach. She saw Toni and Keira by the window and made her way there, past empty tables, and decided that today she wouldn't order the cheapest cocktail. She would order what she wanted, and it was going to have gin in it. Lots of gin. Wasn't that a healing drink?

Toni stood. "You clean up good. Drinks on us, Mands." She had subdued her makeup today, which gave her an unusually soft look, but when she spotted a waitress, she waved her over with all the subtlety of an airport marshaller directing a 747 to its gate. Keira stayed seated, floating in her angelic aura.

The server appeared—bright smile against tanned skin. Her youthful face made Amanda feel like an old bag, but she wasn't going to let that stand between her and an infused pink gin. She wriggled onto an upholstered chair, tucking the makeshift sarong under her, and doffing the wet shoes as Toni snapped her menu closed, saying, "Make it two." Keira demurely held up a finger and Toni added, "Make it three." Then she slapped the table, making the others jump. "And a plate of nachos." She looked at Amanda. "I'm sorry, should we have something more . . ."

"Respectful?" Keira asked.

Toni screwed up her face. "Elegant?"

Amanda smiled. "Nachos sound perfect. Comforting."

Toni pointed a finger at the server. "Don't be cheap with the cheese. Or the guac." The waif responded with an uncomfortable laugh. Toni made others uneasy with her hard exterior, but Amanda knew she was a softie inside. "How you doing, Mands?"

"Taking off the shoes helped," Amanda said, wriggling bare feet under the table, and looking out at the water. A gentle surf welcomed those who waded into its shallows, sandals dangling in their hands. Swimmers bobbed in the calm water and Amanda realized that she hadn't been for a swim this summer. Aside from this morning, of course. *Hardee har.*

Keira clasped Amanda's hand. "Aye, T'was a lovely funeral service last week. So many people, and a lovely reception. A right proper send-off." She grimaced, re-arranging the pattern of freckles on her face. "Even if today was a bit bonkers." Toni shot her a look that screamed, *shut up*. "Oh, Mother Mary, I'm sorry! I reckon you don't want to discuss it." A delicate hand tugged at her bangs as if she were trying to hide—her nervous trademark gesture.

"No, it's okay," Amanda said, experiencing a familiar flood

of stomach acid. None of this was okay. What was life going to be like with no daily phone calls from Mum or about her? "I don't know what I'm going to do with myself."

She thought they'd have more time.

Keira was quiet for a minute, then said, "I have a wee idea." She blinked big eyes. "At the Mums and Tots group, I heard that the local retirement home needs volunteers." She cast her glance to the table, running a hand over it. "It might be hard to be there but could be therapeutic."

Amanda scrunched her nose at the thought of pushing around a trolley of afternoon tea and coffee. It made her shudder, for the sadness of what her life had become and because her sweet Mum had been robbed of old age. "You mean be a candy-striper?"

"No!" A blush crept over Keira's delicate face. "Take O'Keeffe there to visit. She must be lonely. You would be an ace visiting team."

Amanda sensed it might be wise to find activities to occupy her time and mind. "Let me think on it." The server returned, angling herself away from Toni as she set down three icy glasses of pale pink. Each drink was topped with a delicate flower. Amanda picked up the crimson nasturtium and held it in the palm of her hand. She had originally planned the ashes sprinkling to be private and was surprised at the surge of relief when her friends offered to join. Had she been worried she wouldn't be able to go through with it? Afraid to face the fact that her number one person in the world had been reduced to a box of ash? She forced a smile. "Thanks for coming with me today."

"In the end, we got it done and in the perfect spot," Toni said, eyeing the drink in front of her.

"It was straight class that you tipped the skipper after his cock-up," Keira said, "And the sea otter certainly had a grand time." Keira received another shaming look from Toni.

Toni hoisted her glass. "To Laura." She looked at her friends. "Independent, wildly creative, loving—"

Keira added, "To Laura, a true original, who raised her daughter in her lovely image."

"To my sweet Mum. I had her for forty plus years, I know that should be enough, but. . ." Amanda trailed off.

Toni pushed Amanda's glass to her lips and raised her own glass, saying, "Take some medicine." It broke the relapse of grief and Amanda obeyed as Toni added, "She was a great mum, and she had a good life, lived on her own terms."

Keira clinked her glass to Amanda's, saying, "That's near as good as it gets."

As the words settled, Amanda reflected on her mother's life, her passion for literature and painting, good health, close friends and one true—although brief—love. It *was* as good as it gets.

So, where the hell did that leave her single, kid-less, middle-aged only child?

Three

The lobby of Singing Swans Lodge featured a statue of a swan, its neck bent towards a harp, as if it were about to pluck out a tune with its beak. The room was dotted with wing-back chairs, a few marble-topped bistro tables, and a smattering of seniors. The front desk demanded, 'Visitors Must Sign In', but punctuated the sign with a smiley face.

The receptionist rushed over to them. "Oooo, your dog is so cute!"

Amanda wasn't used to having a dog but couldn't deny her serious cuteness. "This is O'Keeffe." The dog's tail spun propeller-style. The five-year old mix (what was the combination again?) had turned out to look like a Golden Retriever in permanent puppyhood. Amanda remembered her mother Facetiming from the breeder's the day she had found her "perfect match."

The receptionist got Amanda signed in then directed her to the second floor, but by the time Amanda stepped off the elevator, she'd forgotten the directions. She saw a Nursing Station, a tall desk in front of a bright clinical room, where a stout and sturdy nurse greeted her and the dog. "That's a sweet lass." Her accent was Scottish, and an easy smile revealed a gap between her front teeth. As nurse and dog tousled, Amanda thought that this volunteer dog-visiting might be a good idea after all.

With fresh directions, Amanda headed down the hallway, the dog snuffling every inch of the dark floral carpeting until they found the door marked, 'Elaine Wetcomb, Manager.' A woman in an outdated business suit, complete with shoulder pads squealed, "This must be O'Keeffe!" The dog's swirling tail picked up speed. "Who da pretty girl?" The woman got down on all fours. "Oh, yes she da good girl!" When she realized her position, she quickly stood, smoothed her suit, and extended a hand to Amanda. "Well, that was embarrassing. How unprofessional!" She tucked short dark hair behind her ears in a nervous gesture, offering a laugh.

"Happens a lot." Amanda swatted the air. "She's a sweet dog. Good-natured. I think she could bring a lot of happiness to the residents." They stepped into the office, which seemed too small for the chief administrator of a large retirement home.

"I was thrilled to hear you wanted to come onboard!" Elaine said.

"We're excited to volunteer," Amanda said. "Of course, we still need the dog visitation training." O'Keeffe wore a grin. "But I think we'll pass that."

"Let me take you on a tour," Elaine said, pulling the office door open. "Leave your bag here."

Amanda didn't need to tug at O'Keeffe's leash since the dog was already at Elaine's side.

~~~
~~~

On the main floor, they walked past the glass doors of the dining room, where sunlight bounced off bone china set atop white tablecloths. "We have two daily sittings for lunch and two for dinner. And we have a bar." Elaine pointed across the hall where a brass plaque announced 'The Long Neck Pub.' It featured dark-paneled walls and crown moldings. A row of liquor bottles shone behind the bar. "It's a beautiful place," Amanda said.

"Thanks, we try." Elaine stopped at the stairwell door and pulled out her ID badge, swiped it and popped the door open. "Stairwells are locked, so you'll need a fob. Residents use the elevators, and you certainly can too, but only staff and volunteers can use the stairs. Except in an emergency, of course." The battleship grey stairwell was clean and quiet. Elaine's voice echoed as she said, "The residences are on each of the five upper floors: studios, one and two-bedrooms, most have their own kitchen. Each floor has a lounge too. Plus, there's a small gym on the main floor."

"Sheesh," Amanda said, "I wouldn't mind living here." Lately, she'd sure felt old enough for retirement.

When they reached the landing of the second floor, Elaine opened the door without needing to fob. "This is our special care floor, with separate dining room and the central Nursing Station. "Hello Sal!" Elaine waved to a woman in a floral housedress big enough to cover a sofa, then said to Amanda, "One of our residents."

Up close, the woman, Sal, stood around six feet tall, and towered over Amanda. She wore a silver wig, styled short and soft. O'Keeffe dove at Sal's feet as introductions were made all around. "What a little sausage roll!" Sal said, holding out the back of one fleshy hand to the delirious dog. Amanda scooped the dog in her arms and brought her as close to Sal's face as she could reach. "Hello, O'Keeffe. Aren't you a morsel?" Sal's voice was gravelly, and Amanda remembered once reading how human voices got deeper with age. "This boring place needs some cheer." She winked at Elaine.

Minutes later, back at the Manager's office, Elaine stopped to strip off her high heels. "These things are murder." She let her feet sink into the carpet outside her office, satisfaction settling on her features. "So, what do you think?" She unlocked the door and ushered the duo in. "I don't mean to rush you, but I'm off to Hawaii for two weeks." A dreamy look coated her face. "Cannot wait."

Amanda sensed it would be a good fit for them but was she ready to commit?

"Of course, you don't need to decide now, but while I've got you here, I'd like to check your size." She slid a clean folded blue smock across the desk. Amanda put it on, finding the fit good. Elaine nodded. "Keep it on today as you look around. Makes you look official." Elaine looked for O'Keeffe, finding her curled on the carpet. "Do you remember your way around?"

"I'm sure we can manage," Amanda said. "After all, look at the schnozzle on this dog."

Elaine crossed to the dog. "Oh, it's a pretty nose! Yes, she da pretty girl. Oh, kisses! Thank you." Elaine turned into pudding. Once she'd had a good dose of affection, she saw them out, saying, "Enjoy exploring."

"Thanks. Enjoy Hawaii."

~~~

Amanda had barely rounded the corner when she slammed into a woman racing down the hallway. "Omygod, I'm so sorry! Are you okay?" Amanda yelped, as the twenty-something woman hit the wall then struggled to regain her balance. Dull brown hair framed a face that might be considered pretty if it wasn't fixed with such a severe expression, if the brown eyes weren't so hard.

"Vatch your step!' The order was issued with an Eastern European accent.

The dog growled, low and loud. "O'Keeffe, stop it," Amanda snapped before turning back to the woman. "Sorry. We're just here to–" But the woman was off, her chic dress flapping, leaving a faint smell of cigarettes in her wake.

"Jeez." Amanda muttered to O'Keeffe, who caught an enticing scent in the distance and pulled her away with more power than a short 20-pound dog should have.

~~~

Minutes later, Sal caught up with them and suggested they go *walkabout*. The trio hit the hallway again, touring past resident's doors, some of them decorated with wreaths and artwork that looked handmade by the grandkids. Sal chatted away, describing this person and that, pointing out various details of the residence. Once they'd looped around the second floor, they ended up back at the Nursing Station. Sal greeted the Scottish nurse. “Hullo Mary. Have you met my new friends?”

When Mary nodded, saying that she had, Sal pointed to the clock. “Thought your shift was over.”

Mary shrugged, giving Sal a pointed look. “It would be if someone wasn’t late.”

Something caught Sal’s attention, causing her silver brows to shoot up and her voice to drop to a whisper. “Uh-oh, here comes Miss Sour Pants.”

The woman marching toward them was none other than the one Amanda had collided with moments earlier. Despite the marching step and unflattering scrubs, her willowy figure was obvious. But what wasn’t so attractive was the bad energy that surrounded her, and made the hairs rise on Amanda’s arm. She couldn’t know if the nurse always held a negative charge or if she was angry. O’Keeffe began to growl. Nurse Mary moved her sturdy frame a step closer to the other nurse, asking, “Oxana, is everything alright?”

The dog’s growling intensified, but before Amanda could shush her, Oxana executed a military style clap at the dog. She turned to Mary, raising a hand to retrieve a clipboard, a hand that was shaking. “Before I begin za shift, Mary, ve review Mrs. Schneider!” She rammed a hand onto her hip and stared Mary down.

A faint smell hit Amanda’s nostrils, and she turned to find the dog peeing on the carpet. “O’Keeffe, stop it!”

“Stupid dog!” Oxana slammed the clipboard on the desk and rushed off into the back room.

“She’s not stupid!” A mortified Amanda snapped. She had never known the dog to have an indoor accident.

Mary chuckled. "Dinna fash, I've seen much worse."

Sal produced a gym sock from who-knew-where. "Use this to sop it up."

"Thanks." Amanda knelt and padded the wet carpet with the sock. The dog wore a look of shame as Amanda whispered, "I know. It's okay, Girl."

Something smacked Amanda on her nose, startling her. Oxana stood above her, holding out a bottle of disinfectant spray, before dropping it to the floor and walking off.

Tears pricked at Amanda's eyes. "Give me a break!"

"Ach. Worse than usual, she is," Mary murmured, handing Amanda a wad of paper towels. "Not the first girl she's made piddle." She clucked at the dog, petting her head. "And likely not the last."

~~~

Once Amanda's upset had faded and the carpet was clean, Sal escorted her to the lobby and pointed at the Long Neck Pub. "You might want to knock one back then head home." She turned towards the elevators with a wave. "I'm off. Time for mani-pedis. I don't want to miss out."

The pub, like all The Singing Swans Lodge, was tasteful in its décor. O'Keeffe pulled them in when she spotted the sole patron, an elegant senior in a Chanel suit, who offered them an encouraging hello. Amanda introduced herself as did the woman, Lillian, who sipped her drink, saying, "Old family tradition to have a pre-dinner martini." Her expression softened. "It's also my time to visit with Tom." She nodded toward the
~~~

uniformed older man who was busy polishing glasses.

"A pre-dinner cocktail sounds very civilized," Amanda said, taking a seat and suddenly becoming aware of her fatigue.

Lillian patted O'Keeffe's head with age-spotted hands that held beautiful rings. "We always had dogs on the estate. Precious beings."

Amanda felt bedraggled in comparison to Lillian's elegance. Gawd, she had let herself go. She needed a haircut, some primping. The dog probably needed a bath too. How often did dogs need baths? She settled into the seat, politely refusing Tom's offer for a drink. She'd probably fall asleep if she did, the dinner patrons would find her drooling, her face on the bar. After a few minutes of visiting, and once Lillian's martini was nearing its end, Amanda excused herself, saying, "Time to get home."

As soon as they left the pub, Amanda remembered she'd left her backpack in Elaine's office. She looked at the stairwell, knowing that it would be locked. As luck would have it, the receptionist was exiting the dining room, a cup of tea in her hand.

"Oooo, hello again cute doggie!"

Amanda nodded at the stairwell. "I need to go back to the second floor—" The receptionist bobbed her head, pulling out her fob and swiping it across the panel. Amanda turned the handle then rested the door against her hip as the receptionist petted the dog. After their goodbyes, Amanda pushed the door open and stepped into the stairwell, O'Keeffe's snout in the lead. The dog yanked the leash so hard that Amanda's feet left the ground. She landed on something large and warm as the air was knocked out of her and a pain vibrated through her solar plexus.

O'Keeffe's barking began, clipped and shrill. Amanda winced and took a minute to catch her breath. When she opened her eyes and managed to lift her head, she found herself staring directly into another face, one that was ashen and perfectly still. The head lay twisted at a grotesque angle, blood oozing from it.

She tried to get up, using her hand for leverage, but it slid in the blood, and she fell again. Eye to eye.

Just keep calm.

Her scream was loud enough to be heard in the vacuum of outer space.

Somehow, she scrabbled herself up to standing. She leaned over the woman and asked in a hoarse whisper, "Nurse?"

No response.

Quiet now, O'Keeffe was diligently sniffing the nurse, sussing out the puddle of blood. "O'Keeffe, get away!" A spinning began in Amanda's head, she raised a palm to still the sensation but found it covered in something warm, sticky and red.

"Helllp!"

It took her a minute to realize that the thundering voice ricocheting off the walls was her own. Her throat stung and she bent over, hyperventilating. When she straightened again, the body was still there, the only motion the widening pool of blood around the head. Amanda noticed clumps of grey matter in it. Disgust flared and she swallowed hard. O'Keeffe looked up at her, smiling, a swath of red clinging to the fur around her snout. Amanda couldn't help the eruption of vomit that sprayed from her own mouth, all over Oxana.

Four

Two cops, a male and a female, bolted shut the doors of the Oak Lounge as soon as they arrived, locking them all inside. Amanda shivered on the chintz sofa. Sal sat down beside her and eased a blanket over Amanda's quaking shoulders. Close-up, Sal's face was pale despite a heavy layer of foundation over thick features, her grey eyes filled with caring.

A smell of coffee and freshly baked cookies infused the air and Amanda felt her gag reflex kick in again.

Elaine paced back and forth, heels sinking into the floral carpet. She shouted into her cell phone, "The police have the entire home on lock-down!" Her face twisted as she listened to whoever was on the other end of the line. "But what am I to tell our residents about what happened in their stairwell?" She tucked her cell phone between ear and padded shoulder and ran both hands over the front of her suit, leaving a streak of moisture. "Of course, we'll keep it out of the news!" She collapsed into an over-stuffed wingback.

O'Keeffe slurped water from a soup bowl, although Amanda couldn't remember who got it for her. When the dog finished drinking, she wagged her tail and looked at Amanda, her maw still covered in blood. The sight of it set Amanda's shaking into overdrive.

"I'll get it." Sal stood, walked to the coffee station, grabbed a handful of paper napkins, dousing them with water. She cleaned up O'Keeffe's face, using her body to block the sight from Amanda. When she finished, the male officer took the garbage from her, stuffed it in a plastic bag and handed it to his cohort. Amanda fingered the empty paper bag that rested in her lap in case she had to throw up again. O'Keeffe settled in against her feet.

The cops stood over Amanda, pens, and notepads ready. The female officer wore an oversized uniform that made her look tiny and farcical. Her youth and timid manner made it hard for Amanda to believe she'd finished the police academy. She held the bag of bloody tissues away from her, as though it contained radioactive material. The male cop was big, angular, and close in age to Amanda. The fact that he used a cane exacted a ripple of sympathy from her.

"Mrs. Sunderson, I'm Officer Beaton." A clipped voice matched the clean-cut appearance.

Amanda's sympathy evaporated. She hated being called *Mrs.* nearly as much as being called *Ma'am.* She held up her left hand to correct the cop, rotating it in her best Beyoncé move. "Miss." She offered him a long blink. "Amanda."

He cleared his throat. "Amanda. Me and *Officer* McIver have a few questions." There was a note of disdain when he used the word, as if he didn't deem her worthy of the title. Strike two against the guy.

"I have a question." Amanda pointed a shaking arm towards the stairwell. "What the hell happened?"

The cops exchanged glances. Officer Beaton straightened his cap. "The nurse seems to have hit her head. All we know so far. Why we're here." He looked down at McIver, nudged her and hissed. "Here's where we start the questioning."

McIver tilted her barely-there chin towards him. Her eyes were wide as she stuttered, "Oh. Okay. Right." She continued, "A- Amanda? What happened?"

Officer Beaton rolled his eyes at the limp opener. McIver gazed up at her partner, her face awash in self-doubt. "Ugh, yeah, dumb question."

"Relay the events, in order, according to you, please Miss Sunderson." Beaton shifted his weight from one foot to the other. Was he being impatient with her?

Throughout the ensuing interview, Amanda described what happened, according to her, her perspective being the only one she had. She tried to recount everything she'd witnessed, but her memory was as shaky as her shoulders, and she turned to Sal for support. "You're in shock, Lamb. Just take a breath and try to remember as best you can," Sal said, patting Amanda's back. The police kept their line of questioning neutral, cautious. They never used the word *dead* when referring to Oxana. It occurred to Amanda that the nurse might still be alive. After all, people recovered from head injuries, or broken necks, or both.

Didn't they?

She ventured the question, "Are you sure, I mean, are you positive that she's actually—" but her words sputtered to a halt when she saw the expression on Officer Beaton's face.

"Nurse Oxana is en-route to the morgue," he said, then he winced, levelling his gaze at her. "How does that make you feel?"

Was that a snarl from Sal?

In an involuntary reaction, Amanda's lip curled upwards. "It horrifies me. That's how it *makes me feel*, Officer." She was done with his rudeness, she decided, doffing the blanket from her shoulders. Her shock had lifted, her body had warmed, and the shaking had stopped, but when she tried to stand, her legs wobbled, and she slumped back onto the sofa.

Sal put an arm around her, a mama bear protecting her cub, and snarled, "If there are no other questions officers, we need to get our girls home."

Officer Beaton pulled a card from his notepad before slamming it shut with such force it woke O'Keeffe with a *woof* of surprise. Seconds later, she started scratching at the carpet. Sal recognized the cue and turned to the police. "May I take this Sausage Roll out for walkies or is she needed for questioning?"

Amanda held her breath, watching the policeman's face shift from annoyance to consideration and finally, decision. "Fine, Ma'am. Go ahead."

"I'll take doggie out for a bit, while you finish up here," Sal said to Amanda then stood and clucked at the dog, before squaring her substantial shoulders to Beaton. "You will please allow her to go home as soon as possible as it has been a harrowing day." O'Keeffe stretched and yawned, seeming unaffected by the day's trauma, then followed Sal out of the Oak Lounge, tail wagging.

Beaton pulled his fellow officer away from the sofa, towards the snack table, opened his notebook and conferred with her. Elaine sat down beside Amanda and immediately threw a hand to her nose. Amanda looked at her shoes to find them splattered with vomit, a sight that generated a new wave of nausea. "Sorry Elaine. I need to clean up."

"Not to worry." Elaine put a hand on Amanda's shoulder. "Are you alright?" She rolled her eyes. "Oh, of course you're not. Nothing about this is all right." She wiped her hands along her suit. "This is bad." They sat together in silence as Amanda's adrenalin ebbed and fatigue settled in.

The police returned to them, and Beaton said, "Amanda, you're fine to go." He seemed more polite as he turned to Elaine. "A few questions for you, Mrs. Wetcomb." He caught himself, and asked, "Miss Wetcomb?"

"I prefer Ms.," Elaine said, straightening her back. "And, of course I'll stay for questioning."

Beaton nodded, despite the perplexed look on his face. He made a note in his book as Sal and O'Keeffe returned.

Amanda had a flicker of happiness when she saw the dog wriggle into the room. "I believe I'm cleared to leave, Sal."

"I'm already on it." Sal winked. "Taxi will be here in five."

Amanda gathered up her knapsack, jacket, and O'Keeffe. She nodded to the police and Elaine then followed Sal into the lobby, which was packed with gawping residents. She felt eyes on her, heard whispers. No matter how hard Elaine tried to keep this thing quiet, the talk had already begun. O'Keeffe bounced over the floral carpet, a smile on her clean face.

Sure enough, a cab was waiting for them outside. "Missy, you get home, pour a stiff drink and shut your noggin off. Watch an episode of *The Big Bang Theory*." Sal snickered. "That show is a hoot."

Amanda turned to Sal and leaned in for a much-needed hug. "Thanks for everything." O'Keeffe stood up on her hind legs to join the embrace. "Oh, and thanks for walking O'Keeffe too."

"She had a grand poop, so you needn't worry about another long outing tonight."

"Great." Amanda turned to the main doors. "Did you find somewhere to throw out the doggie bag?" She didn't want it left in the lobby trash to make a stink.

"The police took it," Sal said, punching the panel to open the door.

Amanda ground to a halt as the automatic doors slid open with a *whoosh*. "The cops took the dog poop?" Her words came out sharper than intended, but the afternoon had been hell and she wanted it to be over. She tugged O'Keeffe 's leash, and they all stepped out into the mild evening. "Why would they do that?"

Sal spread her hands. "Don't know. The kid, McIver, stopped me and Beaton asked what I was holding. When I told him what it was, he barked at McIver to bag it." Her ample shoulders rose and fell in a shrug. "I told them it already was." She giggled at her own joke. "They didn't laugh," Sal said, pulling open the taxi door.

Five

Amanda savoured the sun on her back as she climbed the steps of the lacklustre old house that held her flat.

Last night, once the shock had evaporated and the emergency scotch had worked its magic, she had felt only empathy for Nurse Oxana. Her life had ended too soon, and in a lonely and unceremonious way: a quick slip or trip on the second-floor landing before tumbling down the stairs to her demise. It was sad. The only good thing, Amanda had thought, was that it all must have been over with so fast that Oxana wouldn't have realized what was happening.

Once she set the grocery bags on the landing, a thumping sound began before her key was in the lock. As she twisted the doorknob, a wet snout wiggled its way through the slim opening. The dog's nose guided her straight to the groceries and she got busy snooping. "Get out, you nosy beast." Amanda stepped inside, locking the door behind them.

The living room was plain but large, the high ceilings giving the one-bedroom flat a sense of spaciousness. She had meant to fix the place up, give it some pizzazz, but hadn't ever gotten around to that. The style remained o*utdated cozy.* She trudged down the hallway, dog at her heels. In the bright kitchen, she unpacked the food, which was dearly expensive in the overinflated city. "Bananas for breakfast tomorrow." Amanda pulled out a tub of plain yogurt then opened the fridge. She paused, wondering why it was so bare.

Then she remembered. And she didn't want to.

The image of her mother in that last month drew a claw of anguish to Amanda's throat. It merged with a vision of the bloody and lifeless Oxana. She tried to stifle a sob, but it was all too much, so she lay on the floor, letting the cold air embrace her as she gave into grief.

~ ~ ~

The ringing of her cell phone roused her. She used a sleeve to wipe her face and answered the phone to a gentle voice asking, "How's my Manda Panda?"

It was a voice Amanda had known her entire life, and one that flooded her with comfort. "Joyce." Amanda imagined her sitting at her vintage desk, dressed in immaculate business attire, pearls resting at her clavicle. Joyce and Amanda's mother had gone through university together. Strait-laced Joyce had specialized in pre-law, while bohemian Laura had studied literature and art. The unlikely pair had become lifelong friends. On the rare occasions when she needed a lawyer, Joyce was the only one that Laura would consider.

"Holding up all right, thanks," Amanda said, petting the dog who'd come to check on her.

"I'm so sorry I was out of town for the sprinkling of the ashes. I hope it went as well as possible."

A terrorist sea otter, Amanda's near drowning, her bedraggled state when she finally dusted the water with her mother's remains. Heaviness sunk into her body. "It went pretty well." One day she'd recount it to Joyce, but right now she couldn't.

Joyce took a second before asking, "Thought I'd see how you're getting on with the executor tasks."

Ugh, that. Amanda sighed. "It's going slowly." She strolled into the kitchen and glanced at the mountain of paperwork on the table. A mountain that she'd worked hard to avoid. "I can only manage a little at a time." She slumped against the wall. "Sorry I haven't called." There was a catch in her voice.

Joyce made a shushing sound. "I know. I miss her so much." She sighed. "Perhaps it wasn't the best idea for me to be her lawyer. . ." Her voice trailed off.

"Or for me to be her executor." Amanda's world grew blurry. "But here we are."

Joyce's tone shifted, lightened. "Que Sera Sera."

A smile tugged at Amanda's face as she wiped away a tear. Her mother had loved word play, sneaking literary quotes into conversations, and getting into rampages of idioms, which drove her friends nuts. "That's how the cookie crumbles."

"Such is life," Joyce hammed it up.

"Alas poor Yorick–" Amanda couldn't finish before Joyce joined and they spit out the line together, "I knew him well." They shared a chuckle before Amanda's sadness returned. Even the annoying things about her mother struck a chord of pain since she'd been gone.

Joyce let the silence expand before continuing, "She left

things in good order, and the sale of the condo can wait a while if need be. But you need to get through the executor tasks as soon as you can."

Terrific. No pressure.

"Then you can move on."

Yeah, right. Amanda thought, spotting a vase of wilted flowers, the last of the bunches from the funeral.

"She'd want you to move on, Mandy. Life is meant to be lived."

Amanda's eyes had welled into a swollen river, and she spat out a quiet laugh.

Joyce cooed, "Have you been eating properly? Let me take you for lunch."

For some reason she couldn't face that. "Can I take a rain-check?"

"Rain or shine, the offer stands Panda. I'll call you again in a week or so." Joyce signed off. The hollowness within Amanda filled with an unfamiliar pang of hunger.

~~~

The afternoon sun angled through the blinds, drawing knife-like stripes on Amanda's kitchen table. A pot of coffee and remnants of tuna sandwiches sat between the three friends. "Was the nurse's death an accident?" Keira's eyes were as big as the rim of her coffee mug.

"Of course!" Amanda said, her voice cracking.

Toni leveled a stare at Keira, speaking in a clipped tone. "Of course, it was an accident." Her eyeliner was as thick and black
~~~

as rails of iron.

Keira shrugged. "Okay, just asking. . ." Her eyes bulged again. "Maybe she's a narcoleptic."

"Maybe she had a seizure, you know, from epilepsy." Toni nodded, taking a slug of coffee.

"Or a secret pregnancy gave her a fainting spell," Keira said, as her phone pinged from the depths of her mammoth pleather bag. She fumbled through it, bringing out a package of baby wipes, a onesie, and a tattered teddy bear. She dug further into the depths, pulling out a princess-themed colouring book, a small pink t-shirt and a bag of apple slices that had turned brown. The carry all was the clown car of bags. "Aha!" She found her cell phone.

Amanda reached for the bag of apple slices. "I'll toss that." She got up to put it in the garbage as Keira read the message.

Worry spread over the freckled face. "Piece of Lego. Up the nose." Keira scrolled further then nodded in relief, "Object retrieved. Crisis averted." She sent a quick text then dropped the phone back in the clown bag. "No blood." She bowed her head and whispered, "Sorry, Mands."

Toni plunked her elbows on the table. "Was it Princess or Butterball?"

Keira flushed a shade of pink. The names were accurate descriptors of her offspring. With a frown, she said, "Princess."

Amanda smiled at the repartee, a welcome break from recapping the traumatic event. But Toni seemed to want to continue. "So, Mand, what happened after your shrieks for help?"

"I wouldn't say they were shrieks. I think I was fairly—."

She stopped herself, remembering being so loud that her throat had hurt. "You're right, they were shrieks." She tucked her hair behind her ears. "Anyway, I can't recall what happened after that." She raised her hands in futility. "A vague memory of hearing a door open. It startled me. . . There were more screams." She stabbed the air with her index finger, adding, "which I'm positive weren't mine." She slumped in her seat. "Next thing I knew I was being interrogated by those cops."

"Was the male cop cute?" Toni asked.

Two perplexed faces looked back at her.

"Sorry. Not *approp.*" Toni turned her focus to the multiple rings on her pale hands.

Amanda pulled up an image of the cop and gave some thought to Toni's question. "Officer Beaton. I suppose he wasn't un-cute." She recalled that his features were nice enough and he did fill out his uniform well, but there was his personality to consider. "He was bossy, irate, kinda mean." Amanda picked up the coffee pot to refill their cups, but her hand shook so much that Keira took over. "Thanks."

Keira looked pensive as she poured. "When's your first volunteer shift?"

Amanda blinked hard twice. "I'm not going back there after what happened." How could anyone even ask that?

Keira nodded, exchanging glances with Toni then asking, "Anything we can do for you, Mands?"

"Don't think so, but I'm not thinking clearly. All I saw in my sleep was Oxana's twisted neck and bloody head surrounded by bronze swans."

"So, was it a broken neck or a head injury?" Toni asked.

"I don't know," Amanda said. "Could it be both?" She grabbed the hem of her t-shirt and twisted it in contemplation.

Keira pointed at the front of Amanda's t-shirt. "How about I get at some washing?"

Sure enough, Amanda saw the coffee splashes on her top. "I probably need a load of laundry done."

Keira leapt to attention. "Great. I'll grab your basket from the closet." She hesitated at the kitchen door, "What of your clothes from Singing Swans Lodge, do you still have them?"

"Of course, I do. Where else would they be?" Amanda remembered the cops taking O'Keeffe's poop bag and the napkins used to clean her bloody snout. But nobody had asked for her clothes or volunteer smock. "Threw them in the bathroom hamper. Showered the minute I got home." She'd scrubbed her shoes too and left them on the back stairs to dry. Her lip curled at the memory of that disgusting job.

Keira went off to hunt for dirty clothes as Toni took a closer look at Amanda and asked, "Are you trying to be trendy?"

Amanda snorted. "With my dirty clothes?"

"No," Toni said with caution. 'With your single earring."

"What?" Amanda's hands flew to her earlobes where she found one, just one, earring. "No!" Panic spread through her, as she searched over her clothing, on the kitchen chair. "Toni, where the hell is my other earring?" She crawled under the table, growing frantic.

"Chill a second, Mands," Toni said. "You defs were wearing both at the Beach House. I remember how much they contrasted your red eyes."

A bob of auburn curls popped into the kitchen. Keira held

an armload of dirty clothes. When she saw Amanda under the table, she asked, 'What's this then?"

"Amanda lost an earring." Toni helped her friend up from the floor. "Must have happened when you made a flesh sandwich with the dead nurse."

Oh God, she was probably right. Amanda felt her chin quiver. But Toni was fixated on something in Keira's arms. "What the hell is that?"

Keira looked at the tumble of clothes in her arms. "It's the washing."

Amanda recoiled when she saw Toni point to the t-shirt she'd worn yesterday. The Singing Swans Lodge stairwell flashed in her mind. She didn't dare cross the room to be near that thing. "Oh God. Tell me it doesn't have blood on it."

'No." Toni extracted the t-shirt. "No, but it has this on it." She pointed to a long strand of wavy red hair, leaning in for closer inspection. "And, yup, this thing has blood on it."

Keira's arms went loose, and the pile of laundry collapsed onto the floor.

"Careful," Toni yelled then hunched over the heap of dirty clothes, arms spread wide as if to protect it. "Might be a clue."

Amanda waved her hands in the air. "There's no mystery here, so no clues!"

Keira glanced around as if searching for what to do. She noticed something else in the pile of laundry and pulled out the volunteer smock.

Amanda clapped her hands over her eyes, peeking between her fingers. "I know there's blood on that."

Keira looked to Toni before tilting her head at Amanda, as if she knew something Amanda didn't. A look of decision crossed Keira's face. "Let's collect these." She reached for the t-shirt and smock, adding, "We canna be too careful."

Six

Amanda knew as soon as she walked into the gig, this one in a cavernous gymnasium, that it was a mistake. Scents of rubber, floor polish and synthetic fabric triggered a ripple of nausea. It was too soon to return to work. Why oh why hadn't she cancelled this gig? What was so great about being reliable anyway?

She stood behind the registration table as Daniel, founder and trainer of Fight and Flight Self-Defense Method, issued last-minute instructions. Over-inflated pecs strained against his t-shirt as he motioned from the door to the registration table to the mats that Amanda had set up in the middle of the basketball court. "Open the doors in, say, two mins," he said, checking his sports watch. "Sign 'em all in, hand out nametags and notebooks." He pointed to the mats. "Then send 'em over to me and Kel." He wiped his hands over his t-shirt, branded with their motto, 'Fight or Flight, just don't freak out.'

"Will do. I'll point out the washrooms too. And you might need this." Amanda handed over the whiteboard eraser she'd used to clean the board for the workshop itinerary.

"Thorough. Appreciate that." Daniel grinned. "Your boss said you were one of his top workers. I can see why." He turned to join his wife Kelli, who was twisting her long brown hair into a knot as she reviewed the whiteboard, her lips moving as she read. She let out a giant sneeze, probably coating the board in germs.

Top worker? His comment surprised Amanda, but she was glad to hear it, even if it came from her weirdo boss at Timely Temps. Reputation was important to her, but then it always is to people who've had it ruined.

"One other thing," Daniel twisted around and said to her, "Bring in our sign? Don't want it stolen. It cost a bunch. Careful —we haven't gotten it laminated yet." He gave her a thumbs up and sauntered over to Kelli.

Amanda punched open the double doors to a cluster of women in the hushed corridor. "Welcome! Everyone ready to knock them dead?" Her enthusiastic grin ebbed when she saw the blank faces looking back at her. After a moment, one that felt rather long, a teen floral Lycra growled, "Yeah, let's knock the bastards on their asses!" And the group let out a little cheer as Amanda directed them to the registration table, stepping aside for one noticeably pregnant woman.

Once the dozen women had been registered and joined Daniel and Kelli on the mats, Amanda sat back and took a breather. Maybe it was for the best that the gig agency had booked her to work this weekend. There had been too much time alone lately, too much focus on the events of recent months. It was good to be busy, to be needed. She remembered the sign, got up and went out to the corridor.

Fight and Flight had been around for ages and had branches throughout the country—she remembered them from when she lived in Toronto. They were the ones whose trainers wore full body padding for practice attacks. The padding around the helmet created a massive head, one that made the trainer look like a blockheaded Michelin Tire man, but without the trademark smile. It was this image that stared back at her from the oversized and glossy sandwich board, which she picked up, noting its flimsiness. She carried it into the gym, set it beside the table, then closed the double doors, quietly so she wouldn't disturb Kelli and Daniel's welcome speech.

Geez, the way they gazed at one another. The couple looked as if they actually liked each other. Amanda knew that was no small feat when you worked with your partner. Her face twitched into a snarl, not that anybody noticed. The group of participants, strewn over the bright blue mats, were focused on the uber-fit couple who were alternating commentary and tender looks. So, everyone seemed surprised when Daniel took a step closer to Kelli and she began screaming.

"Stop!" Kelli looked around to make sure she had the audience's attention before turning back to Daniel, hands raised. "I said stop and back the hell away!"

Once the shrill cries had stopped reverberating off the rafters, Kelli and Daniel smiled, looking very pleased with themselves. Kelli said, "Step number one in dealing with a threat. Use your voice. Loudly."

Daniel tapped a hairy knuckle on the whiteboard. "Assertiveness is the top strategy to keep you safe." He hugged his wife, adding, "Good job, Kel. Way to set a boundary." Then he clapped his hands together, like a football coach. "We're gonna practice eye contact and assertive body language."

Amanda ran her hand over the table's rough wood, which asserted itself by ramming a splinter into her finger. She managed to stifle a yelp and then squeeze the shard out before stuffing her finger in her mouth and reaching for her backpack.

Kelli coughed, then continued in dulcet tones. "Tomorrow, we're going to get on our feet and practice fighting." The group offered a tinkle of applause.

There must be a tissue in here somewhere, Amanda thought as she reached into the backpack. She pulled out a water canister —top notch with a rubberized base—then continued rummaging around until she found a used paper napkin, which she twisted around her finger. She unscrewed the water canister and took a sip before setting it down on the table.

Daniel cleared his throat. "Over these two days, our techniques will get progressively harder. As you advance, your confidence will grow." He threw to Kelli with a coo and a wink that made Amanda roll her eyes. Dulcet Kelli waved a toned arm, saying, "You'll see that you have options, choices. There's no one right way to fight. Each situation is unique, and the decision rests with you."

Amanda pulled out her phone to check for messages. There were exactly zero. She'd called Singing Swans yesterday to report the lost earring. The receptionist reminded her that the stairwell had been a crime scene—an idea that Amanda found ridiculous for an accident—so it might be with the police but promised to call if she heard anything about it. Amanda shuddered to think that the earring might have become lodged somewhere on Oxana's scrubs, only to end up in the morgue.

"Open your notebooks," Daniel said, "And a sidebar," his

face melted into a soft expression. "Some of you might have been in a bad situation. We're gonna take it slow and easy." He angled his head towards his wife.

Kelli's doe eyes blinked. "If it's happened to you, know that you did nothing wrong."

Amanda reached for her water but fumbled and tipped it over. She had a sense of time slowing as the canister tumbled, flooding the cheap table. But the somersault was only the beginning of the routine. The canister's rubber base bounced it upright in a move as well-executed as an Olympic gymnast. It continued its trajectory, vaulting into an aerial cartwheel. In slow motion, it twisted, showering its remaining contents in all directions, making its final approach.

Towards the sandwich board.

"No!" She clasped a hand over her mouth.

In a final move—one sure to get it a place on the medals podium—the canister punched clean through the poster with a celebratory *thwack,* leaving a ragged hole where the face of the Michelin Man should be.

Seven

On a scale of success to failure, Amanda had to rank her first day at the Fight and Flight gig as a hard fail. She slumped on the sofa, fixated on the empty wall opposite. Staring at walls or ceilings had become a bit of a hobby lately. There was something soothing about it. Blank space, blank mind. This spot was on her top five list. The bedroom ceiling ranked high too, especially at night. When hunger snuck up, making her stomach growl, she finally had a good reason to get up.

After gnawing on cold pizza, she decided it was time to confront the stack of bills, subscriptions, contracts, identification cards and other documents that created Mount Executor. Crowning the peak was a document issued by Bailen's Funeral Homes, citing an extensive list of tasks required to carry out the instructions of the will.

Her duties had begun as soon as the funeral director had registered the death and ordered the death certificate. When it arrived, Amanda stared at it trying to process its details. *Laura Sunderson, deceased.* The death certificate brought a new level of reality to the situation, one that was too overwhelming to fully comprehend. In the days and weeks that followed, Amanda's brain felt swathed in layers of cotton batting. She'd had a sense of watching herself from a distance, high-above. There she was sitting in a funeral parlour planning a service. There she was going to the bank, death certificate and will in hand, withdrawing money to pay for a funeral. There she was receiving guests who had embraced her and whispered condolences.

When the last embers of the sunset extinguished, she flicked on the kitchen light and picked up the document. Joyce had kicked off Amanda's executor duties by delivering the box of Mum's financials from the condo that Amanda couldn't bear to enter. The place held every personal item of her mother, and Amanda couldn't handle going through that. It might be wasteful to let the condo sit, but for now that was the best she could do. Joyce made it clear that the executor duties took priority.

How hard could it be?

She read the first item and smiled as she realized it could be crossed out, even if it was only because the item was inapplicable. There was no need to 'get approval from other beneficiaries' when there were none. Next, she had to 'inventory and valuate all assets and debts, take control of them, transfer ownership registrations and collect debts.' A surge of relief came at the realization that Joyce had ensured most of this was done, although how she'd anticipated the tasks was a mystery. Someday Amanda would take a good look at those assets, which were now hers. Really, all she had to do right now was to check recurring or preauthorized payments: insurance, hydro, utilities, phone, etc.

Easy peasy. She pulled out her day planner, transcribed the tasks, adding an ASAP, but she kept running out of space and having to erase the note and rewrite it in smaller and smaller scrawl.

The next requirement was to file her mother's tax returns. She slumped in the chair. Doing her own taxes was monumental, and now she would have to double that. But wait —there was no reason that couldn't be put off until taxes were due, next April. Happily, she flipped to the back of the day planner and made another note.

But the list stretched on. 'Empty and cancel safety deposit box. Pay off and cancel credit cards'—that one triggered a ripple of urgency even if there wouldn't be many charges since Mum had been bed-ridden at the end. Amanda swallowed hard, pushing the thought away and made a notation in the day planner but ran out of space and had to loop the note down along the margin and onto the next page.

More? Yes, there was more. Amanda was like a magician pulling endless silk scarves from her pocket. *Now a blue one, now a green one. Where will it end?*

Her stomach complained. Maybe cold pizza hadn't been such a good idea.

'Redirect mail. Cancel all subscriptions and store reward cards.' She'd have to make calls to cancel her mother's yoga membership, dentist, chiropractor, EFT healer and acupuncturist. None of them were conversations she looked forward to. The good news was that she'd come to the end of the page.

The bad news was that there were more items on the flipside.

"Are you kidding me?" she yelled, slapping the table until

her hand stung. How could any one person get through all this?

'Cancel Canada Pension Plan, Old Age Security, Revenue Agency. Fax a copy of will and death certificate. Each department to be notified separately.' She snorted—of course, the government couldn't make anything easy. 'Sell assets, as necessary.'

The thought of the condo set the pizza churning again in her stomach. She'd need to go through every item. Clear everything out. Get a realtor. Set a price. Put it on the market.

'Wrap up other personal matters.' What personal matters would her number one person need now that she was no longer a person?

But it was the last item that was a hand closing over her windpipe with the chokehold of the Boston Strangler: 'Shred passport and driver's licence.'

That would be like destroying evidence of her mother's existence.

She couldn't do that.

Rising from the table, she crumpled the list into a ball and threw it against the window with another scream. She took a lap around the flat, closing blinds, flicking on lights, picking lint off the carpet—anything to distract herself. Halfway through the tour, she found O'Keeffe nestled on her living room mat. She sat on the floor to join her. The dog lifted her head, enjoying having her fur stroked. Amanda leaned in close, kissing the dog's head. Suddenly they were surrounded by the familiar scent of *Jo Malone's Lime Basil Mandarin*. Was it on the dog bed? Was it sense memory? Or was her mother with them?

Once Laura had been released from the hospital, she'd

needed in-home care. Amanda couldn't understand why her mother wouldn't let her move into the condo to help with the recovery. "I want you to have your own life, Love," was the only explanation. Nevertheless, Amanda had spent most of her time at the condo she'd been raised in, tending to the patient as best she could. It turned into a revolving door of care aides, nurses, and physiotherapists. Amanda thought her mother was recovering and told her, "We just need to get you strong." But Mum must have sensed what was coming because she became adamant about end-of-life details.

Remembering the minutiae of those final moments was salt on her wounds. If she let herself recall the feel of her mother's soft hand in hers, the slash of sunlight on the quilt her mother had bought in Mexico, the smell of something that could only be called sickness, she wouldn't be able to control the flood of emotions. Better to just stay with the fact: her mother's second stroke was massive and ended her life at age 70.

O'Keeffe tapped a paw on Amanda's knee, as if trying to pull her back from the brink, even though it was hopeless. When the dog's sleepy head descended onto her bed, so did Amanda's, her weeping soon accompanied by gentle canine snores.

Eight

What struck Amanda most about Toni was how much she was like a cannoli. Hard on the outside but soft and sweet inside. Most people didn't get past the brittle shell, the one Toni had carefully constructed as a protective layer.

They sat on the deck of Café Milo's, a pricey place overlooking an urban park and the distant North Shore Mountains. The morning sun was bright, not that it mattered since they were huddled in the back corner behind a cluster of giant yuccas, Toni's face obscured by a flurry of tissues. She had called the emergency meeting a half hour ago, and Amanda had been relieved for something to do. She'd been up early after a lousy night's sleep on the living room floor, had taken O'Keeffe on her walk, and was wondering how to fill the morning when the phone had rung.

Toni's flushed face appeared from behind the tissues. "And then out of the blue he texted, 'I need us to bulk up.'" She shook her head. Her raven hair remained frozen in place, what with all the spiking gel, but her eyebrow rings quivered.

Poor Toni, with another sad dating story. Amanda was too familiar with this routine, but this wasn't the time to point out Toni's destructive pattern. This was the time to soothe her friend.

The pair had met when they both worked at a sleazy downtown bar, about a hundred years ago. Toni was the broke student working towards a master's in chemistry, a degree that led her to a solid career as a biochemist. Amanda had been a flailing actor but terrific bartender. That was before she'd moved to Toronto, upgraded to become a casting director, met he-whose-name-shall-never-be-spoken, bought a darling home in the Beaches, started a business and then. . . Before her life had skidded sideways and shot off the local scenic bluffs into the chill of Lake Ontario.

Amanda reached across the marble-topped table, noting how her hand shook. She narrowly missed toppling her $7 latte. "He said he needed you both to bulk up? That's weird. So, what did you say?"

Toni took such a ragged breath, Amanda expected her to break out in the hiccups. Spittle shot out of her mouth, "I'm always trying to lose weight, why would I want to bulk up? What kinda guy wants his girlfriend to get bigger?" She wiped her nose with one black cotton sleeve. "I'm such a jerk."

"No! He's the jerk," Amanda petted Toni's arm. Why was Toni always so soft on undeserving men? Or was it that Amanda was too hard on them? No, she decided in a millisecond. "Then what happened?"

"So, I texted, um, I dunno, something like, 'I don't mind hitting the gym,' and there was this pause before he replied. Remember this is all by t – t – text," she let out another round of tears before calming down enough to say, "Break up. Not bulk up." She sucked in some air. "Auto-correct."

"Coward. Breaking up by text." Amanda hated these stories. She knew there were lots of good men out there, even if she and Toni never seemed to attract them.

"And he didn't even bother to check his spelling. B-bad enough I'm not worthy of a face to face, but not even a spell-check?" That only made her cry harder. The tears, combined with the heat of the café, turned her swoops of black eyeliner into rail-lines along her cheeks.

Amanda contorted her face into a sympathetic shape, grabbed a stack of coffee napkins and held them out. Toni always went into confidence overdrive in the early stages of dating, another protective device. It made her blind to the guy's faults, in this case, the fact that Mr. Right Now was a player. Amanda never knew the right thing to say when Toni got man desperate. In the past, she'd tried using her mother's wisdom, *you don't need a man to be happy*, but that had backfired and made Toni fume. Who could blame her? Not everybody was raised by that kind of mother. Despite losing her beloved husband early in their marriage, she'd become independent and advocated that Amanda do the same.

Too bad Amanda hadn't listened.

"I'm done with them a- all!" Toni's hiccups began. "Damn it!" She slapped the table in frustration, hiccupped again, then punctuated it with a good nose-blowing. "They can all just f-f-," Toni slapped the table again, trying to spit out the words, "forget about it!"

Nine

An hour later, Amanda was back at the gymnasium, confronting the Fight and Flight sandwich board in the hallway. Scotch tape crisscrossed the face of the Michelin Man, leaving him looking distorted. Her fault. Guilt flared as she entered the gym.

Daniel waved her in. "Hey, Amanda. Kelli's out with a bad cold." He made a gung-ho sign with his arm, as if trying to conjure Amanda's can-do attitude. "I'm gonna need your help for the demonstrations today."

It was a statement, not a question. "Okay," Amanda sputtered. How could she deny his request? "Can-do."

"It'll be fun," Daniel angled his jaw towards her with a wink.

Sure, Amanda thought. Fun, wow.

~~~

Amanda stood in the centre of the mats beside Daniel, who said, "Today is 100 percent participation, ladies. You'll be up on your feet fighting then down on the mats fighting." The women stared at him with tense faces, suggesting they were afraid of his demands. Or maybe they missed Dulcet Kelli.
~~~

"You all look scared," Daniel said, leaning into the circle. "That's good. Fear releases adrenalin, and training with adrenalin ensures that your body will remember our maneuvers when needed."

"Question?" The wispy teen in flowery Lycra asked, "Wouldn't it be smart to just, like, carry around some brass knuckles?"

The pregnant woman piped up, a tremor in her voice. "Yeah, I mean you know, maybe a can of mace—"

Daniel waved his hands to quiet them. "Remember, we're teaching you how to use your body as a weapon." He leaned into the group. "Mace or brass knuckles or any object can be used against you. We don't want that."

Nobody could argue with that one, and nobody did, judging by the bobbing heads.

He pointed to the whiteboard where he'd drawn a man's face and torso. "This morning we'll learn some upright fighting techniques: basic releases, punches and strikes. These will allow you to disable an assailant and get away safely."

He motioned to Amanda. "We're going to demonstrate some basics."

Close-up, Daniel seemed huge. What had she agreed to? Amanda didn't know how to fight. Sure, she'd yelled at a few people in her time, but they had very much deserved it. But fight this guy—Daniel was about 6'2" and 200 pounds—that was going to be a stretch. She forced a smile. At least those decades of acting training were good for adapting to the ever-changing and often weird needs of the gig economy.

"We're gonna focus on vulnerable spots, rather than make

you compete with a guy's strength," Daniel said, then took his hand to the drawing on the whiteboard and slowly mashed his hand under the nose, then into the eyes. "Amanda. Slowly, push the flat of your hand under my nose." She complied, feeling the damp of his lips then the chill of the underside of his nose. She pushed his head back with ease. "Done at speed and strength, that move will hurt your attacker like hell and disable him."

The next demonstration was to aim the flat of her hand into his eye socket. Simple. From then on, Amanda added her verbal command, "Stop, back away!" and an intentional grunt to her movements. When Daniel grabbed her from behind, she swung an elbow into his side, "Ha!" Another time, she stomped on his foot, "Hiya!" Turned out that it actually was kinda fun.

~~~

The lunch break left Amanda refreshed, raring to return to combat and the scheduled 'take down techniques.'

Daniel wore the Michelin Man suit, making him look giant, puffy and a bit ridiculous. He held the padded helmet under one arm as he spoke. "Let's move onto the final techniques. In the suit I'm protected, so don't hold back. I'm also anonymous —because I know you wouldn't want to punch your beloved trainer," he chuckled. "Ok, ladies. Any guess what the best weapons of your body are?"

Titters from the crowd. Lunch had left them feisty.

"Get your minds outta the gutters everyone! Women hold their strength in the legs, so we're gonna learn some basic kicks. Everyone on your feet."
~~~

They spent the next few minutes practicing front, back and side kicks. Amanda felt empowered to know that she could topple an attacker with a few targeted kicks. Plus, it was killer cardio, and she mentally ticked *workout* off her list of things to do.

"Time to demonstrate." Daniel motioned Amanda to the middle of the circle. "I'm going to come at you, slow and easy. Okay?"

Amanda nodded, mentally preparing for the side kick, which she executed, stopping just short of contact.

"Good," Daniel said, turning to the group. "You see how that one would get me in the kidneys."

"When do we get to knee you in the nuts?" Someone asked, and the group roared.

Daniel held his hands out in a full stop, "That is the ultimate take down, the total knock out." He turned to Amanda, "First, you need to be close to make the move successful." He stepped into Amanda's space, mere inches from her. "I'm going to grab you." Daniel put his hands on her shoulders, staring her down. Without his helmet on, he wasn't anonymous, and her heart began to canter. His grip on her shoulders made it impossible to move her arms. Daniel turned to the group. "She could try kicking me in the shin or the ankle because her arms are immobilized. But that's not a strong move in such a compromised position. She might only succeed at making the guy mad." He nodded at Amanda, "Shift all your weight onto one leg and use the other to knee me in the groin." Heart galloping, she slowly moved her knee as directed, stopping short of contact.

Daniel raised his eyebrows. "Well, I can't see what you're doing, but I sure didn't feel anything. This is your chance, make it count."

"You mean really do it?"

"Yup."

"Like, hard?"

"Yes. I'm well padded. Drive your knee in there so hard that my whole family feels it. "

Maybe it was the heart palpitations, but Amanda couldn't bring herself to do it for real. No matter how much fear or anger she'd ever had towards a man, including he-whose-name-shall-never-be-spoken, she couldn't do *that.*

"Hell, I'll do it!" Floral Lycra leapt up to take Amanda's place. She probably needed a way to purge her anger, Amanda thought, gratefully stepping aside, allowing the teen to get into position before snapping her knee upward into a sickening *thud.*

Daniel coughed out his words, "Okay, I felt *that.*"

~ ~ ~

To prepare the participants for the final take-down attacks with him, Daniel had them practice in pairs, with Amanda overseeing half the group. She took her role seriously, suggesting minor technical tweaks and cheering the fighters on. The gym, noisy with battle-cries, soon reverberated with power and confidence.

She rooted for the angry teen, "Aim for the kidney." At the successful move, she clapped, yelling, "That's right, that's it!"

The pregnant woman couldn't bring herself to aim for her

mock-attacker's face, despite Amanda's coaching, "Nice and slow. Under the nose then drive it up." The woman's energy was flagging, which was unsurprising since she was growing an entire human being inside her. Amanda increased her encouragement. "Yes, you can do it. Get him. He's a *fucking asshole!*" The pregnant woman stopped, mid-punch, a shocked look on her face.

Amanda felt a tap on the shoulder. She spun around, and with the maneuver safely programmed into her body courtesy of training with adrenalin, she drove the flat of her hand into the nose in front of her.

Ka-thud.

Daniel twisted on the gym mat, the padded helmet nowhere to be seen. He held both hands over his nose, which was seeping blood, as he spat out his words, "Just wanted to say—watch your language."

Ten

The call came in that morning, the Singing Swans' receptionist telling Amanda to come in as soon as possible, before asking her to please hold. Amanda sagged with relief—they found the earring! Questions chased each other around Amanda's brain like frisky squirrels. Where had the earring been found? Was it damaged? Did the police need to inspect it before she could bring it home? She leaned against the kitchen counter, sunlight flooding through the window. When the receptionist—by now Amanda had learned that her name was Mai—returned to the line, she apologized, saying the phone was crazy this morning and specifying that Amanda come in to see Elaine.

Come in? After discovering a dead body and being grilled by the police? No way Amanda was going there. "Can I send a courier or a friend please?" She heard the incessant trilling of incoming calls on the other end, as Mai politely repeated the request, then signed off.

~ ~ ~

Amanda reluctantly stepped into Singing Swans Lodge, the heebie-jeebies filling her body. There was a charge in the air and it wasn't the positive kind. Once the front doors swished closed behind her, the lobby fell quiet. She sensed the stares of residents. A sign rested on the reception desk. 'Please note the east stairwell is temporarily closed.'

Mai was patiently speaking into her headset when Amanda reached for the Visitor Log, grabbing the pen tethered to it by a ribbon. She scrawled her signature, time of entry, and cited Elaine as the person she was here to see. It would be a quick in and out. When Mai finished the call, she turned to Amanda with a sympathetic expression. "How are you?" She stood up, but at a mere five feet tall she could barely see over the reception desk. A frown slackened her porcelain skin. "Where's O'Keeffe?"

"I'm doing all right. Amanda leaned against the counter. "I didn't bring O'Keeffe. Wanted to keep this visit quick and simple. That dog complicates things."

"A cute and sweet complicate." English wasn't Mai's first language, but her kindness was clear as she squeezed Amanda's hand before tapping her silky bob. "I almost forgot, they said to meet them in the boardroom on the second floor." The phone rang just as Amanda registered the word, *they.* Who else would be with Elaine? And why would Elaine choose the boardroom to hand over her earring? There was no chance to ask. The electronic trilling created another sense of urgency. Mai pulled her face into a professional smile and answered the call as Amanda headed to the elevator.

~~~

She heard Officer Beaton's voice before her hand touched the
~~~

doorknob, and her irritation surged. What in hell was he doing here?

Elaine and Beaton sat at the boardroom table, which was covered with stacks of file folders. Elaine's face was pale against a plain navy dress. She avoided Amanda's gaze, choosing to focus on the pen she held, as if it were full of secrets. Amanda stiffened. A distant memory flashed of her as a disobedient kid called to the principal's office. What had that been about? She couldn't remember the event—she'd always tried to be such a good girl.

Beaton leaned on the table and hoisted himself to a standing position. "Hello Miss Sunderson. We have a few things to discuss with you."

"Do you have my earring?" Amanda asked, and his confused look told her that he didn't. She explained, watching the cop scribble detailed notes.

He pointed at a chair. "Take a seat."

Gawd, he was annoying. Case in point: it was irritating to be told to sit. She wasn't a dog. But his stare bored into her, so she pulled out a chair and slid into it. Beaton got straight to business, picking up a sheet of paper and saying, "First, we heard that you and Oxana were in a duel."

She flinched. "A duel?" She looked at Elaine, who stared at the table. "As in five paces at sunrise, choose your weapons?" Her forehead crinkled.

"Yes, a duel." Beaton shrugged his muscular shoulders, "A fight, an argument."

"Of course not. We had no problem. Only met twice."

Beaton scanned another piece of paper. "Miss. Sunderson,

could this have anything to do with—how do I say this delicately?" He turned to Elaine, who cowered in her chair, looking appalled. Without any help from the home's manager, Beaton forged ahead. "Several people think you might have had a breakdown." He didn't meet Amanda's eyes as he spoke.

She couldn't stifle the laugh that shot out of her mouth, riding on a spray of spit. Was this a joke? "A breakdown? Who on earth said that?" She waited for a reply, looking between Elaine and Beaton, as though she was watching a tennis match, and a bad one at that. But they gave nothing away.

"Can't disclose who told me." Beaton rearranged himself in his chair.

"Yes, you can." Amanda didn't know the rules around this kind of thing, but she didn't care. Her shock had made her bold. And why the hell would they have so many questions when the nurse's death had been an accident?

Beaton turned to Elaine, who nodded her consent. He continued, "Mrs. Hyde-Bowles."

"Who is that?" Amanda's throat tightened and her skin prickled. "Wait. Is she the one that wears her bra outside of her sweater?" Sal had pointed her out, even though it was a hard sight to miss.

"Don't know, Ma'am."

A low growl began in her throat. Was this really happening? Amanda turned to Elaine, who sat slumped in her chair, fingers pressed to her lips. "Do I have to do this?" Amanda's words sounded pleading, even to her.

Elaine's chin quivered as she said, "Legally, not without a warrant or court order. But refusing could make things worse for you." Tears seeped into her bloodshot eyes. "I already called our lawyer."

"Moving on," Beaton barked, fussing with the papers. "The upshot is that we have been told that you pushed Oxana from the second level of stairs, and it was no accident."

Amanda's face couldn't have stretched wider if she had a set of elastic bands connecting her ears. "You have got to be kidding me." She twisted around in her seat, looking everywhere for cameras. "Am I being punked?"

"No Ma'am."

"Right." This was just a bad dream, and she'd awake shortly. Meantime, Amanda knew she must stay cool. "And who, pray tell, announced that little gem?"

"Can't say Ma'am."

"Yes. Yes, you can. And for the love of God stop calling me Ma'am!" She slammed her hands on the table so hard that all three of them jumped.

Elaine nodded her consent.

"It was Mrs. Pendergrass," Beaton said.

Amanda recognized the name, and an image blossomed along with Sal's commentary about her wig, *some days she has a middle part, some days it's on the left or the right, other times she looks like Donald Trump*. "She can't even get her wig on straight. How can she get a story straight?" Amanda pushed her chair back and stood. "This all sounds like idle gossip." Her head spun and she fell back onto her chair, took in a deep breath, let it out. "Listen, I really don't know how any of this happened. But I barely knew Oxana. I did not, repeat, did not push her anywhere, any time." A flashback: the horror of finding Oxana.

O'Keeffe snuffling, licking, and pawing around the body. Amanda vomiting everywhere.

Beaton met her eyes, and she saw them soften. "We see your point, it's not the most reliable crowd here. But I must pay attention to testimonials. We're still corroborating stories and gathering evidence." He tapped his fingers on the stack of folders. "But what we have doesn't add up to anything good for you."

An icy sensation reached Amanda's hands and feet. How could anyone possibly think she was involved in the nurse's death?

Eleven

Implicated.

The word bounced around in Amanda's brain as she and O'Keeffe walked along the Kitsilano beach seawall. That's what she was—implicated in the accidental death of someone she didn't even know. The events of yesterday had left her stunned, and Beaton's words haunted her, *several people think you might have had a breakdown.* Maybe she did have a breakdown or was in the middle of one. People probably weren't aware that they were breaking down. Wouldn't that be part of the process, not being able to see yourself clearly? And who could blame her if she was, after everything she'd been through?

It was all too much, so she was doing what her mother had always said was the remedy to any problem—going outside for some fresh air.

O'Keeffe was aquiver with excitement, sniffing every inch of grass and sand they passed. Warm air buffeted Amanda's sundress as she strolled the asphalt path, the salty breeze and scent of coconut suntan lotion filling her lungs. They ambled past a row of volleyball games, dodged a swooping seagull, met a Great Dane the size of a pony, and navigated around couples pushing baby strollers. The Prussian blue water was dotted with sailboats, and a few orange and black tankers. The sky held soft clouds that drifted with the offshore wind. She welcomed the small measure of relief, shoulders dropping, face relaxing. Did she feel the tug of a smile?

Across the harbour rose the downtown residential area, The West End, studded with apartment buildings in a hodgepodge of architectural styles. A few rainbow flags hung over balconies and an occasional palm spiked the skyline. Below that was a stretch of the seawall, and she let her gaze follow the curve of the shoreline past the high-rises, towards English Bay Beach and the emerald expanse of Stanley Park.

She could have stopped her gaze there, maybe she should have, but she didn't. Her vision swept further west until her eye landed on the distant landmark she'd been seeking. She came to a halt when she saw it, the lighthouse rising from its perch.

The night before the funeral, Amanda had held a viewing at the funeral parlour. She'd opted for a closed casket, not being able to bear the sight of her mother in it. When she first walked into the viewing chapel, her legs nearly gave out under her. She whispered to the ceiling, *I can't do this without you*. Logically, she understood the reality, but the bigger part of her knew that the body in the casket was nothing but the shell of the warm loving mother she'd always known.

Sure, some people had found it odd that a grown woman would be so close to her mother. But, at just over twenty years apart, they were more best friends than mother and daughter. Unlike the men who'd come and gone through Amanda's life, her mother had been a constant. Unlike the men, who seemed to want to knock her down, or who ran hot and cold, Mum had always built her up and made her feel cherished. Images of that sweet face, the slim perfect nose, the soft eyes, that knowing expression that said she was for Amanda and knew that Amanda was for her. Memories of vacations, celebrations, and all the quiet moments in between. Even the distance that separated them during Amanda's years in Toronto hadn't loosened their bond. Since the death, Amanda had hoped her mother would communicate with her: in a dream, a waking vision, a voice in her head, something. But there'd been none of that. Amanda was truly alone. Adrift.

O'Keeffe pulled them onto the sand to snuffle around a log, but when she saw something interesting in the distance, she made a leap towards it, yanking the leash. Amanda's foot caught under the log but the rest of her kept going until she landed with a thud and a yelp, which was muffled due to her face being in the sand.

"Hey, you ok?" A guy in dreadlocks, smelling of patchouli, towered above her.

"Yes." No, she wasn't alright. Even though she was grateful that her chin landed in softness, her teeth hurt. So did her pride. The guy held out a tanned sinewy arm to help her up. She pushed into the warm sand, raising herself into a pathetic version of Cobra pose before taking the proffered hand. A small crowd had stopped and were watching her awkward attempts to get up. She wanted to scream, *everyone stop staring!* Instead, she spat out a mouthful of sand, and thanked Patchouli Guy. Then she noticed that she didn't have the dog's leash in her hand. "O'Keeffe?!" She scanned the area and found a pack of teenage girls leading the jouncing dog toward her.

"Like, is this your dog? It's, like, so cute! The cutest, ohmygod, I can't even!" The girls handed over the leash and Amanda thanked them before turning to O'Keeffe. "Even you didn't stay with me, Girl. What would happen if I *really* got hurt?" The dog offered slow blinks of liquid brown eyes in response, then returned to her snuffling.

Who was going to be there for Amanda?

That was a problem that all the fresh air in the world couldn't solve.

She brushed the sand off herself then steered the dog towards the shore. The expanse of sea and sky unfurled around her and the gentle surf beckoned. Sandals in hand, she strolled to the water's edge and stepped in. A chill coursed through her and with it, Beaton's words, *we're still corroborating stories and gathering evidence.*

Her eye was drawn to Lighthouse Park, and she heard O'Keeffe begin to *woof* insistently. The dog was sidestepping each wave, her nose pointing to the lighthouse. Amanda pulled off her sundress, adjusted her bathing suit then tied the dress to the dog's collar. "Stay, Girl."

She turned to the surf and waded in. Another echo of Beaton's words, *what we have doesn't add up to anything good for you.* Water swirled around her calves, then her thighs. She waded in further, being pulled by something she couldn't name, couldn't hear, couldn't see. Her breath caught as the water hit her belly, but she kept going, further and further out, then plunged deep into the same water that held the last vestiges of her mother.

Moments later, she re-emerged, returning to the smiling

dog at the shore, and knowing what to do next.

She was going to clear her name.

Twelve

Timely Temps' office was in a sleek skyscraper at the northern edge of downtown. Inside the building's cavernous marble lobby, Amanda waved to the security guard who sat behind a monolithic console, then breezed into an elevator that whisked her to the twelfth floor. She exited into a cool quiet hallway and walked the few steps to the office.

The waiting room of Timely Temps was elegant and minimalist, a new look for its owner, Jeremi, who'd recently hired an interior decorator to help attract a bigger and better clientele. The decorator had made him promise to keep his clutter—of which there was a lot—hidden away in his private office, leaving the waiting room clean and professional. The artwork changed every few months in some sort of rental program. This round was a series of abstracts in the style of Jackson Pollack. Amanda confronted the one across from her, its mashup of bleak colours and random slashes of paint echoing her own inner canvas.

The office's best feature was its floor to ceiling windows overlooking the sparkling waters of Coal Harbour and the evergreen North Shore. She watched as a seaplane taxied into the channel, gathering speed before lifting into the air, heading to Victoria or one of the small islands that dotted the rugged coast. Too bad she wasn't on that plane. She sighed and poured a glass of cucumber-spiked water before settling onto the Italian leather sofa.

The gig economy was the perfect fit for her. As a generalist, she could step into any number of roles the temp agency might need, especially any administrative or hospitality task. Her acting background gave her the ability to appear as if she could do anything. The second career of running a casting agency had developed her business skills, also helpful in the gig economy. She sure didn't miss all the responsibility of owning a business. But it was the freedom she loved best, being able to pick her schedule and assignments, without being tied down.

She smelled Jeremi's cologne before she saw him, a sickeningly sweet mix of disinfectant and rawhide. He stepped into the sunlight with a magician's flourish. Tall and thin, Jeremi looked older than his 50-something years, even if he kept his grooming and attire immaculate. "Amandear." He pulled her towards his designer shirt.

Amanda gripped the water glass with one hand, her knapsack with the other and reluctantly leaned one shoulder against him. She hoped he would take the hint to back off. He didn't. Jeremi clutched her like she was a life raft, he a drowning man. "My dearest. I'm so sorry about your *Mommy*," he said in a babyish voice.

She pulled away, his scent mixing with a fresh swell of emotion. "Thank you."

Although she'd extracted herself from the hug, Jeremi didn't catch the social cue. He leaned toward her, donning a sympathetic face as if he reveled in the drama of the moment. A lanky arm petted her shoulder. "She's in a better place."

Amanda took a step back, anger flaring. People said the stupidest things to her, as if they didn't know how to deal with others' grief. Hadn't everyone experienced loss? Was it really so hard to just listen, or say *I'm sorry*? If anyone said *it's for the best,* or *everything happens for a reason* one more time she was going to smack them.

"Let's see what's coming up, okay?" She pointed to Jeremi's office and corralled him towards it. He followed, seeming oblivious to the offence he'd caused.

E-Gads. Stepping into his office was like entering a musty junk store. The room overflowed with knick-knacks salvaged from thrift stores and yard sales. The desk was stacked with files, bookends, and dusty bric-a-brac. Tangled stems from unruly plants wove a web of greenery over the walls and furniture. In one corner stood an antique bird cage containing a taxidermy cockatiel named Lola. A crowning yellow plume and dot of orange on its white face reminded Amanda of a Copacabana showgirl, frozen in time. Lola gave her the willies.

"Any good gigs for me?" She brushed off the seat of a sagging brocade chair before sitting.

Jeremi sat behind his desk and moved a stack of files out of the way. Dust motes flew into the air. "What have you been up to lately?"

She had no interest in small talk and wondered why he'd changed the subject. She sighed and told him that she and O'Keeffe were volunteering in the local retirement home.

Jeremi gasped, "OMG, Amandear, tell me it's not the one

where the nurse died."

That got her attention. How could he know about that? Unless there was another nurse who'd recently died at a retirement home, something she'd missed on the news.

He must have seen the look of confusion on her face so he said, "Never you mind." He turned his attention to the desk. "Now, what were we doing?"

"Looking for work." Amanda took a ragged breath and let it out in an exaggerated sigh. Why was he stalling? He'd known that she was coming to the office, so why wasn't he ready with assignments?

"Ah, right. Work." Jeremi tugged at his greying goatee then smiled, exposing yellowing teeth. "Here's the thing." "You know our clients adore you. . ."

Amanda's Spidey-senses kicked into high gear. She couldn't wait to hear what was coming next, but damn it was a long time coming. "Go on." Her face stretched, eyebrows rising. Seconds ticked by. "What?"

"You knocked out Daniel at the Fight and Flight workshop."

Oh, that. She thought back to the tap on her shoulder that had triggered her already amped self-defense response. She tilted her chin high. "He didn't actually lose consciousness."

"You bloodied his nose!"

"I didn't hit him that hard. He probably has thin blood vessels."

"Plus, you ruined their expensive sign."

"It was flimsy—" Oh God, she hoped Jeremi wouldn't take that out of her pay. "They must be insured for such mishaps."

"Amanda!"

Embarrassment seeped into her. "Listen, I'm sorry about that." She thought of that awful moment, how bad she'd felt, how it took three of them to hoist Daniel to his feet, his nose dripping blood. "And I apologized." About a hundred times. She drew in a belly breath. "But I have a great track record here."

Jeremi was nodding in agreement before she finished her sentence, eyes squeezed shut in deference. "I know, I know, of course." His nodding head sent a fresh wave of cologne into the atmosphere, like a Chernobyl cloud. "That's why I'm giving you another chance. Just not right now. We must let things cool off a bit. Let the talk die down."

There was talk? She slumped into the squishy chair.

He averted his gaze and silence filled the room for a few seconds. "Let's chat again in a few weeks. Okey Dokey?" A smile curled his lips.

Amanda had learned to be cautious around Jeremi. First, he did have power over her income stream, at least until she figured out her next career move. Second, there was something *off* about him, something she couldn't trust. She realized he was staring at her. "Right, of course. I understand. We'll revisit this later." She stood so quickly that she rode a wave of light-headedness.

"Hugs." He walked around the desk, arms outstretched, cologne wafting.

Amanda held her breath, using the last of it to whisper, "Thanks." She imagined a classic villain film, the bad guy clamping a handkerchief of chloroform over the damsel's mouth.

Thirteen

The next afternoon, Amanda stepped off a bus and into the Downtown East Side, to make a long overdue visit. Waiting for the traffic light to flick to green, she witnessed a shoeless man stagger onto the busy six-lane road. Car horns blared and the wheels of a pick-up truck squealed as it swerved around him. But the shoeless man continued his zigzag across the lanes, as if he didn't care if he got to the other side of the street alive.

Life was cheap for some people, and nowhere in the city was it more apparent than here. The area had the dubious honour of being the worst postal code in the country. As she walked towards the address that Officer Beaton had given her, Amanda experienced a wave of sympathy as she stepped around a homeless person tucked in a filthy sleeping bag. She passed cheap coffee joints and a soup kitchen with a line outside that extended around the block. Above the streets rose a flashing neon sign to one of the area's biggest attractions, The Jewell Strip Club. A tacky logo of a shapely leg kicked up and down. She'd never known if the club's name was mis-spelled, or if it was the name of its owner or a top dancer.

As she settled into a good walking pace, she reflected on Toni discovering the bloody red hair on her equally bloody volunteer smock. Toni had soothed Amanda's freak-out before requesting a plastic sandwich bag and tweezers. She and Keira had bagged the hair, smock, and t-shirt separately, as carefully as a couple of forensic scientists. Then Amanda had called Beaton's number and left a message that she'd bring the items to him today.

Who at Singing Swans Lodge had long wavy red hair? None of the nurses fit the bill, all of them were austere and tidy. The residents leaned towards short grey hairstyles or wigs. Cleaners and kitchen staff wore hairnets. She figured it must belong to a visitor and had somehow found its way to her t-shirt and clung there.

Even though she remained convinced that Oxana's death had been an accident, Amanda understood that the police would have questions. Singing Swans' insurance company would surely demand it. And what about Oxana's next of kin? They'd want answers. A wave of sadness hit when she thought of the next of kin. Even if Oxana was disliked at work, there were people who loved her. Or at least, Amanda hoped there were. Everyone deserved that, didn't they?

A minute later, she wrenched open the heavy door and stepped inside Vancouver Police Headquarters. The air smelled like iron and sweat, with a top note of misery. She found the reception desk, where an officer asked the reason for her visit, before making a phone call then pointing her to the waiting area. She was headed there when a ragged voice cut through the air, "Oh, no you effing don't!" Amanda jumped out of the way as two cops dragged a handcuffed guy through the door. His t-shirt was covered in unidentifiable stains. "Get your mitts off me, you effing Po-Po!," he screamed as he struggled against them. But his squirms were no match to the pair who hauled him across the lobby like a rag doll. The cops led him to a steel door and punched numbers into its keypad. The door opened with a *thunk* and the suspect's invectives continued until the door slammed shut behind them all.

Once the commotion passed, Amanda walked through a wake of body odour to the waiting area and sat on a chair hard enough to crack any case, or rear end. Over the next few minutes, she watched cops shuffle in and out of the steel door, the gateway to their inner sanctum. They barked orders at each other and traded good-natured insults.

More time passed. She hadn't set an appointment to meet Officer Beaton but had assumed he'd want to see her, to retrieve the items, ask more questions. But as the minutes ticked by, she wasn't so sure. Was it stupid to deliver a dirty smock and sweat-stained t-shirt? As for the stray red hair, well, that could have been from anywhere. Was she just wasting the cops' time?

"Ms. Sunderson?" A plain-clothed guy towered over her.

Amanda leaped to her feet, an innate respect for authority flaring in her.

"Officer Beaton asked that you leave the items with me." He shook open an over-sized Manilla envelope. "He's sorry he can't meet you in person."

Amanda wasn't sure that she believed that, but she handed over a sandwich bag in which the red hair clung, along with her t-shirt and smock, which was folded to hide the blood stains.

"Thank you." He placed the items in the envelope. She noticed the label on its front, *Evidence*, and her stomach sank.

"I will ensure this gets to the appropriate place." He smiled and nodded, as if to dismiss her.

It was a slight that Beaton hadn't come out to meet her, although why did it matter to her? She'd done her civic duty. So, she smiled and nodded. "Tell Officer Beaton that it was lovely to meet him at Singing Swans Lodge the other day." Sure, it was a lie. She pivoted and made her way to the exit, unsure why she was ruffled, but happy to offer a little quid pro quo.

~~~

Amanda was halfway down the block before she realized her bus transfer had expired. If Police HQ hadn't kept her waiting so long, she'd have been able to make the round trip on the one ticket. Damn. She stopped, stepped to the edge of the sidewalk, leaned against a building, and reached into her backpack. She had a tenner in her wallet, and enough coin to buy half a bus ticket. Double damn. She looked around: soup kitchen, flea-bag hotel, safe injection site. The Jewell Strip Club was the best option, and one hard to miss with its emerald-green exterior and neon sign. She crossed the street before she had time to change her mind.

After the bright mid-day sun, the club's interior was gloomy. She stumbled up a few stairs, past a display case of promotional photos. Even in the dimness, the place looked run-down. Old wood paneling lined the walls. The carpet, once a chevron pattern, was patchy. An elevated stage, empty, sat in the middle of the room, surrounded by seats that would be prime viewing during a show. The place smelled like stale beer and desperation.
~~~

Her arrival garnered attention from a smattering of men who sat bobbing their heads to the drones of *Stairway to Heaven*. She headed towards the bar, passing a table of guys in coveralls having a bitching session. She caught a few snippets: "How much the Goddamn freight on my rig weighed… Think I got paid for all those fucking miles?" Their hostility set Amanda on edge, and she yelped when a greasy guy holding a wet rag stepped in front of her. The men had a good laugh at her expense, while the greasy guy grinned in pleasure. "Mamacita, come on in."

Amanda turned and scurried out the front door. She got a bus ride home with nothing but her expired transfer and an enormous smile.

Fourteen

O'Keeffe huddled in attack posture, haunches tensed, eyes focused, teeth glistening. Her growls were a low constant rumble.

"Just toss her the frickin' stuffy!" Toni yelled, stumbling into Amanda's living room with a second bottle of wine. Keira tossed the stuffed octopus, which flew through the air, landing at Toni's feet. O'Keeffe pounced and Toni jumped high enough to compromise the wine. A splash of precious liquid landed on her hand. "Ah, bad dog!"

Keira yelled from her position cross-legged on the carpeting. "Dunna get mad at her, she's just playing." Her brogue got stronger depending on how much wine she drank. She tapped her hands on her thighs to call the dog back for more toss and fetch. "And pop another light on, will you Toni?"

Amanda lay flat on her back and didn't move even as O'Keeffe rolled the octo-stuffy over her feet, begging her to play. "Where's the wine?" She moaned.

"Toni do this, Toni do that. Sweet Jesus." She made fast work of refilling Amanda's glass then handed her a pillow.

Amanda pushed herself up to sitting position. "Thanks. Might as well enjoy it while I can. In prison I'll have to drink that junk they make from rotting fruit."

"Pruno. La vin du prison." Toni poured for Keira and herself. "Made from whatever fruit inmates can get their hands on. If they can't get fruit, they use ketchup. Add Wonder bread to ferment it." Toni raised her glass in salute. "To Pruno!"

Keira raised her glass. "I dunna even care to hear how you know that."

The soothing nectar of an Okanagan Pinot Gris filled Amanda's mouth and she realized how much she took freedom, and wine, for granted. Tears pricked at her eyes. O'Keeffe dropped the toy in Amanda's lap, curled her lips and growled in demand to play. It was a great distraction ploy, and it worked. Amanda wiped her nose on her sleeve and picked up the damp toy. "Okay. Here you go." She wound up the pitch and tossed the stuffy to the end of the hall, into the kitchen then wiped her hand on her jeans.

Toni stuffed the cork back in the wine bottle, facial piercings trembling with her movements. "What I don't get is how Officer Beefcake came up with those weird ideas when he and Elaine ambushed you in the boardroom." She dug her hand into a bag of potato chips. "I mean, you're pretty likeable Mands, why would any of the residents taat smat abow you?" She raised a ringed finger while she finished chewing then swallowed hard. "Talk smack about you?" She licked her fingertips, one by one.

"No idea, but I'm going to find out." Amanda wiped the residue of tears away, leaving a smudge of makeup on her fingers, which she wiped on her jeans. What was that blob on her knee? Yech—her jeans were dirty. She glanced around her living room. The place was a wreck. How did that happen? She reached up to her hair. Yup, dirty too. "Guys, I'm a mess, aren't I?"

Keira leaned in to pat her friend with a gentle, "Not at all," at the same time as Toni shouted, "Totally." Keira shot Toni an incriminating stare for a change, saying, "Amanda, it's been an awful time for you." She held her glass to her lips. "It's been a stink." When she saw that her glass was empty, a sadness fell over her face. She snapped her fingers at Toni, who passed her the bottle.

Toni said, "That's what I meant: a *totally* awful stink time." She was in a stare down with O'Keeffe who had tired of the octopus and retrieved a dirty tennis ball from under the sofa. "But you were responsible enough to take the evidence to the cops. Even if Officer Beefcake didn't bother to show up."

"Plus, it's a shame that Jeremi put you on hold, but I'm sure he'll come around soon." Keira was starting to slur her words.

"I'm sure it'll all work out fine." Toni narrowed her gaze at the dog, which only seemed to incite her more, setting her tail a-whirl. "All right. Go fetch!" Toni faked a throw which sent the dog in quizzical circles before finding the thing wedged under Toni's black jeans. O'Keeffe burrowed below Toni's legs before snagging the ball in her teeth, then pulling it out with the strategy and force of a mechanical engineer. Toni said, "Mands, don't worry, you won't end up in an orange jumpsuit drinking Pruno and being some bull-dyke's bitch."

"Thanks, that's a relief." Amanda drained her glass, then held it out for more.

Toni poured a refill and topped herself up. "Take a lesson

from O'Keeffe. Nothing bothers her. Animals are so in the moment, you know. They don't worry about what might happen. That's why all the orphans at the animal shelter are so happy."

"When were you there?" Keira asked, a furrow creasing her forehead.

"Last week, after I gave up men." Toni threw her hands in the air. "Thought I'd be less disappointed if I was in a relationship with a dog." She crunched another chip. "Or a cat." She ran a hand over her black hair. "Maybe a ferret. Ferrets are cute."

"Ferrets smell!" Keira said, "And don't you go telling my kids if you do get one." She reached out for the potato chips, muttering, "They'll bloody want one too."

"So, what happened at the animal shelter?" Amanda leaned in as Toni described that she had found it all too sad. "All those rejected animals. I just couldn't do it" She sighed, "So I went home and signed up for online dating."

Amanda and Keira swapped exasperated looks.

Keira slurred the words, "A cat might be nice," as her cell phone pinged. "In the name of all that's holy—it never stops!" She wrestled the phone from her bag, checked the message and read it aloud, "All fine but when you coming home?" She held the phone at arm's length, yelling, "Leave me be Liam, I'm not on the clock." She saw her friends staring at her. "It's his turn to mind the chiselers. I do it all day long while he's playing in his office in the sky." She turned back to the phone and yelled, "While you're having a *life*." She tossed the phone across the room, it landed on the sofa then slid to the carpet. O'Keeffe followed it and gave it a good sniff. Keira lay down. "I'm not trying to be funny or anything, but there are times I think an orange jumpsuit and Pruno sounds quite relaxing."

"You're right," Toni said, "Men. Who needs them?" She pulled her cell phone from her back pocket and punched in her passcode. "In support, I'm deleting my online dating account." Her face morphed into a scowl. "I mean, look at these guys. Seriously, these are my choices?" She scrolled. "Hamster." More scrolling. "Forty years old? Try sixty." She held the phone out to her friends, "This one looks like an axe murderer."

"Ugh."

"Ach."

In a show of bravado, Toni punched a series of buttons. "Bye bye sucky dating site."

The phone made a sound like a Vegas slot machine paying out.

"Wait. Why is it making that noise?" Toni glared at her phone. "Why am I seeing balloons and confetti?" She held out the screen for the others to see. "What the hell?"

Amanda squinted to better see the screen. It had been ages since she'd used the online dating site, but she remembered one thing for sure. "Tell me you didn't hit the big pink button."

"What? I don't know, I just told it to delete my account!"

Amanda twisted her face in sympathy. "No Toni, I think you accepted all requests. How many were there?"

Panic flattened Toni's face. "No. Please be wrong about that." She put her fingers on the screen, widened them to zoom in on the dashboard. "Total requests." She dropped the phone with a resounding thud. "147."

"Feck"

"Fuck."

"Oh mother-bleeping Fuuuckk."

Fifteen

Keira's doorbell squealed a tinny rendition of *It's a Small World.* The sound bored into Amanda's skull. Her hangover was full-fledged now. She plugged her ears and squeezed her eyes against the sight of a quaint wooden heart that hung on the door. Keira answered the door in flannel pajamas, spotted with vomit, or maybe apple sauce, it was hard to tell. Her auburn curls stuck up at an angle that made her resemble a Who from Whoville. She squinted into the sun. "Come in for a cuppa?"

Amanda put a hand on the foyer wall to steady herself. "Yes, please." It hurt to talk. She followed Keira over the gleaming hardwood foyer, past the tv room—a riot of kids' toys—and into the recently renovated kitchen.

"Take a seat, mind you don't scrape the leg or it will–" Keira's hands flew to cover her ears as the stool screeched against the tile flooring. "Screech. That's what it'll do Amanda. It will screech." Keira pointed to the tiles. "Just like that." Her hangover had made her punchy.

"Sorry."

"Not to worry." Keira planted a tall mug of tea in front of Amanda. She sat at the marble island then wrapped her hands around her own mug, saying, "I have a headful. Too much langering last night."

"God. Me too." Ringing echoed from Amanda's jacket pocket. "Right." She pulled out Keira's phone and handed it over. "Why I'm here."

"Thanks." Keira sighed as she read the screen. "The quiet was bliss while it lasted." She stabbed a finger at the phone and said, "Hello Liam, how's your day?" She settled into her stool, listening to her husband.

A tiny voice, tinged with her parents' Irish accents, came from the doorway. "Hullo Auntie Mands."

"Well hello Princess." Amanda slid off her stool and wrapped little Essie in a hug. "How's the life of a fairy princess?"

The girl shook her blond head. "I'm not a princess Auntie Mands. I'm a stretchy superhero—Elastic Girl!" She opened her cardigan to reveal a red E carved out of construction paper. "My superpower is that I can stretch *really* far." Essie flailed her arm out so fast and far that Amanda feared a dislocated shoulder, but she seemed to be fine. Maybe she *was* made of elastic.

Keira had finished her phone call, left the room, and returned with the baby snoring in his basket.

Essie watched him sleep. "I hope he wakes up soon. We're in a duo, and we have missions to accomplish!" She thrust her arm in the air—a superhero about to take flight.

"You're in a what?" Keira set the basket down on the marble island.

"A dynamic duo."

Keira sounded relieved. "Oh, I thought you said you were in a duel."

A frisson of electricity surged in the back of Amanda's fuzzy brain.

"Essie what did you do with the baby's soother?" Keira scanned the room lethargically.

"That's on the other storey. Elastigirl can reach it."

"I've told you Missy, do not make up a story." Keira banged her mug of tea on the table.

"I mean it's upstairs, Mama." She blinked at Keira as if to ask what was wrong with her today.

Keira slumped in her seat, "I'm sorry, Honey. I thought you were making up a story. You know Mummy doesn't like that. I was wrong."

Another ripple passed through Amanda's synapses. The thought gelled. "That's it—a game of broken telephone!"

"What?" Keira's look was blank, probably remnants of her hangover.

Amanda pushed her mug aside. "It's a game. Whisper something to a person. They repeat it to someone else. But things get misheard and change. By the time the last person gets the words they're quite different."

"The broken telephone game," Essie squealed.

"That's it." Amanda petted the girl on her head.

"I got the answer!" Essie did a celebratory dance.

Keira's freckled face remained in a blank stare.

"If you and your progeny can't understand each other, imagine how much trouble any confused or hearing-impaired seniors would have." Amanda pushed her stool back with a screech and stood. "Gah—get these things fixed!" She took a deep breath, shook her arms out. "Sorry. What I mean is that maybe the residents weren't talking smack about me. They didn't accurately hear or didn't understand what someone said." She stabbed a hand into her jeans' pockets but came up empty. "Can I borrow a pen?"

Elastigirl came to the rescue. "Here Auntie Mands, use these." She grabbed a box of crayons and an *Incredibles* colouring book then climbed into Amanda's lap. Amanda stopped the swirl of thoughts for a second, wrapping her arms around the girl, reveling in a flow of love so sweet her eyes stung. She snuck a deep inhale and gave the princess a kiss on her crown.

Sixteen

Last night, as Amanda had stared at her bedroom ceiling, she'd made a plan. She would go to Singing Swans Lodge and figure out the game of broken telephone. Surely Sal would agree to help her. They'd sort out who had said what, how the messages mutated from resident to resident as the gossip spread through the home. Amanda would get all the info needed to clear the cops' ridiculous suspicions against her. It would be a comedy of errors. Oh, how they'd laugh!

With such a good plan and optimistic outlook, Amanda wondered why she continued, long after her breakfast was finished, to stare at the blank living room wall. "What's wrong with me?"

The dog roused from her snooze at Amanda's feet, shook out her little body and offered a meaningful stare. "That's not much of an answer, O'Keeffe." Amanda wrapped a hand around her coffee mug, now cold to the touch. The dog wandered into the foyer, returning seconds later with her leash in her mouth and another profound stare.

"You're right, Girl. I can do this."

~~~
~~~

In front of Singing Swans Lodge stood a fountain of two swans spitting streams of water to each other in an arch that formed a heart. The installation must have been expensive, Amanda thought, saving it from being even more tacky. She pulled O'Keeffe to heel—a trick Amanda had finally mastered. The automatic doors slid open, and she tugged the leash, saying, "Let's go."

The mood inside was bright, as if maintenance had installed higher wattage lightbulbs. A colourful sign announced 'Button-down Bingo. Dust off your tuxedos and evening gowns!' Were these tactics to distract the residents? Help them move past the recent trauma of Oxana's death? Or was the place brighter because Oxana was gone? Amanda shuddered, signing in at the unmanned reception desk. What good was it to require visitors to sign in and out if there was nobody at reception to ensure that happened?

As if reading Amanda's thoughts, Mai rushed out of the back room, a pile of envelopes and packages in her slender arms. "Hello there, I had to get the mail," Mai said in an exasperated tone. "Too much to do since cutbacks!"

Cutbacks. Amanda hadn't heard about these and wondered if they might have somehow contributed to Oxana's accident. Maybe the cleaners were too rushed to set out their wet floor sign and the nurse slipped to her death. "Mai, do you think the cleaners have been cutting corners?"

Mai gave this some consideration as she dumped the mail on the reception desk. "Don't think so." She lifted one bony shoulder. "Not that I noticed."

"One other question." Amanda leaned on the desk, watching Mai sort the envelopes. "Does anyone who works here, or visit, have long red wavy hair?"

"Let me think," Mai said, shuffling the envelopes. "Ah, we had a Fun Day here a few weeks ago. There was a clown doing a magic show. He had red hair." She crinkled her nose. "Probably a wig. At least I hope so." She frowned.

"Was it long?"

"Very." Mai released a sigh. "And boring too. Should cut the act to a half hour."

Amanda mimed long waves on either side of her head. "No, the hair, the hair."

"Are you having a seizure Amanda?"

"No!"

"You keep saying the hair, the hair, and seem to have no control over your arms."

The dog gave a firm bark, announcing her need to move on to fresh territory. A frustrated Amanda said goodbye to Mai, and let O'Keeffe pull her along the main floor, searching for edible bits as Amanda searched for Sal.

Amanda wondered if Sal knew about the interrogation in the boardroom. Maybe she'd run into Elaine, still mortified from the meeting and needing a confidant. Or maybe she'd run into Beaton and dragged it out of him?

What if everyone in the home knew that Amanda was a suspect in Oxana's death?

They found Sal in the dining room, finishing a late breakfast. Amanda tapped on the glass door and waved as Sal threw down her napkin and rose from her seat. Today's outfit was another tent of a housedress, this one dotted with a pineapple print. Her silver wig stuck out a bit at the back as if she hadn't combed it. The dog tugged at the leash, the wafting aromas of brioche and bacon torturing her. "You had breakfast already. Apples and kibble." Amanda commanded her, "Sit. Be a good girl." A set of big brown eyes stared back at her, but the dog didn't obey. She was off like a cannon shot as soon as Sal entered the hallway, nearly pulling Amanda off her feet. "Ow—my shoulder!"

"Oh, Sausage Roll," Sal said, hunching over to grab the dog's leash. "Have you hurt your human?" She petted the excited dog, who made figure eights around her ankles, then shifted her focus to Amanda. "My Dear you appear pained. Either that or you're sucking on a lemon."

"That bloody hurt," Amanda rubbed her shoulder. "Damn." Her mood shifted from pain to regret. "I'm sorry Sal, that was rude." Her outburst had attracted the attention of a few residents who were staring.

"No mind, my Dear. I used to be a trucker you know." Sal winked.

Amanda cocked her head. "You did?" Sure, women were truckers today, but in Sal's working days?

"Let's just say that my cussing can keep up with the truckers. Hello Amanda. Glad to see you both. Are you here to spread puppy love?" Sal scratched O'Keeffe's rear end, setting the dog trembling with joy. O'Keeffe twisted herself around, trying to reward the scratching hand with kisses, but even her long body couldn't manage.

"No, this isn't a doggie visit. I need to ask you a favour,"

Amanda said, as the late breakfast crowd spilled out into the hallway, making it hard to talk. "We're here to figure out a few things. Can you help?"

Sal's eyes widened, "Oooh, how thrilling," she said over the hubbub then pointed to the Oak Lounge. "Let's find a quiet spot."

As the trio headed to the lounge, Mai's voice cut through the crowd. "Amanda. Good news!" She waved something in the air, yelling, "Your earring!"

A flush of happiness filled Amanda as she raced to the reception desk and took the earring, saying, "Oh my God, where—" She stopped herself. Did she really want the answer? She held up the earring, inspecting it for damage. Or blood. Or brain matter. Much to her relief, it looked clean, sparkling even.

"Cleaners found it in the hallway, not on the dead body you found!"

Terrific, now everyone within a ten-kilometre radius knew who had discovered Oxana. Amanda felt the heat rise on her face.

But did it really matter? The talk had begun long ago, surely all the residents knew by now. Besides, she had her earring back! She thanked Mai then turned to join Sal and O'Keefe. Together they headed to the Oak Lounge, barely aware of the guy who leaned against the reception desk, hovering over the Visitor Log. The one who pulled out his cell phone so he could discretely snap photos of them.

Seventeen

Anxiety pricked at Amanda as she entered the Oak Lounge, the memory of that initial police interrogation surging. But the memory was cut off when Amanda heard a snort and noticed a square-faced woman with tight blue curls scowling at them.

"What's that mangy mutt doing in here?" She didn't wait for an answer but shook her head then turned around as fast as her walker allowed. Thick Frankenstein shoes slowed her further and Amanda thought how hard it must be to make a dramatic exit when your body is so slow. The scowling woman punctuated her sluggish exit with a threat, "I'm going to report you to the health department, young woman!"

Only in a retirement home would Amanda be called young. She felt downright ancient most days.

Ka-thud, ka-thud.

Amanda turned toward the doorway and saw that the cranky woman had a wheel of her walker stuck in the doorjamb. Sal and O'Keeffe were busy exploring, so Amanda raced over to help.

"I'm going to turn you in right now." The cranky woman grimaced as she pulled her walker backwards, slowly, aiming for a better angle, but ending up ramming the same spot.

"Let me help." Amanda bent down, assessed the situation then freed the wheel. She stood, offered a smile, and received a snort in return.

"Hrmph." The tight face made it hard to tell if she was grateful to Amanda or still angry. "I'm going to report you now."

Still angry, Amanda decided, watching the woman totter out of the lounge.

Sal offered a wink. "Don't let that old biddy bother you. She's always unhappy" She sighed, adding, "Must be the shoe inserts, custom orthotics."

"She's certainly has mastered the scowly face," Amanda said cutting off the last bit of Sal's comment. The overlapping words created a moniker, Scowly Orthotics, which sent them both into a fit of giggles.

"She's got a point," Amanda said. If she wanted O'Keeffe to keep joining her on these visits, they'd need to get her certified as a visiting dog. It would be a lot of work though, and she still sat on the fence at the idea. She sighed. For now, just being able to return to the Lodge felt like progress.

Sal pointed to a corner table, before getting two cups of coffee for them. When she returned, she said, "I've a confession to make."

"Uh oh." Amanda tore open a package of sugar.

"I heard about that bully Beaton and his accusations against you." Sal stirred her coffee, thoughtful.

"Right. That." Amanda focused on her own coffee. She wanted details but was unsure she could handle them.

Sal belonged to a gracious generation, and she didn't make Amanda ask. Instead, she volunteered the story. "Elaine told me.

She was tortured by the grilling Beaton put you through. That he might possibly think . . ." Sal balled up her hands. "I told her it was Beaton's lucky day since he didn't run into Sal the Pal." She shook one fist. "I smuggled Elaine a shot of whiskey, she tossed it in her herbal tea. Asked me to keep the incident under my hat, and I have. Even though I don't usually wear hats." She sipped her coffee, "Never looked good in them."

~~~

One by one, Sal helped Amanda knock off the conjectures that Keira and Toni had put forward.

"She did not have narcolepsy or epilepsy, to my knowledge. Those ailments would be hard to keep under wraps," Sal said, setting a plate of cookies between them, organized from biggest to smallest. She reached for a huge oatmeal raisin. "Besides, would a governing board offer a nursing license to someone who might need to be nursed?" She held the cookie to her lips, her frosted lipstick smudged. "As for a fainting spell due to a secret pregnancy," she said with a shrug, "I suppose even ice queens can get knocked up."

O'Keeffe rose from her post under the table and stared longingly at Sal eating the cookie. Amanda reprimanded her. "No beg."

Sal reached for a stack of napkins, rested the uneaten half biscuit on it. "The slip and fall theory is another one that I can't buy. Have you seen the treads our nurses wear? And the cleaning staff always sets up one of those yellow caution whodads after mopping any areas."
~~~

"But what about the cutbacks Mai mentioned?"

"Haven't heard of any. Haven't seen any." Sal knocked the half-eaten cookie to the floor and O'Keeffe dove on it. "Besides my Dear, it was not the Work Persons Compensation board or the Nursing Union that corralled you in the boardroom." Sal gave her a pointed look. "It was the police."

Amanda reached into her jean pocket, running a finger over the returned earring. "You're suggesting this wasn't an accident? Because if not—"

"How be we start with asking questions around here?" Sal cut her off with the wave of a fat hand then reached for the second largest cookie that sat on the plate, nodding in encouragement for Amanda to join in. "I have relationships with most of the residents and I'm here around the clock."

"Good idea. Me asking questions might seem out of place." The dread of confronting the residents clung to Amanda. How could they suspect her of wrongdoing? But the list of statements in front of her, on Essie's colouring book, said exactly that.

"Don't worry about what that beastly officer said. It's twaddle. Complete poppycock." Sal's expression was soft, kind. "We'll get this sorted."

"Okay." Amanda bit into a peanut butter cookie that was crazy good. "Let's recap." She straightened herself and read from her crayon notes. "One. Find out how this got started. Someone heard that Oxana and I were in a duel. Odd choice of words." She shook her head, "But a smart friend of mine, we'll call her Elastic Girl—"

"Oh, I like that name, sounds like a superhero." Sal bit into a gingersnap. "A very stretchy one." After taking a bite, she passed the rest under the table.

"Good deduction. And please stop feeding O'Keeffe cookies," Amanda said. "Elastigirl suggested a mix up between the words duo and duel. Inquiries to be made along that line."

"Duel. Check." Sal confirmed against her own list, scrawled on a paper napkin.

"Two. The superhero also referred to the second storey of her house, but her mother thought she was telling a story."

"Easy enough to confuse those two words, I suppose."

Amanda continued, "Next. Mrs. Hyde-Bowles claims I had a breakdown. What made her think that? Oh, make sure she's awake." Amanda squinted at her notes, struggling to read her thickly drawn words. "Aware. Right. Make sure she's *aware* when you question her."

"If she's wearing curlers at the lunch table, I'll come back another time." Sal made a notation on her napkin.

"Finally, Mrs. Pendergrass says that I pushed Oxana from the second level of stairs, and it was no accident."

"Could be the storey versus story confusion," Sal raised a fleshy finger. "I must also be wary of possible disorientation with Pendy. If I find her talking to her reading lamp, I'll cease and desist."

"Lastly, the biggest question of all. Why would anyone want Oxana dead? Snoop for any and all information on that."

"Bear in mind that, truth be told, most everyone wanted her dead." Sal said then shrugged in response to Amanda's grimace. She fluttered her napkin. "We might consider getting proper notepads too. My list is disintegrating." Sal tapped Amanda's notes with a grimace. "And yours is done in a colouring book with bright crayons. These scream *amateur*."

"I'll check petty cash." Amanda smiled. "Thanks so much for your help. It means the world to me."

"Oh, what else am I doing here in God's waiting room? I'm bored silly. You've spiced things up for me." She folded the napkin carefully, tucked it down the front of her dress and patted her bosom, adding, "Been a while since that's happened."

Eighteen

'Veuillez appuyer sur deux pour le Français.' Amanda listened to the phone menu then pressed number one on the keypad.

The morning's task was to cancel her mother's OAS, government speak for old age security. Amanda found herself zoning out during the lengthy recitation of phone menu choices. She'd already sat through a protracted greeting in both English and French and was fuzzy headed with the number of options, none of which seemed suitable. Old enough to remember the days when human beings answered business lines, listened to a person's needs then cheerfully patched them to the right department, she longed for that simplicity, that care.

But more than that, she longed to make any kind of progress. While Sal was questioning residents about the gossip that had led to Beaton's interrogation, Amanda was determined to cross at least one more item off Mount Executor.

What number was she supposed to press now? Gah! The information had been repelled by her brain, like a GorTex rain jacket in a Vancouver winter. A push of the star key repeated the encyclopedia of choices. 'Changes to your account' was the best match, so she pressed the corresponding key and was immediately told that her call was 'very important to them' and an agent would answer shortly. Muzak began, a cover version of *Forever Young,* a choice she didn't think was particularly appropriate. She put her phone on speaker and nestled it in the tracks of the kitchen window. Might as well suffer through some dish washing while suffering through the song.

What seemed like days later, a clerk answered, reciting her ID number and name in a tone so depressed that Amanda considered calling the Distress Centre. She explained her executor status and asked to cancel her mother's Old Age Benefits. The phrase, old age, still didn't sound right to her. Was 70 even considered old anymore? Wasn't it the new 60?

"Wrong department." The clerk sighed, "transferring now."

Amanda heard a series of clicks before the line went dead. So much for getting transferred to the right department. Eyes squeezed shut in frustration, she hit the redial button and endured the welcome greeting in English, then again in French. Ah the joys of having two official national languages. This time, she heeded the list of options with the focus of a dog on a bone then chose 'Cancel an account.' She was told again that her call was 'very important but a high volume of calls meant wait times were longer than usual.' Longer than she'd already been on hold? She'd be fossilized at her kitchen sink by the time someone realized she was missing. What happened to her call being important?

Deep calming breath in, then out. Three, four, five.

Well, what the hell else did she have to do? Might as well keep on with the dishes, enjoy the birds fluttering around in the backyard. She cleaned all the cutlery and was reaching for a glass when a fresh song began, its strains recognizable from somewhere in the deep past. It was another bad song from the seventies, *Seasons in the Sun.* The lyrics wailed about how hard it is to die while life goes on around us.

She wanted to smash the glass in her hand.

The dispensation of her mother's will could have been much more difficult, she knew. While her mother was supposed to be recovering from her first stroke, she'd been busy behind Amanda's back. She'd enlisted Joyce to tackle everything possible to get her estate in order, so that Amanda would be spared the lengthy and expensive process of probate. They'd made Amanda a joint holder on every bank account. They'd updated the will, ensuring that Amanda was sole beneficiary on all investments, annuities, the life insurance policy, and private pension. The condo was put into a joint tenancy, ensuring it would pass automatically to Amanda when her mother died. Why had her mother invested time and energy to get her estate in order when she should have been focusing on her recovery?

The sensation of a hand wrapping around her throat, finger by finger, overtook Amanda, squeezing with increasing force. Intuitive Laura must have sensed that another stroke was looming. She must have been so scared.

Amanda gripped the counter as the edges of her vision blurred; the view through the window nothing more than a swirl of green. Her mother had ensured that Amanda would be taken care of, whenever the time came.

Now it was too late to thank her for that selfless act.

When a voice erupted from the other end of the line, Amanda juddered back to reality, taking a second to swipe her cheeks with the sleeve of her t-shirt. This civil servant was less despairing than the first, but possibly manic. He rattled off his ID number and name as quickly as a hungry vagrant diving into an open dumpster. When Amanda stated the reason for her call, she got no response and implored, "Please tell me I have the right department."

"You do. Have you sent us the death certificate?"

Those words still hurt, still made her loss feel so final, what with it being *certified*. "Well, seeing as it was the government that issued it, you will have it on file."

"Records. Different department."

Oh, for the love of God. "Fine," Amanda said, "What's the best email address to send it to?"

The clerk rattled off a fax number.

"I don't have a fax machine," Amanda said. Did anyone have one anymore? "I can scan it then email." She moved to the kitchen table and grabbed a pen.

"Has to be faxed." The clerk was emotionless.

Damn it all, she'd forgotten about the faxing note beside this task. "How about a local office? I could bring the original to show someone."

"Can't you just fax it?"

It was a stalemate, one that strained Amanda beyond her wits. She couldn't stifle the eruption of sarcasm. "If you have a time machine I could borrow, I could travel back to the era of faxing. Perhaps I might hear another cheerful song from that epoch too."

"Transferring you to a manager."

There were a series of clicks before the line went dead.

Amanda sat, dropped her head to the table and wept.

Nineteen

Finding a local dog training program had been a simple Google search. Amanda found an opening for that weekend and registered at once, grateful to make the decision, and have something to fill her time. The slim price tag was appealing too.

Saturday was for dog owners only, and a dozen hopeful volunteers filled the borrowed office spaces. The trainer Ben was a grizzled older guy who looked like he'd followed the Grateful Dead around for a few summers. He spoke with a hint of a drawl and Amanda imagined he'd be in his element with a long stalk of grass to chew on. He introduced the other trainer, Jared, who was tall and shapeless, with a personality to match. "People call us Ben and Jerry," Ben said, winking. That drew a few chuckles and set Amanda on a craving for ice cream.

During introductions, most attendees waxed poetic about giving back, wanting to contribute to those less fortunate. Amanda wished she had a more altruistic reason for signing up, something better than, "My Mum just died, and I'm wracked with grief and need to get out of myself. And I have her dog, who doesn't understand why her mistress is gone and she has to live with me. Oh, and I got suspended from work and have too many empty hours. . ." So, at her turn, she decided to keep it general, saying, "I have a dog with lots of energy and love to give, so thought this would be a good fit."

They spent the morning discussing basic training videos about best practices in hospitals, treatment centres or senior residences. At the lunch break, everyone gushed about their dogs. *Basil is a small guy with a giant heart and funny face – he'll make the kids so happy. . . Juno is a big lug who just wants to rest his anvil-head in anyone's lap. . . Madame Coco doesn't realize how good she has it, it's time for her to do some work!*

In the afternoon, the group role played scenarios, with the trainers playing the sick or elderly, exhibiting a wide range of emotions. Jared's lanky body waved back and forth like an inflated tube man promoting a used car lot. "You need to be sensitive and careful. You and your dog will be visiting people in an unfamiliar environment or a tough situation. They might be lonely or scared, angry or distraught."

Madame Coco's owner was left completely rattled when Ben pretended to be an enraged patient. In another scene, Jared imitated an unresponsive patient, and it was sad to watch. At one point, Amanda asked herself why the hell she'd signed up for this when she had enough pain in her life. Then she remembered the tower of executor duties on her kitchen table, the empty condo that she couldn't bear to step foot in, the void in her life, and she rallied.

~ ~ ~

On day two, the volunteers brought their dogs. Amanda and O'Keeffe arrived that morning to a room in utter chaos. A brown cockapoo cowered in the corner, the bright polka dots on its sweater shaking. Amanda suspected that was Madame Coco. O'Keeffe was so excited to be in a new place, and one that had a table of muffins, she could barely contain herself. In between meeting the other dogs, and a lot of intrusive butt-sniffing, she cleaned the area around the snacks table, like a fuzzy blonde vacuum cleaner. Then she grabbed a corner of the tablecloth in her mouth, attempting to bring few remaining Morning Glory muffins directly to her. Amanda was grateful to catch her in time. A Ridgeback made a show of peeing in the middle of the carpet, as if asserting his rule. The mortified owner screeched, "He never does that!" as several people nodded in commiseration. Amanda was one of them, remembering the day that Oxana had screamed at her when O'Keeffe peed at the Nursing Station. While the Ridgeback owner scurried for an armful of rags and bottle of carpet cleaner, Ben called a timeout.

"An indoor whiz is always a problem, but it's worse in a volunteer situation," Ben said as he tugged on his scraggly beard. "The dog is there to bring happiness, not demand a clean up."

"But accidents surely happen," Madame Coco's owner said with a wave of her manicured hand.

Willow branch Jared, stepped in. "You can prevent accidents by making sure to take the dog out on frequent pee breaks."

Ben chimed in, "Usually it's a behavioural problem." He pointed to the Ridgeback, "This here dog was marking his territory, probably 'cause there are other dogs here. If he does that on the job, he'll be fired."

The Ridgeback owner didn't try to hide a look of upset as he mopped up the mess. "Can't we give him another chance?"

"Yessir," Ben drawled. "But just the one."

Uh-oh. O'Keeffe already had one strike against her at Singing Swans. Amanda hated the thought of them being rejected because of another accident. It couldn't happen again. She whispered against a furry ear, "No piddling inside, Girl, especially at the Lodge."

"What if the dog gets scared?" The human attached to Basil, a timid Pug with bulging eyes, asked.

"Yup. That happens. Scary person. Or maybe the dog smells fear on someone," Ben's words twigged a memory for Amanda. The raised hackles, the low growling—had O'Keeffe been scared by Oxana, or had she smelled fear on the nurse? The thought tickled her brain for a second until Ben continued," But if you got the sorta dog that scares easy, he might not be a good therapy dog."

"Please be a good therapy dog," Amanda whispered to O'Keeffe and the dog responded with a shiver of delight.

"Today we train 'n test," Ben said, "And we're gonna use bribes." He held up a family-sized bag of liver treats.

Jared waved his lanky arms, like Elmo the Muppet gathering children to hear a story. "Form a circle with your dogs." He held up a pencil-like finger. "But do not let them interact with each other." The participants did as told. Their dogs sat looking from owner to trainer to the dogs on either side of them as if they didn't know what was coming next. But they all stayed in their spots and stayed quiet. They all passed that first test, and that earned them their first dehydrated liver treat of the day. After that, all the dogs became surprisingly well-behaved.

The trainers discussed how important grooming and hygiene were. Amanda learned dogs needed wash and cuts, nail trimming and anal gland draining—whatever that meant. She sure was learning a lot about having a dog, and she made a mental note to find out what groomer her mother had used.

Ben and Jared set up simulations of arriving at a new facility. This round of train and test was to ensure that the dog obeyed commands and would behave if their owner stepped away, in an unfamiliar setting. Bug-eyed Basil seemed to panic when his human left him on his own although Amanda didn't know why since the little guy must have excellent peripheral vision. The dog calmed, and once again, the entire group of canines passed the test before turning drooling mouths in the direction of the liver treats. Ben tossed them out like a dolphin trainer at Marine World, and not a single dog missed catching theirs.

The next round gauged whether the canines would endure strangers petting them, and how they coped with multiple strangers at once. Amanda watched as dog after dog handled the onslaught of attention, some with more cheer than others. She felt a wave of pride at O'Keeffe's turn, the sweet dog delighting in the affection and rewarding every pat of her fur with a lick of gratitude.

"Let's try some triggers like sudden loud noises," Ben said, proceeding to have a great time banging utensils against pots and pans. "A dog who starts to barking at the sound of a rolling crash cart or other commotion, is gonna be a problem." Madame Coco did not like the concert. She cowered against her owner's feet.

Amanda learned a few things about O'Keeffe. First, she really was an easy-going dog. Her gentle temperament and friendly nature shone through. Second, she was much more cooperative and obedient when there was a liver treat on offer. Third, she could only master two tricks, offering a paw or lying on the floor. They might need to expand that repertoire, Amanda thought.

After lunch and walkies, they were back to work, testing reactions to unusual situations like dealing with people on crutches, with a walker, or in a wheelchair. To ensure realism, Ben and Jerry coughed, moaned, and let out the occasional shriek. Unfortunately, the combination of yelling and a chair on wheels was too much for nervous Madame Coco. After nearly getting caught in the chair's wheels, she shrieked, teeth bared, the polka dots of her sweater vibrating like an exploding box of Skittles. When her owner reached out, the dog snapped at her hand. The woman yelped, "Madame!" in shock. Jared issued his first fail, leaving the owner insulted and furious. She scooped up her dog, swirled around and exited the offices with a volley of insults over her padded shoulder.

"That ain't a therapy dog," Ben said, "That's a dog that needs therapy."

Ben retrieved a Tupperware container, saying, "Now we got to ensure they don't eat anything off the floor. Don't want 'em to get any meds." He placed a row of breadcrumbs over the carpet while the pack salivated from a safe distance. Amanda was sure that O'Keeffe would fail but Ben showed how to entice the dogs with a liver treat. She was so proud when O'Keeffe passed the test, she laughed out loud, making another mental note to buy liver treats.

Testing the dogs' reactions to children was the next item on the docket. It was the limp Jared who awkwardly pretended to be a kid, yelling, throwing things, hitting the dogs, and pulling their tails. This was the end of the road for the Ridgeback, who was issued a firm fail mid-stream of his second carpet pee. The owner was good natured about their failure, shaking his head and sitting down to watch the rest of the trainings.

Amanda had suspected that O'Keeffe would pass her tests, but what she hadn't expected was how much fun the dog would have. Ben's banging on frying pans delighted her. Jared's pretend kid tugging on her tail was an invitation to play. Being screamed at was nothing more than a game. She endured the noise, abuse, and physical obstacles with a grin on her face. Nothing flustered her. She had a ball.

~~~

They went home at the end of the day exhausted but carrying a certificate of completion. Amanda made a pit stop at the grocery store. When she returned to the dog, she held up the heavy bag, saying, "I couldn't decide between Vanilla Praline and Rocky Road, so I got them both." O'Keeffe's eyes widened and Amanda told her, "Don't judge me."

Once back home she rewarded O'Keeffe with a dinner of leftover beef and kibble. "You're a working dog now. Mama's so proud." Her choice of words surprised her—she'd never thought of herself as O'Keeffe's mama and wasn't sure how the idea sat
~~~

with her. She sunk into the sofa that night with two tubs of ice cream and a deep sense of sadness.

Twenty

Amanda's heritage neighbourhood was looking its best as she and O'Keeffe stepped out into the morning sun. Towering cedars and cypress trees, some reaching six stories high, filled the air with their resinous scent. Rhododendron bushes, some as big as sheds, dotted the area in bursts of pink and purple. Vancouver was downright slutty in its summer showcase of flowers.

A few original homes still stood, with generous lawns separating them. But most had been demolished, rebuilt in mock turn-of-the-century style then resold as multi-unit strata. Developers made a killing on those projects, selling them for prices beyond the reach of most mere mortals. Amanda was one of those mortals but counted herself lucky to have snagged a great rental unit when she moved back to her hometown two years ago. Careful to sidestep the tiny fallen plum—or was it a cherry—she let O'Keeffe pull her across the street. While the dog had a piddle, Amanda looked back. Pretty as the area was, the house which held her flat was the scourge of it. Rundown and tilting at a slight angle, it stood out in stark contrast to its peers. Even the yard screamed neglect compared to its well-manicured neighbours. She'd tried to make improvements, but her landlord persevered with his love of dilapidation and cheapness. Boy, was it ugly.

What had her life become?

She sighed. At least the exterior gave her a sense of safety. What kind of burglar would target that ruin when there was such luxury nearby? Besides, the upside to her landlord's general inattention was that the rental was below the current, crazy market price.

O'Keeffe pulled her along the block. Despite her growing love for the dog, there were days when three walkies cramped Amanda's style. She remembered casting for a tv commercial that had promised to train cats to use a human toilet. Maybe O'Keeffe could learn that? She was long enough to twist around from a sitting position and reach the flush handle. After another quick pee, the dog slowed to do some serious sniffing and catch up on the local news.

The smell of rosemary and lavender bushes filled Amanda's lungs. She inhaled deeply, happy to be in nature, a welcome chance to de-stress from recent events. She examined the sky, dotted with fluffy clouds. But when thoughts of her executor tasks intruded into her thoughts, sadness zapped her. She slumped onto a shaded patch of grass. The dog sauntered over and gave her a good snuffling. "I'm alright, don't worry. I just miss Mum so much." She thought of how much O'Keeffe must miss her too, how disorienting it must have been to suddenly lose her mistress. A vibration in Amanda's jeans pocket signaled an incoming cell phone call and a welcome distraction. What wasn't welcome was the voice on the other end of the line.

"Checking up on my suspended worker bee." Jeremi

snickered at his own joke. "Get it? Bees fly, so they're always suspended." Getting no response, Jeremi cleared his throat then continued, saying, "Are you still volunteering at the retirement home?"

An image of Beaton's interrogation flashed in Amanda's brain. *We can't ignore evidence, Miss Sunderson, and these testimonials point to you.* She sucked in a breath, chasing images of Beaton, and prison, from her mind. How fast does someone go from suspect to prisoner? "Um, not sure about that."

"Well, a little birdie told me that the place is a hotbed of activity, because of the you-know-what." Jeremi's tone was conspiratorial.

O'Keeffe got out her morning poop, which Amanda had the dubious pleasure of picking up. "I really don't." She sneered at the warm squishiness she felt through the poop bag.

He hissed, "I'm talking about *the murder*."

"What?" The word came out more sharply than she intended. "What murder?" She tied off the bag and followed O'Keeffe onto the edge of the next lawn, where the dog sniffed under a laurel hedge.

Jeremi's voice grew light, almost musical. "The nurse at your retirement home, Silly."

The puzzle pieces snapped together in Amanda's head. "Oh, that." She exhaled in relief. "No, no, no, that wasn't a murder!" She laughed. "God. Jeremi, you gave me a shock." She pulled a thick stalk of grass from its casing, enjoying the satisfying action. "A nurse died because she fell down the stairs and hit her head."

"Tsk, tsk. You can be so naïve, Amanda." Mockery tinged

his voice. "It was no accident. It was a straight up murder."

The images flashed: O'Keeffe pulling her off her feet, the thud as she landed on something lumpy, the sight of Oxana's grotesque face, the pool of blood. A shudder passed through her until Jeremi's chatter pulled her from her thoughts. She realized he'd been talking through her flashbacks and had to ask him to repeat the last thing he said.

"I was wondering how things are there, I mean, for you." She imagined him tugging at his goatee like a villain from the nineteenth century. Cue the chase music.

Suspicion wormed its way into her thoughts. Why should she tell him anything? "Things are, okay." She felt her eyes narrow. "By the way, what made you think it was a murder?"

Jeremi paused. "I caught it on the news."

"Which broadcast?"

"My goodness the questions, Amanda! You are a suspicious Silly Billy, aren't you?" His speech raced. "Gotta go, filling positions for the Wedding Show." He cut himself off, maybe recognizing that this would be a sore spot for Amanda, and it was. His voice shifted to a cheerful tone. "I know they'll miss you but there's always the winter session. Toodles!" He rang off.

As O'Keeffe led the way up the concrete stairs to their flat, Amanda couldn't shake the weird feeling. The death of nurse Oxana hadn't been broadcast on any newscasts, had it? She knew how hard Elaine would try to keep the story quiet. Even if a journalist had caught wind of it, there was no foul play to be reported. A shiver ran along her spine.

So, how could Jeremi, who had no link at all to the retirement home, possibly know about any of it?

~ ~ ~

She unclipped the dog's leash in the foyer, headed to the kitchen table and fired up her laptop. She tried every search she could think of, ending up with three video clips from the local news and five snippets on local news blogs or e-newspapers. The reports each had their own angle, as reflected in the headlines: 'Are Retirement Homes Safe?', 'Unfortunate Accident Leaves Nurse Dead', and 'What Really Took the Police to Singing Swans Lodge?' Amanda took in all the coverage. Not one of them mentioned foul play or suspicious death. Not one of them suggested murder.

So why had Jeremi sounded so sure?

Twenty-One

Despite foreboding skies, Amanda chose to take the bus to Singing Swans. The temperate climate was known to be erratic and changeable, so today she'd packed an umbrella, sunglasses, and sweater, just in case. Halfway along her route, the storm exploded, and she was grateful to have left the driving to someone else. It was unusual for Vancouver to have a rainy day in August, and rare for lightning and thunder. The storm exhilarated her, until she had to step off the bus and dash a block and a half to the Lodge, arriving wet as a sewer rat, and equally jumpy from the flickers of lightening and claps of thunder.

She shook off her umbrella and raincoat then headed to the reception desk, offering a wave to Mai and Elaine who chatted there. Talking to Elaine was tops on Amanda's list. She wanted to confirm what the news results from her internet search had found, that no coverage hinted at a murder. That Jeremi must have lied about hearing that on the news. That he was yanking Amanda's chain, spooling another one of his melodramas.

Amanda was signing the Visitor Log when Elaine waved and rushed off to the elevator. Amanda chased after her. "Elaine, I just want to ask something about the recent news reports."

A flush rose on Elaine's pale face as she stabbed at the elevator button. "We tried to keep it quiet," she said as the elevator doors slid closed, leaving Amanda behind.

Sure, Elaine was stressed and tired. Having to cancel her Hawaiian vacation must have really hurt. But why had she wanted to get away from Amanda? Maybe Sal would know. Number two on Amanda's list was to find out what intelligence Sal had gathered. Where would she be at this hour? The lunch seating had just let out, residents were exiting the dining room, but none of them were Sal. The crowd trickled around her, slow as molasses in a Quebec winter. It was impossible not to overhear conversations. One snippet of dialogue, from a pair of women walking arm-in-arm, tickled her subconscious.

"I said she had a break, downstairs."

The other woman chuckled. "Jiminy Cricket Madeline, I thought you said she had a breakdown!"

The words swirled Amanda's brain before snapping into place like puzzle pieces. Break downstairs could be misheard as breakdown on the stairs. She silently congratulated herself on decoding another part of the broken telephone riddle.

Eager to share her news, she peeked into the Oak Lounge. No Sal. When her cell phone rang, she smiled at the thought of how much she and Sal were in tune, even if they only met two weeks ago. She hit the answer button just as she remembered she'd never given Sal her phone number.

"Officer Beaton here. Are you at home?"

Beaton? Beaton! Why would it matter to him where she was? "No, I'm at Singing Swans."

"One moment, please." He put her on hold.

Why would he call? None of the scenarios that flitted through her mind eased a mounting concern. She walked around the corner towards the gym, the alcove offering a bit of privacy. Through the window of the gym doors, she saw a half dozen residents in loose t-shirts and khakis doing chair yoga. It looked like the world's easiest workout class.

Finally, the line clicked, and Beaton said, "The coroner's report came in."

Oh God.

"Nurse Oxana's death has been ruled a homicide."

Double Oh God. Amanda slumped against the wall. "Is the coroner sure?" It was a dumb question, she knew, but couldn't help asking.

Beaton grunted. "Jack is the best in town, maybe in the whole country. Doesn't get it wrong." He cleared his throat. "This is a courtesy call."

A puff of laughter escaped Amanda's nostrils. Beaton being courteous? Hang on. Why on earth would he call and disclose this?

"We need to formally interview you. Get fingerprints and DNA."

"Me?" Her adrenalin took a sharp turn north. "Why?"

"Because you were not only at the scene, Miss Sunderson, you were actually on the body." He cleared his throat.

Oh, that. Her pulse throbbed in her neck. She pressed a finger onto the wall, tracing the outline of swans on the wallpaper.

Beaton continued, "Need to match all prints and DNA at the scene. Ensure, for example, that there's been no tampering of evidence."

"I didn't tamper with any evidence." She recalled when Keira, Toni, and her found the bloody hair on her equally bloody smock. Oh wait—she *had* tampered.

Beaton's voice was loud, "You removed a red hair from the scene."

"I did not remove it. It clung to my t-shirt." Amanda leaned against the gym door. The class must be wrapping up since all the participants had moved into Namaste pose. It must be relaxing to do that while seated in a chair, without having to sit on the floor and cross your legs. Realizing that the corridor would soon flood with residents, she felt her agitation spike. "You already have my t-shirt. You have my permission to formally interview it too." Her words had a bite she hadn't intended.

Beaton let out a sigh. "We'll see you soon." The line disengaged.

What the hell did that mean?

Was she supposed to go to the station? No, he would have demanded that. Her resentment swelled. Oh God, he must be coming to Singing Swans to interview her now. She couldn't handle another boardroom investigation with him.

What should she do?

Sal would know.

She raced to the elevator and headed to the third floor. Her knocking was sharp, but there was no answer at Sal's door. Good God, Sal was out more than Amanda was. What did that say about her social life?

Time to check the second floor. It was silly to take the

elevator to travel one measly floor, but there wasn't enough money in the world to get her back into that stairwell. She rode the elevator alone—except for the leviathan of fear. Finally, into the hallway. Check the lounge. Coffee, cookies. No Sal. Check the patio, empty but for the wrought iron furniture and a breeze ruffling some potted petunias.

Back inside. Past Elaine's office, its door closed.

To the Nursing Station. A new nurse on duty. Oxana's replacement? She smiled at Amanda, and a shadow crossed her face. "Miss, are you alright?" The nurse wore oversized glasses and a hint of nervousness, although she might have been picking up on Amanda's own panic.

"I'm, I'm trying to find Sal," Amanda stuttered. "Can I get her phone number?" Did Sal even own a cell phone?

The nurse's nametag said 'Nelly,' and she asked, "Sal? What's the surname?"

Amanda searched her frantic mind for a surname. She realized she didn't know it. "Sorry. Just Sal." She slapped her forehead. Stupid, how could she not know?

"Okay." Nelly seemed to register Amanda's sense of urgency. "I'll look." She unlocked a file cabinet, rifled through a forest of files. "Hard to search by first name." An apologetic smile.

"Room 308." Amanda remembered that much.

"I haven't learned how to search by room number." Nelly knit her brow. "It's my first day."

Terrific.

Nelly glanced sideways at Amanda and sighed. "Y'know, even when I find a phone number, I won't be able to give it to you." She brightened, adding, "But I could call her and ask her to call you."

"That would be great." Amanda needed to reach Sal before Beaton showed up.

Nelly leaned over the filing cabinet, pushed her glasses up her nose, but they slid down again. She kept one hand on them as she rifled through files. "I'm going through each label to check the first initial, S." She pulled one out. "Bowen. Stephen. Nope." She re-inserted the file too slowly for Amanda's racing heart. Another try. "Here's one. Delmont." Nelly threw a shaky smile over her shoulder. "Sandra. Ugh." She returned the file, then walked her fingers across a few more.

A noise from the end of the hall made Amanda snap her gaze in that direction. The stairwell door slammed shut and Nurse Mary offered a wave. Another tickle in Amanda's brain. She hadn't seen Nurse Mary in a long while. Amanda shivered. There were too many weird things going on today. She watched Nurse Nelly still poking her way through the filing cabinet. Had time shifted into slow motion?

"Golly, I found it!" Nelly beamed at Amanda, an open file in her hand. "Falconetti. S." She stood and blinked rapidly, sending her glasses down the slide again. "Oh, you didn't tell me. . ." Nelly used the back of her hand to push her glasses up. "I assumed Sal was short for Sally."

Sure, Amanda thought. Made sense. What else could it be?

"It's not though." She pointed to the top of the chart. "Sal is short for Salvatore."

"Huh?" Amanda couldn't compute. "Her name is Salvatore?"

"Not her, *his*." The nurse pushed her glasses again. "Sal is a man."

A man. Amanda tried to process the information, quickly deciding that she was either having a bad dream or had stepped into an episode of *The Twilight Zone.*

Ping! The sound of the elevator's arrival stole her attention, which turned to alarm when it spat out two police officers.

Amanda raced around the desk, fingers pressed to her lips in a *shhhh* pantomime to Nurse Nelly who stood motionless, eyes wide, open file clutched to her chest. Amanda scurried into the bright exam room, huddling behind the door. There was a murmur, but it was tough to hear anything over the galloping of her heart.

"I said, we can see your shoes, Ma'am." One of the uniforms said, pulling open the exam room door and exposing Amanda who cowered like a trapped deer in a Rocky Mountain autumn. The other uniform, a guy with a swagger, pointed at her. It was a calculated look, the hunter lining up the doe in his telescopic rifle. "Yup, that's her." Satisfaction bloomed on his face.

Every part of Amanda was frozen, except for her lip, which was suffering an involuntary muscle spasm and must have left her looking like Elvis on opioids, as the police escorted her out of the Nursing Station and into the elevator.

Twenty-Two

The rainstorm enshrouded the squad car like a traveling cartoon cloud. Inside, the air was humid, rank. Amanda could feel a bad juju, as if the car held in its custody the negative energy from every criminal it had ever transported. She noticed a spot of something unidentifiable beside her on the cracked vinyl seat and her stomach turned.

Beyond the dirty window, the urban landscape drifted by in a haze. A faint reflection stared back at her. Who was that woman and how did her life get so messed up? Wasn't it enough that she'd lost her number one person? Now she was ensconced in a real—no kidding, actual murder. The glass was cool as she rested her forehead against it, feeling even more alone than her mother's death had left her. Stopping the tears was beyond her control, so she gave into them, steaming up the window in the process.

When the crying jag ebbed, she pulled back and gazed at the filmy window. Soon the condensation would clear, and the reflection would reappear.

Who would be staring back at her?

Hang on.

What was the charge against her, exactly? Surely, she wasn't being arrested for murder. There had been no formal charge, no waving of a warrant, not even a set of handcuffs when the cops came for her. They'd only said that they were to take her to Beaton for questioning.

She slid to the edge of the vinyl seat, tapped on the smeared plexiglass that separated her from the officers in front. One of them slid open the dividing panel. What had he said his name was? Riley. "Ma'am?"

Clearly Riley was a man of few words. Amanda asked, "Do I need a lawyer?"

He shrugged. "Up to you."

She pulled her cell phone from her backpack, grateful that they hadn't confiscated it.

~ ~ ~

Next thing she knew, Amanda was in a sparse office, equipped with a desk, some chairs, a few filing cabinets, and an industrial wall clock. There was no two-way mirror, although she noticed a camera hanging from the ceiling. The main feature was the man seated behind the desk. Beaton. Amanda hated that her first thought was how good he looked, even if his stocky frame was thinner than she'd remembered, and his dark hair seemed to have a few greys.

"Thanks for coming in, Miss Sunderson."

Her anger flared. As if she'd had a choice to come in. A snort erupted from her nose. Simply being in the same room with the man was irritating. A long rumble from her stomach was too loud to hide and she felt her cheeks flush. She hadn't eaten this morning and it was pushing noon.

Beaton smirked. “I’m afraid we have no food to offer, but would you like some water?” He reached for his cane, which rested against the wall. Officer Riley stopped him, volunteering for the task. “I’ll get it, Sir.” He slipped out of the room. Riley might have had a swagger and an attitude when he picked up Amanda, but in front of Beaton he’d downgraded from cowboy to cowpoke.

Beaton settled back into his seat and opened a file folder that held a lot more papers since Amanda had last seen it in the Singing Swans boardroom. “Just a few questions.”

It might be that she was hangry, or it might be the newfound privacy she and Beaton shared, but she snapped, “No, it’s not. You could have asked me *a few questions*” (she inserted a set of air quotes) “over the phone. You knew I was at Singing Swans Lodge, so you could have gone there. This is more than *just a few questions*.” She started coughing. Damn her dry throat and the emotions she tried to stuff down it.

The door sprang open, and Riley returned, handing her a bottle of water. She nodded thanks while patting her chest to calm the coughing fit. She tried to untwist the cap, but it wouldn’t bulge. Why were these things so hard to open? Bloody hell, was the plastic welded together?

A shadow crossed over her. Riley hovered, hand extended. He popped the cap open in one swift snap. “Thank you,” she said, angling her chin high. She saw Beaton watching them, a faint grin spreading across his strong features. She blushed, realizing how her angry tirade, her fleeting moment of power, had been deflated by her inability to open a stupid water bottle.

The desk phone buzzed. Beaton grabbed it, nodded then mumbled, "Ok. Send her in."

Riley took his cue from Beaton and opened the door. A moment later Joyce swept into the room and Amanda experienced such a surge of relief that she flung herself at the poor woman, inhaling a deep draught of Chanel Number 5 and a sense of safety.

Joyce stepped back from Amanda, "I came straight from the office." She pulled off her suit jacket and held it out to Riley. He snapped to attention and took it, but didn't see anywhere to hang it, so he slung it over one arm. Joyce had a way of commanding a room and her entrance shifted the energy, bringing a sense of confidence to Amanda. Joyce winked at her, took the seat Riley offered, then reached a manicured hand into her designer bag and retrieved a cell phone. At 71, the same age that Amanda's mother would have been, she remained beautiful, and could give Catherine Deneuve a run for her money with her smooth complexion (no help from Botox), thick golden hair and regal frame. But her head for business was more impressive than her looks. She turned her gaze to Beaton. "Are you filing charges against Miss Sunderson?"

He hesitated. "Not exactly Ma'am."

The air turned brittle. "Women find the moniker *Ma'am* offensive. I'm Ms. Kinkaid." Joyce narrowed her eyes. "So, this is merely a detainment?"

Amanda reveled in the power that was Joyce.

Beaton cast his eyes downward. "Yes, a detainment."

"And this was fully explained to my client?"

"Of course—" Beaton looked at Riley who stood mute,

holding Joyce's jacket like a mannequin butler.

Riley's eyes widened, and a look of fear crossed his face. "Uh-oh."

Beaton slammed his hand on the desk. "What in hell? His face bloomed a shade of red that might signal a medical emergency. "Riley, you know the drill. It's policing 101!"

The room fell silent.

"Apologies Ms. Kinkaid." Beaton nodded to Joyce, then to Amanda, adding, "Miss Sunderson." He pointed at Riley, staring him down with the focus of a laser beam, then curled his finger ever so slowly. The guy walked the few steps to his superior, looking much like O'Keeffe that time she'd peed on the carpet in front of the Nursing Station.

While Beaton tore a strip off Riley, Joyce pulled her chair alongside Amanda's and shifted from hard-nosed lawyer to gentle godmother. "The police can detain you if they have reasonable grounds to suspect you're connected to a crime they're investigating. You don't have to answer their questions, but it's smart to do so."

Congestion flooded Amanda's sinuses. "But I did nothing wrong." Her chin twitched.

Joyce patted her hand. "I know."

"What am I supposed to s-s-say to them?" Amanda's voice was ragged.

Joyce glanced toward the lecture Beaton was giving his junior. "I suspect that some rules have been broken." She turned her gaze back to Amanda. "Just answer their questions and I'll get you out of here ASAP."

"But it's become a m-m-murder investigation." Hot tears

spilled onto Amanda's cheeks. She turned her face toward Joyce's shoulder, as Riley returned to his post by the door.

A light went on in Joyce's eyes and she called out, "Officer Beaton, how was the nurse's death determined to be a murder?"

Out of her peripheral vision, Amanda saw Riley jerk his head. Beaton glared at his officer for such a long moment that both Amanda and Joyce twisted in their seats to see him. This guy was in big trouble, but Beaton wasn't going to deal with him right now. Instead, he focused on the file in front of him. "Miss Sunderson, which is your dominant hand?" He picked up a pen and pressed its retractor button up and down, as if trying to click away some of his anger.

"I'm right-handed."

Beaton made a check mark on a page. "And how much do you weigh, roughly?" He looked at her and returned to the pen-clicking, creating a sound that Amanda thought might be a form of psychological torture. As if being asked your weight wasn't bad enough. She looked at Joyce, who cocked one perfectly threaded brow.

"About 120 pounds."

Beaton scribbled a few notes, then looked back at the ladies. "Um, there's also the issue of your volunteer smock, t-shirt and the red hair." He tapped his pen against the desk in a rhythm strong enough to set a musical baseline, maybe having tired of his first irritating habit.

"Please explain," Joyce said, leaning forward in her chair. "And stop with the noise."

Beaton did as commanded, fixing his eyes on Amanda. They were nice eyes, Amanda thought, too bad they were attached to his personality. "We'd like you to sign a disclaimer stating that you brought these items to us three days following our interview, having kept them in your sole custody, the entire time." He tapped a piece of paper.

Amanda remembered Beaton and timid McIver, taking O'Keeffe's poop bag into custody, but not her clothes or volunteer smock.

"That is unorthodox," Joyce said.

"Well, you think on it." Beaton extended the paper, but Joyce sat still, not making a move toward it. The two of them engaged in a stare-off.

Tick tock.

The power balance could go either way.

It was Beaton who broke the silence, and Amanda gave the point to Joyce.

He said, "Miss Sunderson, we need to collect your fingerprints, get some photos and DNA swabs."

How quickly the tides of power shifted around here!

Beaton reached for a hard-sided suitcase, opened it, snapped on a pair of latex gloves, and pulled out what looked like a swabbing kit. "Please open your mouth."

It had been a while since a man had said that to her, and never so clinically. He slid his chair so close to her she could feel his body heat. She shot a pleading look to Joyce, who lifted both hands in the air and nodded, a gesture recommending compliance.

Amanda wished she had practiced more meditation, so she was skilled enough to mentally leave her body.

Beaton continued, "You were at the scene, and we must

identify all DNA found on the body." He looked at her, she at him. Then she opened her mouth. He slid closer and inserted the testing swabs.

The ick factor was off the charts. "Id my dod a subec too?" Amanda knew it sounded childish, but it humiliated her having Beaton running the swabs along her inner cheek. It was intimate and awful.

"Pardon me, Ma'am?" He must have seen Amanda's eyes narrow to cat-like slits, and corrected himself, "Amanda." He dropped the swabs into a test tube, capped it, and scribbled on its label.

"I asked if my dog is a suspect too?" She smirked.

Beaton raised a finger and reached for another vial and set of tweezers. "Ah, thank you for the reminder." He swept his gaze over Amanda until he saw something on her t-shirt sleeve. "May I?"

She followed his line of sight and found a few dog hairs clinging to her sleeve.

"You have got to be kidding me."

Beaton dropped the dog hairs into another vial then leaned back in his chair and sighed. "It's unpleasant, I understand." He looked from Amanda to Joyce. "I'm sorry, but this is my job." He put the DNA vials into the case. "We'll have more information after the autopsy report is complete." He squinted at his officer whose face was dewy with sweat. "Riley will escort you to Imaging, for fingerprints and a photo of your hands."

Why did they want a photo of her hands? Amanda held them up, considered that they were nice enough, but not model calibre. No, they must have found handprints at the crime scene. Of course, hers would be among these, the bloody ones near the body, maybe even *on* the body. That was a detail she couldn't pull up.

Beaton checked the clock and scribbled the time on his paperwork, before closing the file. "Thank you for coming in today and co-operating, Miss Sunderson. You can go." He leveled his gaze at her. "Just don't go far."

Did he steal the line from a movie of the week? "What does that mean?" Amanda felt Joyce's hand on her arm, but she ignored it.

"Oxana's family is anxious for us to release the body. We must solve the case before they arrive from Ukraine to collect her." Beaton's look was all business.

A knot began to twist in her stomach. "When do they arrive?"

Beaton held Amanda's gaze. "Don't know for certain. Aiming to wrap this up within two weeks."

Two weeks? Didn't murder investigations take months, even years to solve? How could they rush this when it was Amanda's neck on the chopping block? She thought she might throw up, even if there was nothing but water in her stomach.

She had less than two weeks to prove her innocence, or someone else's guilt.

~~~

At Imaging, Amanda had her electronic fingerprints taken, which was little more than placing her fingers on a screen. The tired-looking police photographer then positioned Amanda's
~~~

hands on a cold gridded slab with rulers inlaid along its four sides. He pulled a monster of an overhead camera into place and snapped her hands from various angles. Once it was done, Amanda knew she'd be put in the police database. What awful possibilities could that lead to? She envisioned her future, routinely being called into police lineups—one of the usual suspects, along with her fellow felons.

Riley escorted them through the *thunk* of the security door, to the main doors of the station. "Good day, ladies." He tipped his cap, holding the door for them. Amanda and Joyce walked in silence until reaching Joyce's Mercedes. The storm had passed, but the air hung heavy as the sun was fighting to shine.

"Can I take you for a drink?" Joyce asked. "I'd love one." She raised both eyebrows, "Besides, I need to hear how you ended up tangled in this mess."

A few blocks away, the marquis of The Jewell Strip club flashed, leg up, leg down. Amanda smirked as she pointed it out to Joyce. "Maybe we should go there. I'm sure it's chock-full of criminals." She raised both hands in the air. "Might as well get to know my own kind."

Joyce punched her car's key fob and the doors unlocked with a *chirp*. "Absolutely not." She ran a finger along the car door. "Today's hijinks must be countered with some elegance." She smiled and nodded to Amanda. "Get in."

Twenty-Three

Joyce had belonged to the Vancouver Club for as long as Amanda could remember. Built in the late 1800s, the Club was one of the oldest buildings in town, dominating a sliver of real estate among the glass and concrete landscape of downtown. It had long been a pillar to the business community, a hub for those determined to move or shake. Amanda wasn't one of them. But she was thrilled every time Joyce took her there. Today, it was just what she needed, she thought, as they swept across the black-and-white tiles of the domed lobby. Despite a stuffy reputation, the place was getting with the times. She'd joined Joyce at a celebrity bartender showdown once and had been beside herself the time the club procured them tickets to a sold-out Lady Gaga concert.

Even the washrooms were elegant, with dim lighting and polished fixtures. Amanda stripped off her smelly t-shirt and wrinkled shorts then wiped herself down with damp paper towels. Changing in washrooms was becoming a new skill and it didn't take long to freshen up. Joyce had magically produced a dress from the trunk of her car, saying she always kept emergency clothes on hand. The dress ensured that Amanda met the dress code, even if the fit was snug. Thankfully, Amanda had put on decent shoes that morning.

She thought back to the morning, which seemed like a hundred years ago. What a difference a few hours make. This morning her optimism had soared, and she was eager to hear what Sal had learned from the residents of Singing Swans Lodge. This morning, she hadn't known that her new friend was transgender, hadn't been taken into police custody, hadn't needed a lawyer to help her out.

Her phone vibrated from the depths of her backpack, and she picked it up to hear Toni shriek, "Jeezus, there are so many sad men out there." She was still wrangling her 147 online admirers. "Listen to this. I booked coffee for Saturday with smoking hot Soccer Dad. He texted back, 'want to meet earlier? I can meet you anywhere I am so board LOL.' He spelled board as if it was a piece of lumber. And I'm ever so flattered you want to meet me to ease your boredom, Dude."

Hearing about Toni's love life was the last thing Amanda wanted to do, but Toni sounded so agitated, she couldn't let her spin out solo.

"Here's another one. 'Must live within a 10-minute drive of Lougheed Mall.' Sure thing buddy, don't want to inconvenience you."

Her friend's words vindicated Amanda's choice to stay off the dating circuit, at least for now. A woman walked into the washroom, smiled as she swanned into a cubicle. Amanda lowered her voice, "How many did you meet?"

Toni paused. "These guys? I haven't eaten any of them and I'm not going to! What are you thinking?"

Amanda stifled a laugh, "Meet, Toni, meet."

"Oh. None. Can you believe these guys?"

"I cannot believe them." Amanda ran a comb through her hair.

"Forgot to tell you the best part—I'm sending you a copy of this text, check it out."

Amanda girded herself for the next excerpt, which was, 'You so hot. why no babies? Unfortunately, we don't seem to be a match. Well maybe if you had babies we would be, single women are so fussy. no wonder you are single. tah tah.'

"That's awful," Amanda snarled. "Who says things like that?"

"Apparently Clean & Jerk 15 does." Toni sighed. "And he does so with atrocious spelling and grammar."

Good thing Toni was a scientist and not an editor, Amanda thought. "I'm sorry you have to endure that kind of talk." She was aware that Joyce would be wondering where she was. "I'm just out to lunch with Joyce. Can I call you later?"

"Oh man, I should have asked what you were up to," Toni said. "No problem. Thanks for listening."

~~~

The Grille was full of people, beautiful people, surrounded by the golden aura of success and money. There was a time in her life when Amanda was heading to that place, but her train had derailed. She thanked the maître-d and dropped into the seat he held for her. Joyce held up the wine list. "Is white ok, Mandy?"

White, red, God almighty, brown wine would have been welcomed at this point. Joyce ordered a Chablis, a pricey one,
~~~

and they settled in. Moments later a waiter appeared with a flourish, and their wine, "Ms. Kinkaid," he nodded at Joyce, then Amanda.

"My Goddaughter, Amanda Sunderson."

"Pleasure." The waiter poured the wine with one arm behind his back and the bottle's label, calligraphed and French, facing the drinker, all in a show of perfect service.

Once the waiter was out of ear-shot Amanda said, "Thank you for introducing me that way."

"With your name?"

"Yes, instead of criminal-at-large." Amanda reached for her wine. "Or murder suspect."

Joyce raised her glass and tapped it against Amanda's. "I don't think you need to worry."

The ring of crystal continued resonating long after the toast was over. Curious as she was to hear Joyce's insight, Amanda was more desperate for the wine, and set her mouth to sipping instead of talking. The icy Chablis was crisp and lemony. Perfect. Once she'd enjoyed another sip, she said, "You will help me understand what in hell just happened, yes?" She held up one hand, spreading her fingers. "I still feel the electric buzz from the fingerprinting." She ran her tongue along the inside of her cheek. "And I still feel where he swabbed me for DNA." She shivered. "It was so degrading."

"Legally, he should have had a warrant or court order to collect prints or DNA." Joyce reached out for her wine, picking up the glass. "But refusing could make things worse for you." The waiter returned, and two leather-backed menus floated onto the linen tablecloth. Once the waiter left, Joyce continued, "For some reason, the police's evidence collection was done improperly, and that's their fault." She glanced at the menu, then pushed it away, before finally sipping her wine.

Amanda had to admire Joyce's level of self-restraint. "Evidence. Meaning my t-shirt and volunteer smock?"

Joyce nodded in affirmation, absent-mindedly running a finger over her strand of pearls. "Crime scene evidence must be processed then and there, by the police. Now the chain of custody is broken."

Images of *CSI Miami* sprang to mind—the proper handling of each piece of evidence, the bad acting, the palm trees and pastels of South Beach—damn she needed a vacation. She forced herself to focus. "I took them into the station as soon as I could, a few days later," she said. "Along with the red hair that clung to my smock." Due to the dead woman's blood on it, Amanda shivered.

"A broken chain of custody is bad for everyone, but especially for the police." Joyce smiled, exposing small perfect teeth. "Tough to make any charges stick with that error." She pointed a finger at Amanda. "Do not sign the disclaimer." She sipped her wine, put the glass down, shook her head. "How in the name of the seven mad seas could Beaton have made that mistake? He's a seasoned officer. A sergeant, I believe." She squinted, saying, "Although I suppose that these days a male officer might be uneasy asking you to remove your smock."

"But his partner was female. Officer McIver." Amanda scanned the lunch menu. Everything looked delicious, but her hunger and pain called out for a solid hit of carbs and fat. Spaghetti Carbonara.

"A female. Really?" Joyce whistled. "Well, then she should have collected them."

"Then their screw up would work in my favor if this ridiculous suspicion against me goes any further?" Amanda fought away images of herself in a provincial-issue jumpsuit, brewing Pruno in a smuggled bedpan.

Joyce ran a finger along the base of her glass. "The court could see it as benevolent, that you voluntarily brought the items in."

She liked the sound of that. *Benevolent Amanda.*

Joyce waved to the waiter who appeared in a nanosecond and took their orders. "Or the court could see it as your manipulating the evidence."

Amanda decided to do a Google search for Pruno recipes as soon as she got home. In the meantime, she would enjoy the Chablis in front of her. She refilled Joyce's glass, then her own, took a luscious sip and savoured the blessed wave of relaxation. She rolled her shoulders and neck, stiff from the day's events. Then she remembered. "Hey, did you catch Riley's gesture when Beaton said he can't reveal the coroner's findings on an open investigation?"

Joyce said, "I remember him yelling at Riley, then sending him away when I asked the question. My goodness, Beaton's face was scarlet. The man needs his blood pressure checked."

"Yes, well, out of the corner of my eye I saw Riley jerk his head. It was creepy. And it made Beaton's anger rise. Again." Amanda recreated the gesture, cupping her right hand under her left jaw then yanking her face.

"Don't snap your neck, heavens to Zeus!" Joyce's voice was

loud enough to attract attention from the handsome businessmen at the next table.

Amanda thought back to landing on Oxana's lifeless body, how the nurse's neck sat at such an unnatural angle. "She didn't break her neck as a result of the fall." She shouted, "Someone snapped her neck!"

A pair of well-suited millennial women stopped mid-conversation to stare at her. The businessmen shot them another series of looks, this time not so kind. Joyce offered a reassuring wave to them.

"My God, they can't think I did it," Amanda said as her fear rose. "I couldn't even open my water bottle."

"Seems an unlikely M.O. for you," Joyce said.

"Especially since I landed in her blood." Amanda shuddered.

Joyce was quiet, a pensive look on her face. "Blood? Hmm. If she bled on the bottom stairwell, she must have been *alive* when she landed there."

"So, she broke her neck as a result of the fall?" Amanda puzzled. "Then it should be ruled an accident."

"But it hasn't been." Joyce tapped a fingernail against her wineglass. "There's obviously information we're not privy to. And can't get."

Amanda sensed that they were on the verge of a big breakthrough. "Who could give us that info?"

"Nobody. Joyce let out a long exhale. "Beaton won't give anything up. And the preliminary autopsy results can't be shared with anyone except police or next of kin. Even then, the findings are not considered final until the Coroner's Report is issued."

"Only the police and the coroner know?" Amanda had narrowed her options.

"Correct. The police can't and won't say." Joyce laughed, continuing, "And it's not as if you can drop into the morgue and ask questions."

Drop into the morgue and ask questions. The echo bounced around in her head until the waiter set down a steaming bowl in front of her, the heady aroma shifting her focus. "Enjoy, Miss Sunderson." He put a plate of salad topped with a salmon filet in front of Joyce. "Your usual, Ms. Kinkaid."

Amanda dove into her meal, relishing every bite of smoky bacon, creamy egg sauce and al dente pasta. The meal was like breakfast and lunch combined in lusciousness, she thought, twirling it around the silver fork. The rest of the world fell away in those few minutes. She was so focused on eating that she didn't notice the stares from Joyce, who watched her ravenous Goddaughter while she nibbled her salad at half the speed. It didn't take long before Amanda reached the bottom of her bowl. "That was amazing."

Joyce, barely halfway through her meal, wore a look of amusement as she raised a hand. The waiter arrived instantaneously, wafting a dessert menu before Amanda as he removed the bowl that she'd scraped clean. "Glad you enjoyed," Joyce said. "Please have dessert. You're looking thinner than usual." She set her fork on the plate and leaned toward Amanda. "Have you given any thought to selling the condo? When you're ready, I can line up some realtors. The market is strong, but I doubt it will slow anytime soon." She tucked into her salmon.

The carb and Chablis buzz that Amanda was enjoying vanished at Joyce's words. She slumped in her chair. The good thing about finding a dead body, learning that your new friend Sal is really Salvatore, then nearly being detained in a murder investigation, is that it takes your mind off other troubles. Say, for example, your mother's estate and its endless executor tasks, and the condo sitting empty collecting dust and tax bills. Joyce awakened their memory and Amanda's dread bloomed.

Joyce's fork stopped mid-air, and she looked at Amanda with concern. "What?" Amanda pushed the dessert menu away, took a big inhale and slowly let it out. She could rise above her panic. She took another sip of wine then, with a calm that surprised her, she told Joyce all about the disastrous sprinkling of the ashes, her screw ups with Fight and Flight and the suspension at Timely Temps, the Sal/Salvatore story, her failed attempts at finishing any executor tasks, how Toni's man craziness was making her crazy. . .

Joyce took it all in before asking, "Why didn't you tell me?"

"I couldn't handle it." Amanda hadn't realized she'd been holding her breath as she released a long exhale. "Could barely keep moving one foot in front of the other."

Joyce pursed her lips and whistled. "That is a lot." She leaned across the table and took Amanda's hands into her own. "Mandy, it might just be the wine talking, but I think we need to order some more wine."

Twenty-Four

As the elevator doors closed, Amanda knew she'd made a mistake. But it was too late. She was descending into the bowels of the hospital. Visions of bowels, then limbs, then whole bodies, dead bodies, flooded her thoughts. Her flight instinct kicked in, making her claustrophobic in the tight space.

What the hell was she doing?

Her heart had reached turbo speed by the time the elevator doors opened, and she stepped into the basement. A sign confronted her, pointing left for Janitorial, right for City Morgue. A chill passed through her, even though the air wasn't cold. She tried to regain the calm she held when she had approached the front doors of Vancouver General Hospital minutes earlier.

You're already here. Just find Coroner Jack.

She envisioned an old-school pathologist. Jack, the kinda guy who smoked cigars, kept a bottle of whiskey in his desk. He'd slice up a body, eat a sandwich, then crack the case. Beaton had called Jack the best in the country, although she had no idea how many coroners there were in the country. Was Jack the best of ten, a hundred, a thousand?

She'd told nobody of her plan. Joyce, Toni, or Keira would

have tried to stop her or called her crazy, a label she was starting to consider quite possible. On the other hand, Sal would have jumped at the chance to snoop around the City Morgue, without being the wuss Amanda was.

Yesterday, at the Vancouver Club, she'd talked through the Sal / Salvatore issue with Joyce. Getting it all out had helped, even if they got sloppy from the wine. Joyce had reminded her that she and Sal had a very new friendship. "People don't give up their secrets in the honeymoon phase, Mandy." She'd had to agree. Besides, Joyce had presented another angle, how brave Sal was to live an authentic life. Joyce had struck a chord with that, pointing out the fact that people could be anyone they want to be today, could even change genders. "But 30 years ago, it wasn't an option." Joyce had raised her glass to that, adding, "My heavens, just 10 years ago it wasn't."

Man or woman, secretive or not, it was Sal who Amanda wanted now. What did her gender matter? She was still Sal, the one who'd support her, cheer her on. A little encouragement would be nice right now. She had to find out why Oxana's death was being investigated as a murder, not an accident.

The sign for the City Morgue continued pointing to the right. Amanda turned in that direction, telling herself that she could do this. She had to. Her very freedom was at stake.

Her plan was to find out how this Coroner Jack had decided that Oxana's death was not an accident. Murder seemed unbelievable. Sure, the woman had been unlikeable, but nobody got killed because they were disagreeable. Well, rarely, anyhow. If they did, most of the human population would be either murder victims or murderers.

She forced herself towards the morgue, dreading what she might find. Police dramas flashed through her mind: interior windows with a view to a corpse. *Can you identify the body Ma'am?* Cavernous rooms filled with refrigerated cupboards full of cadavers. Cavernous cadaver caves. Oh God, the thought shook her. She reached out a hand to steady herself against the wall. A few deep breaths helped. She was being hare-brained. All that was made up for television. Surely the gruesome things were kept hidden from public view.

The door marked VGH & City Morgue had a window, through which Amanda could see the reception room. A few chairs, a row of filing cabinets, a large desk. Nothing ominous here. She stretched a sleeve to cover her hand and reached for the doorknob. Odds were that they brought in the dead bodies through a back door, but it seemed smart to be careful anyway. As she opened the door a faint whiff of formaldehyde greeted her. The place was empty and deathly quiet. A cardigan hung over the receptionist's chair. Stacks of files stood perfectly aligned. A clean mug, decorated with the outline of a body and the caption 'I'd kill for a coffee', sat on the desk. Were they closed for lunch? She checked the time—11 am, too early.

A loud *clunk* in the distance made her jump. She shouldn't have let the calm reception area lull her into a sense of safety. She was at the morgue for God's sake! The temporary resting place for—an image of her mother, the last image Amanda held—flashed, and she struggled to push it away. Thinking of her frail mother taking her last breath made her heart race. Adrenalin flooded her system. She backed up to the door, fumbling for the knob with icy hands, and threw it open. A red glow promising 'Exit' was an obvious sign from the heavens. She ran to it, pushed through a fire-door, raced up a set of stairs, then another. She was so close to freedom she could almost taste the summer air that wafted in through an open door.

Hallelujah!

The adrenalin was still pumping when she pushed the door, far harder than necessary, and stumbled over something. A small wedge of wood skittered onto the concrete landing and bounced down the exterior steps. But she didn't care, here was fresh air, green trees, living things!

"Don't!" A squawk as the door slammed shut. The woman had short salt and pepper hair, a pasty skin-tone and was clutching her lab coat at the throat. She threw her cigarette to the pavement and a sizzle of sparks exploded. "Christ on a crutch!" She stomped on the butt with one sensible-looking shoe. "Now I have to go all the Goddamn way to the main entrance to get back in," she screamed. "Thank you very much!" With that final wallop of sarcasm, the woman turned on her rubber-soled heels.

Amanda, her back collapsed against the closed door, continued to suck in deep breaths, but she did catch a glimpse of the name embroidered on the white coat as the woman left in a huff. *Dr. Jackson.* Could this be the Jack she'd come to see?

Oh hell. If that was Jack, they were off to a terrible start.

Twenty-Five

"Then there was Jacques from Quebec. Really into old-school romance, flowers and poetry and stuff." Toni ripped her croissant apart and a buttery flake flew into her spiked hair, a speck of yellow landing in a nest of black.

Maybe it was the fact that the week had broken into the weekend, or the warmth of the sun on her face, but Amanda felt like a different person today. It was a good thing she'd kept her plan to meet Toni.

She needed a break from her life.

They sat on the sprawling wooden deck of Café Milo's, overlooking the park that gave way to the city skyline and North Shore mountains. She sipped her designer mocha, pointed to the new accessory in Toni's hair and guided her in retrieving it.

"Thanks," Toni mumbled, letting the crumb fall to the deck before stuffing the croissant into her mouth.

"So, Quebec Jacques. A little old-school romance sounds good." Amanda shrugged. What did she know? She was about as romantic as a placemat, the vinyl kind you can easily wipe clean.

"The date was okay, I guess, until the end, when he kissed me." Toni stopped chewing, some croissant hanging from her lips. "I say kissed, but it was more like a lizard unfurling its tongue into my mouth and wriggling it around in search of insects." She scowled, "His breath smelled like death."

"That's nasty, and I don't mean in the good Hillary Clinton way." It wasn't just the lizard image that made Amanda queasy. The corporeal description reminded her of what she might have encountered at the morgue if she hadn't bailed out. Disappointment in herself flickered, along with the worry that she'd blown any future chance to get information from the coroner. She reached out and tore off a piece of Toni's croissant, stuffing it in her mouth. No way was she ready to tell Toni about the fiasco at the morgue.

Toni paused before saying, "But the days of lame-ass men might be over. I've seen this one man a few times." Her black-coated lips curled into a grin. "Even fooled around a bit." She took in the look on Amanda's face. "Oh, don't judge me."

"Sorry, can't help it, it's my face." Poker faces weren't Amanda's strong suit.

"Anyway, we have a special date tonight, an elegant dinner." Toni pulled out her phone and punched in her pass code. "Normally, I'd say he's not my type, but. . ." She swiped through a few photos. Amanda could see they were profiles on her dating platform. "Here he is. Be open-minded, Mands," she held the phone out.

"Hmm." She took a closer look. "Didn't think you went for older men."

Toni sipped her tea. "I know, but he's really been pursuing me. Sending a lot of sweet messages. Plus, he's nice to be with." She held out her phone. "Check out his pictures, they're kind of cool."

The guy wore a tuxedo well. There were shots of him in various European cities, posed around a massive dinner table with what looked to be kids and grandkids, capturing him laughing it up with friends. "Well, he seems to have a sense of humor. That's always a plus." Amanda inspected a photo featuring an elderly woman. "And it's good to find a man who loves his mother." She squinted. "The woman must be a hundred."

"Ninety-five. Here's the weirdest part," Toni took the cell phone from Amanda's hand and gave her a pointed stare. "He's rich." She spread her hands wide. "And I don't mean a solid retirement fund or expensive home rich. I mean *rich rich*. Look." She scrolled to the profile text: 'My friends warned me I shouldn't say I'm a gazillionaire because I'll attract the wrong type of women. LOL.'

Amanda said, "Well, you're no gold-digger."

"No, maybe that's why he's interested."

"Gazillionaire, huh? That sounds like a lot."

Toni licked her finger and scraped the last few crumbs off her plate. "It's one million more than a fazillionaire."

Amanda shifted her gaze. In the park across the street, a guy threw a frisbee to his black lab. The dog raced alongside it, his tongue hanging out the side of his mouth, ears flapping in the chase. A dog was the perfect companion, Amanda thought. Or was it? The familiar void in her middle re-opened, threatening to pull her in as it had been doing since her mother died. She turned back to her friend. "So, where's he taking you on this date?"

"He said, anywhere I want." Toni spread her hands in

jubilation. "We're going to Le Crocodile."

Amanda smiled. "Good for you." Then, a flash of memory. She'd taken her mother there to celebrate her 65th birthday. The food was rich and delicious, in old French tradition, but it was so expensive that her mother ended up footing the bill. They had a great laugh over that, all stuffed with butter and cream and Pernod. It had been the perfect evening.

It seemed like yesterday.

It seemed a lifetime ago.

"Mands, your face is funny. What's up?" Toni said.

"Nothing. All good." Amanda tapped Toni's arm. "I'm happy for you." She couldn't help but long to have some happy for herself. Something other than police interrogations, a terrifying visit to the morgue, and friends who weren't transparent.

"Listen to me, going on about myself. Sorry," Toni said, pushing her plate aside. "And I'm sorry for what Officer Beefcake has put you through, hauling you to the station and collecting your prints and DNA." She patted Amanda's hand. "It's all routine. Standard operating bullshit. Nobody thinks you're a killer."

Amanda looked back towards the park, feeling her anxiety ratchet up, despite Toni's attempts to comfort her. She thought of the ticking time bomb that Beaton had tucked under her like Wile E. Coyote when he announced Oxana's family was coming to collect the body. She could nearly hear the *meep meep!*

What the hell was she doing enjoying the sun and eating croissants when she had a mere two weeks to prove she wasn't a murderer?

"Is there something else, Mands?"

Amanda nodded, her twitching knee rattling the table, then launched into the story of the revelation of Sal's true identity.

"Woah!" Toni's piercings shook. "Sal isn't Sally but Salvatore!" She tapped a silver ring against her mug. "Wow. I don't know what to say. How do you feel?"

"Stupid." Amanda grunted. "I know I'm bad with men, but not even being able to identify them is a new low for me." She pushed her hair behind her ears. "Looking back, I should have noticed: the Adam's apple, the thick makeup and that terrible fashion sense."

"Sort of a Mrs. Doubtfire type?" Toni asked.

"Yes, now that you mention it." Amanda sat up straight. "I know we just met, and she doesn't owe me any explanations, but we've been through so much already." She shrugged. Who knew that murder investigations could be so bonding?

"She might have the don't-ask-don't-tell mentality." Toni scratched her neck for a second. "Look, I get that this threw you for a loop, but I gotta say Mands, this isn't something that would usually get you all emo."

Amanda swept croissant crumbs off the table. She thought about the grief, fatigue, and the unbelievable events of the past few weeks. Had all that made her overly sensitive?

"You've been through a lot of crazy shit in the past month." Toni drained the rest of her tea. "Nobody would blame you for acting a bit cray cray."

She let that settle in. "I guess."

"I mean, unbelievable stuff." Toni's dark brows arched. "Somebody should write a movie about it."

"Finally, I'd get a starring role." Amanda smiled, winking at Toni. "Let's go, you've got a date to get ready for." She couldn't recall the last time she'd told herself those same words.

Twenty-Six

It was the first certified dog visiting shift for Amanda and O'Keeffe. Mai welcomed them, handing over ID badges with their laminated photos. Amanda draped the lanyard, which also held the fob for the stairwell that she'd never use, over her new smock. She signed into the Visitor Log with their official title, 'dog visitation team'. Even O'Keeffe had a look of pride on her face. Mai allowed them to leave their bags behind the desk, but not before Amanda grabbed a copy of their certificate for Elaine, saying, "C'mon, Girl. Time to spread doggie cheer."

Since hashing out the story with Joyce then Toni, Amanda felt better about the situation with Sal. In fact, she was itching to share recent events. New clues she'd figured out in the game of broken telephone. About that awful call where Beaton had confirmed Oxana's death was a murder. The part where she got hauled into a police cruiser and taken into detainment. Oh, how the good times had rolled!

O'Keeffe lapped up praise and affection from residents as Amanda made her way to the second floor where they found Elaine in the hallway. The manager looked terrible. Her face was pale and slack, and her power suit hung on a frame that looked ten pounds thinner. Amanda tried to hide her shock, but Elaine picked up on it. “I know, I look terrible,” Elaine said then bent to stroke O’Keeffe, “Can dis girl make Lainey better?” She got on her knees and let the dog swirl around her legs, working her canine magic. “Yes, dis doggie makes everything better!” When she stood up and met Amanda’s gaze, there were tears in her eyes. She pointed Amanda towards her office.

“Sorry you didn’t make it to Hawaii,” Amanda said.

Elaine slumped as she walked. Pretty soon she’d be dragging her knuckles on the carpet. “Thanks.” She sighed. “Thank Heavens I had cancellation insurance is all I can say. Don’t think I could handle one more hit.”

They squeezed into the compact office. Elaine shut the door then launched into a frenzied monologue. “I want to apologize for that horrible meeting with Officer Beaton. I had no idea what he had planned, he briefed me seconds before you walked into the boardroom. I was stunned. Of course, nobody here thinks you pushed Oxana down the stairs!” She shook her head as she paced the room, at one-point tripping on O’Keeffe who’d stretched out for a rest, her long frame taking up half the width of the office. “I’m sorry love!” Elaine apologized with some ear-scratching. “You’re so long, like a loaf of dog.” O’Keeffe rolled onto her back, splayed her legs, and allowed Elaine the privilege of rubbing her tummy.

“I appreciate the apology, but it wasn’t your fault,” Amanda said then set the certificate on Elaine’s desk. “I brought you this, to make it official.” She noticed a stack of papers, one letter with a flourish of letterhead announcing, *Barristers at Law.*

In one swift move, Elaine swept the stack of papers aside and put the dog certification on the top. “Congratulations! I’ll put it in your file." Elaine gave an awkward smile. "Aside from that confronting meeting with the police, we've had to deal with the fallout from Oxana's *incident*." She whispered the word, then resumed pacing around the small space. "Two applicants canceled their plans to move in. Oxana's family is demanding answers that I don't have. . . I've had to do things," she slapped her hand over her mouth, dropping into her chair.

Amanda plunked the dog in Elaine's lap. O'Keeffe soothed Elaine by licking her hand, while Amanda gingerly attempted a few questions. When Elaine wouldn't say more about the "things she'd done," Amanda asked whether the news of Oxana's death had been leaked to any broadcasters.

"We tried to keep the story out of the news," Elaine said, "But it was a losing battle." She shook her head, adding, "Gossip is a top hobby around this place."

So, there was a leak to the news, but when? "I need to know when the press announced that the death was a murder."

Elaine sighed. "Well, Officer Beaton confirmed that it was a murder three days ago." She shuddered, shaking her head as if to dislodge that awful truth. "Before that I think that all coverage simply called it a death."

"And does Singing Swans have a public relations department?"

"You're looking at it," Elaine said, raising a hand in the air, before returning to petting the dog.

~ ~ ~

Minutes later the dog visitation team left Elaine's office to get down to the business of visiting. They'd invested in this gig, and it would be good for them both. But as soon as they stepped into the hallway, O'Keeffe tugged the leash so hard that a jolt tore through Amanda's shoulder socket. It was Sal, her masculine frame tented in a floral house dress, her cheeks rouged the colour of an overripe watermelon. She looked as though she'd stepped out of a British pantomime.

Amanda's stomach clenched. She dropped the leash and let O'Keeffe charge ahead, threatening to knock Sal over.

"Sausage Roll! I've missed you!" Sal bent down as the dog made figure eights through her legs.

Why did Amanda feel so flustered?

"My Dear, it's been Yonks since I've seen you!" Sal's voice sure was deep. She folded Amanda into a soft but awkward hug. Her back sure felt broad. Amanda's heart melted just a little at seeing her friend, but then again, she remained guarded.

"I have missed you both," Sal met her eyes with a gaze so direct and open that Amanda knew she was oblivious to Nurse Nelly having exposed her secret. Either that or Sal was an Academy Award level actor.

"I hear you both passed doggie training. Fetes and fireworks!" Sal seemed so happy, but Amanda's lack of reaction changed that fast. "What is it? What's wrong?"

Amanda's fingers itched for something to do. What the hell was wrong with her? She reached into her bag for a bottle of water then shifted her gaze to O'Keeffe, who was a welcome distraction. "Here Girl, have a drink." She unscrewed the water bottle, poured some into the curve of her unsteady hand and let the dog slurp it. The pink tongue tickled her hand. "Good pup."

“I wondered where you’d gotten to this past week.” Sal’s tone had grown cautious. “I never passed along my number to you.”

Oh, the guilt—Amanda knew what Sal knew but Sal didn’t know that she knew!

Amanda needed to get this over with. She wiped the leftover water from her palm onto her jeans, stood and looked at Sal. Then she saw it: the hint of an Adams apple, the coarseness of the facial features, the outrageous height and width, the love of floral fabrics — how could she have missed such obvious clues?

She stuttered, “I. I . . .” as her nerve drained out through her fingers and toes. She tried to say the words, but they were a wad of cotton in her mouth. *Sal, I know you’re a man.*

Nothing but a puff of air came out.

Twenty-Seven

Sal steered Amanda and O'Keeffe into the semi-privacy of the second-floor lounge. A coffee station stood near the door. A man read a newspaper by the window. A few people watched the local news on a gigantic tv screen. The anchorman's drone filled the room, "The man has been missing for two weeks having left Alberta for BC to get work in the trucking industry." A teary woman appeared on the screen, pleading for her husband to call home.

Amanda had her own drama to deal with so led them away from the roar of the television to the far corner. She chose a massive chintz wingback and sank into its depths. Sal joined her, two cups in her hands, and perched on the edge of a companion chair, saying, "I see that the penny has dropped." She extended a cup of coffee.

The gentle tone comforted Amanda—that was her Sal. As she relaxed, she sunk further into the chair and had to grab the armrests to sit up. "Why is this so big? A resident could go missing in one of these!" Finally, Amanda was upright enough to safely take the cup from Sal, who gazed at her with kind eyes.

It was time to talk.

"Why is that filthy mutt in here?" Scowly Orthotics called

out from the doorway. Her tight curls, walker, and Frankenstein boots were backlit from the glow in the hallway, transforming her into a creepy surreal image. She started to make her way towards Amanda and O'Keeffe.

"I'm betting it'll take her ten minutes to reach us." Sal took a deep breath. "My Dear, I said nothing because—" She swept a beefy hand in the air, one that outlined the full picture from the top of her silver do, over the antiquated housedress to the shoes big enough for a circus clown. "It's so obvious."

The unabashed showcasing made Amanda smile.

"At my age, there are very few hormones that my doctors will allow." Sal pulled up one sleeve, revealing coarse dark hair on her forearm. "Like I said, obvious." She crinkled her forehead, pressing foundation into the creases. "How did you finally—"

"Nurse Nelly." Amanda sipped her coffee.

Sal nodded. "Ah, nervous Nelly. No wonder she's been so dodgy around me lately. Poor lamb."

"Poor confidentiality-breaking lamb, who caused a whole lot of trouble."

"Yes, well she is new." Sal twisted her face. "And she does seem a bit screwy." She bit into a cookie. "I'm sorry you found out that way, but I take some time to fess up. And as I said, isn't it all rather clear? I mean really my Dear, look at these ham-hocks." She held out her hands. "Hormones taken late in life can only do so much."

Amanda laughed, a blessed sense of relief sinking in, even as the clunk of Scowly's walker grew closer.

"No matter. I'm still *me,*" Sal said.

"You are."

"Waited my whole life to live my truth."

"I'll tell you the truth," Scowly Orthotics had finally arrived beside them, barking, "I'm reporting you to the police." She pointed at O'Keeffe, who stood, tail wagging, neck stretching out to sniff the angry woman. "You don't belong here."

Amanda held up the dog's ID badge, saying, "Actually, she does." She nodded at O'Keeffe then flipped to her own ID photo. "So do I." She stood and extended a hand. "Amanda and O'Keeffe. Nice to meet you, Mrs. . ."

Scowly sniffed the air, muttered something under her breath, then began the tedious process of turning her walker around. Amanda shot a wink to Sal and rose to help the woman, who immediately shooed her away.

When Amanda sat again, Sal said, "Well done you."

"I'm glad you're living your truth. Proud even." Amanda sighed, adding, "Sorry I pulled away."

"I'm used to it. Not my first rodeo, you know." Sal nibbled her cookie. "Besides, you have had a few things going on, my Dear."

"Thanks for being gracious about it." Amanda said, as O'Keeffe plunked herself atop Sal's shoes.

"I see that the Sausage Roll fully accepts me." Sal snuck the rest of her cookie to the salivating dog, then produced another one from the inside of her sleeve. Before biting into it, she looked at Amanda. "I do hope you are fine with this. I have quite enjoyed getting to know you."

"Me too." Amanda patted Sal's hand. "But we have work to do because our little investigation project has become serious.

Oxana's death has been ruled a homicide."

"Great Scott!" Sal bolted upright in her chair. "Tell me everything."

Finally, Amanda had her chance to debrief Sal, and it was a relief to unburden herself. Sal listened intently, except for the occasional interjection, *that man—we should call him Officer Beaston! The morgue—what a thrill! Jiminy, I wish I had my notebook.*

When Amanda finished, Sal stood. "That is quite the yarn. Come with me to retrieve my notebook." She led the way. "We've got some muckraking to do."

~~~

The trio stepped into the hallway when a voice called out from the Nursing Station. "Yoo-hoo, Amanda, a wee something for you!" Nurse Mary's chubby face flushed as she waved an envelope in the air.

"Mary, are you delivering the mail now?" Sal asked as they approached the desk.

"Aye no, but it was left right here for you." She passed the envelope over, then bent to greet the dog who was sniffing the nurses' desk within an inch of its life. After a quick hello to the dog, Mary patted her scrubs pocket and smiled, saying, "Rounds to do. Too-da-loo!" She scooped up a stack of charts and scuttled off.

A standard business envelope had 'Amanda' typed on it. She pulled out a folded sheet of paper pasted with words cut out of a glossy publication. The text was black on white, and the
~~~

background featured bold splashes of red.

'Wake Up losers!

Don't become fucking Vegetables

Save Yourself or take some pounding

STOP Now'

Odd how the paper was moving, Amanda thought, until she realized her hands were shaking. Her jaw slackened and her mouth fell open.

Sal watched her. "Love letter?"

She extended the quaking note, muttering, "Not quite."

Sal took the letter, holding it close to her face then telescoping it away until finally giving in to the reading glasses that hung around her neck. Amanda watched her face as she read, saw it shift from puzzlement to shock. "My, my, such colourful language."

"Is this. . ." Amanda's throat closed over her words.

"A threat?" Sal tapped a finger against the page. "Most definitely, my Dear." Her finger traced over the cut-out words. "Loosely translated, this is a warning to stop or he will render us into vegetative states."

Goosebumps prickled Amanda's arms. "That's horrible." O'Keeffe, sensing a problem, came and stood guard at their feet.

"The grammar certainly is." Sal folded the letter. "Quite the twist isn't it—someone warning us to stop snooping."

Amanda sagged against the Nursing Station.

Sal tapped Amanda's shoulder as if to comfort her, then folded the letter and stuffed it into her bosom. "I'll keep it safe right here. Beside my gym socks."

Twenty-Eight

"W-w-who would do such a thing?" Amanda stammered as they made their way to Sal's suite. O'Keeffe delighted in the hallway, sniffing at the crack under each resident's door as if they held ancient mysteries she needed to decode.

"The killer, my Dear," Sal said, clomping beside them.

"I still can't believe it's a m-m-murder."

They stopped outside of 308 as Sal reached into the depths of her pocket. "It is, according to the police." She put a hand on Amanda's shoulder, adding, "And I think it's high time you accept that little chestnut."

O'Keeffe's tail thumped against the wall in excitement. Amanda imagined her thoughts: *A new place! I get to go in!* Amanda wiped the back of a shaky hand across her nose. "How would anyone know we've been snooping?"

"Ace question." Sal unlocked the door and pushed it open. "Come in. Welcome to my humble abode."

Sunlight, from a wide expanse of windows, flooded the suite. Amanda tightened her grip on the dog leash that strained in her hand. "O'Keeffe, sit." The dog hunched in a half-sit and Amanda knew she'd have to settle for that. Once Amanda's eyes adjusted to the brightness, she took in the simple elegance of the place. The main area was an open layout: kitchenette, dining area, living room, with a door to a balcony. Off to one side was a bathroom with a stacked washer dryer, then a good-sized bedroom. The furnishings were classic. "What a nice place." Amanda turned back toward the door, alarmed at what she saw. "But what the hell is that?"

A Bristol board hung on the wall. Bits of paper were taped to it: some held Sal's handwritten notes, others were crude sketches. Pushpins pierced the board, coloured yarn linking them. At the centre was an amateur drawing of a woman against a set of stairs, neck crooked, red shading around her head. Below the board was a table with a selection of cookies, assorted teas, and an electric kettle. Sal stood beside it, pride glowing on her face. "I call it the investigation station. All the tv detectives use them."

"Wow. Very professional."

"We'll build on it," Sal said with a shrug. "Snack?"

"Water, please."

"Coming right up." Sal pointed to the dining area, "Take a seat." A vase of lilies rested atop a lace tablecloth. Amanda sat and soon Sal put a glass of ice water in front of her, saying, "Let Sausage Roll explore. She can't get into any trouble here."

"I think she might be able to get into trouble anywhere," Amanda said, unclipping the dog's leash, and hoping for the best. O'Keeffe sprinted to the kitchenette where she snuffled the corners for crumbs and licked the floor in a few spots.

"Where did I put my notebook?" Sal scanned the tidy room, sifted through some magazines on the glass coffee table then snapped her fingers. "On my nightstand." She headed into the bedroom, O'Keeffe in close pursuit. They were in there for mere seconds when Sal said, "How did you get that open?" The dog bounded out of the bedroom, a red feather boa in her mouth, a grin on her face.

"Drop it!" Amanda shouted and the dog happily disobeyed, letting her mistress chase her and the trailing boa around the coffee table, behind an easy chair, around the dining table and into the bathroom, where Amanda cornered her and wrestled it from her jaws. Damp boa in hand, Amanda walked into the bedroom, which held a queen-sized bed littered with animal-print pillows. "Sorry about that, Sal."

"No problem. She's not a bad gumshoe, that dog. Uncovered my secret pronto." Sal pointed to the gaping closet. Half of it held her everyday clothes: floral housedresses, gaudy tunics, and a few bright muumuus. Wedged in the corner were dark suits and a trench coat that looked distinctively male. But the rest of the closet was a cornucopia of sequins, feathers, and fur, straight out of *RuPaul's Drag Race*.

Amanda slapped one hand over her mouth then held out the boa to Sal.

Sal gasped. "Oh, me oh my, have I shocked you?"

"Nope," Amanda spit out the word, along with a rally of laughter strong enough to give her a stitch in her side. "Ouch, ouch, but you sure entertained me." She clutched her belly, struggling to get a breath.

"Well, my Dear, I may no longer be *in* the closet, but that doesn't mean I don't *have* one." Sal winked and wrapped the boa around her neck, saying, "Let's get to work." She shook two notebooks in the air and headed to the dining table, where

Amanda joined her. Sal pushed a notebook and pen across the table. "From petty cash. We can compare notes. You start."

Sal had labeled her notebook, *The Case of the Murdered Nurse who Everyone Hated.* Clearly, she had known that Oxana's death was a murder long before Amanda did. Had Amanda been stupid or merely in denial? She pulled Essie's *Incredibles* colouring book notes from her backpack and began. "In our last meeting—"

"Tuesday. Oak Lounge. Present: you, me, O'Keeffe," Sal read from her notes. "Details: you had a peanut butter cookie and I had a gingersnap."

"Relevance?"

Sal glanced up to the ceiling, her jowls shaking ever so slightly, and then drew a line through the cookie description. "Notes: we established a line of questioning based on what Officer *Beaston* said in the boardroom." She reveled in the malapropism.

Amanda screwed up her face. "Right, when he fingered me as a suspect—"

Both of Sal's silver eyebrows rose, and she stifled a smile.

"Okay, poor choice of words," Amanda said.

"Or was it your Freudian slip showing?"

"No." Amanda shook her head. "Beaton *pointed* at me as a suspect." She ran a finger over a drawing of Elastigirl. "Broken telephone clue number one: Beaton heard that me and Oxana were in a duel."

"We sorted out that that was *duo* misheard as *duel*."

"Right. Since you and I had just met, I assume the duo referred to me and O'Keeffe. I was too stunned to ask who said it."

"Stunned or smitten?" Sal said, sliding the boa back and forth against her neck, mischief in her eyes. She'd probably start humming a porn theme soon.

"Please stop." Amanda took a glug of water. "Broken telephone clue number two: Beaton said that several people thought I had a breakdown. He admitted it was Mrs. Hyde-Bowles who told him that." She tapped her notes and said with pride, "Here's my deduction." Amanda told Sal about meeting Lillian, who was having a martini in the Long Neck Pub. "That would look like me taking a break, and it was downstairs. Mrs. Hyde-Bowles must have heard 'breakdown' and that's what she told someone else."

Sal checked her notes, saying, "Haven't questioned her yet."

That disappointed Amanda, who'd hoped to have confirmation from Mrs. Hyde-Bowles. "Okay," she continued, "Beaton heard that I pushed Oxana from the second level of stairs, and it was no accident." She pursed her lips, adding, "That's when I checked for cameras. Figured I was being pranked, which now seems ridiculous because that man doesn't have a funny bone in his body."

Sal stifled another laugh. "Bone."

Amanda stared her down.

"My apologies."

"I wrangled it out of him that it was Mrs. Pendergrass who offered up that tidbit. So, she must have misheard what Mrs. Hyde-Bowles said as 'down the stairs.' Someone could easily assume that meant 'pushed down the stairs.' What did she say in your interview?"

"I didn't exactly interview Pendy—"

"You only had two people to question. What have you been doing?" Amanda knew her voice was sharp, but she was frustrated.

Sal pointed at the wall behind her, saying, "The investigation station has been a grand amount of work." She shifted in her chair. "And, in all fairness, I *went* to question Pendy but her display of knitting yarn got me thinking about how to improve the investigation board."

Amanda narrowed her eyes. Why bother to hide her annoyance? "What kind of detective are you?"

"No time like the present," Sal said, pushing back her chair. "Let's give Mrs. Hyde-Bowles a visit." Her feather boa slid along one shoulder. She looked at it sadly, adding, "Guess I should leave this behind," She unfurled it and placed it lovingly on the table.

~~~

"Now I lay me down to sleep, I pray the Lord my soul to keep." They found Mrs. Hyde-Bowles on her knees by her single bed, the door to her studio suite wide open. Her petite frame was draped in a flannel dressing gown. "If I should die before I wake. . ."

Amanda nudged Sal, signaling that they should leave, but Sal held up a finger to suggest they wait, whispering, "Nap time." Mrs. Hyde-Bowles' pause left Amanda thinking the woman had fallen asleep mid-prayer.

"I pray He takes me like an earthquake."
~~~

Amanda sputtered a laugh. Sal cocked her head, murmuring, "Not a bad way to go."

Mrs. Hyde-Bowles twisted around in slow motion, her face crinkling into a smile. "Oh, hello Sal. Hello friends." She reached out a hand, and Amanda scooted over to help her get up. "I couldn't remember the rest of the prayer and, well, I found something that rhymed!" She sat on the edge of her bed, patted her blanket. "Time for my Afternooner." O'Keeffe snuffled Mrs. Hyde-Bowles slippers, enjoying a few shaky pats.

"Is it okay if we ask you a few questions?" Amanda asked. "We'll be quick."

"I suppose so. Did you want to talk about the war? Or my husband?" Her rheumy eyes held a faraway look. "Usually, the only things people ask about." She pointed to two occasional chairs, inviting her visitors to sit.

"Thank you," Amanda said. "It's about the investigation of Nurse Oxana's death." She and Sal sat as O'Keeffe calculated a spot equidistant to the three sets of feet, then lay down.

Mrs. Hyde-Bowles perked up. "Such a delicious scandal." "The police reported that you'd said I'd had a breakdown." Amanda was tentative as she continued, "What gave you that idea?"

"I saw you downstairs, in the Oak Lounge, sipping coffee. Isn't that a break?"

"You didn't tell anyone I'd had a breakdown?"

"I wouldn't do that," Mrs. Hyde-Bowles squeaked. "You don't seem like you've flipped your wig."

Amanda whispered, "Broken telephone clue number two. She told someone I'd had a break downstairs. They must have heard it as I'd had a breakdown. That person repeated the new story to someone else." Sal was jotting notes when the snoring began. They turned to see Mrs. Hyde-Bowles, head flopped against her flannel robe, her skinny chest rising and falling.

Sal got up and nestled the woman into her bed, tucking the blanket around her with care.

~~~

The lobby was quiet in the mid-afternoon lull, and the snoops found Mrs. Pendergrass there, a book in her hand and a bag of knitting nearby. True to form, her wig was askew, today's style a back part with a front comb-over. Once they dispensed with greetings, Sal checked her notes and said, "Pendy, the police said you told them that Amanda pushed Oxana from the second storey, it was no accident."

"I did?" Mrs. Pendergrass wore a puzzled expression.

"Perhaps you misheard some gossip?" Amanda asked. "Thought that 'story' meant the second storey of the stairwell?"

"I do recall something about it, but it was so long ago."

Sal squinted, saying, "It was two weeks ago."

"I rest my case," Pendy said, holding up her paperback, which featured a ripped swashbuckler and sensual corseted beauty on its cover. "Have you read this one Sal?" She fanned herself with the book. "Steamy."

Fatigue settled over Amanda. Interviewing the residents was proving a waste of time. She thanked Mrs. Pendergrass for her help.

"Anytime, Alanna."
~~~

Amanda turned to Sal and whispered, “We’ll never get the straight goods from the residents. Let’s piece the testimonials together as best we can.”

Sal winked. “Righty-oh. I’ll stitch them together. Meantime we need to examine other suspects. Who else would have wanted Oxana dead?”

“A lover?” Amanda asked.

“He’d have a lot of ice to melt, but I suppose nearly everyone can find love. I’ll inquire,” Sal said.

Amanda waved a hand in front of her, asking, “What about a resident?” They both had a laugh at that and Amanda imagined Scowly Orthotics following Nurse Oxana into the stairwell, moving at the speed of a starfish, ramming her with her walker, using all the force of her ninety pounds, then making a getaway without getting her walker stuck in the door.

“Who else?” Amanda asked with a sigh. “Elaine, Mary, you, O’Keeffe?” She sunk in her chair, adding, “I’m out of ideas. I’m done for today.”

Sal didn’t seem the least bit tired. “If we’ve dead-ended with the residents, we’ll need answers from the coppers.”

“Don’t look at me, I will not visit Beaston.” Amanda threw her hands in the air. “Great, now you’ve got me saying it.”

“Just say that you have a few questions, because—” Sal scanned the lobby trying to formulate a plan, “because you’re going to sign that waiver he’s salivating over.”

“Lie?”

“Certainly not.” Sal shrugged. “Just tell a little fib.” She ran through a list of outstanding questions: the cops’ failure to collect Amanda’s clothes on the day of the murder, why Beaton wanted a photo and measurement of her hand, how they could release Oxana's body to her family when her murder wasn't solved, and why they were trying to pin the crime on her. Amanda must have looked unconvinced so Sal shifted tactics, "They dragged you in for questioning, it's only fair you should do the same."

"It doesn't work like that," Amanda said, but Sal got her thinking, why not? Telling Beaton that she had a question about the waiver might get them the information they needed.

Sal watched Amanda deliberate, saying, "I'll assemble all our broken telephone clues. You go home and get some rest." She waved a hand. "Don't worry about questioning Beaston. Don't worry about the killer being on our tail."

Damn she was good, Amanda thought, flooded with images of an unknown killer about to sever her spine. "I had temporarily forgotten, but thanks for the reminder."

"Anytime my Dear." Sal winked. "Anytime."

Twenty-Nine

Amanda decided to add one last errand onto her exhausting day, then she'd go home and collapse. Reheat some leftovers, hunker down and binge on tv. She needed comfort, to tune out of her life for a while. And sleep. Damn, she needed sleep.

She pulled into the parking lot closest to Timely Temps, tucking into a spot reserved for the car-sharing service. It occurred to her that she'd been using the service a lot lately and, since being suspended from work, maybe she should curb her spending.

The thought of a paycheque, even a small one, was a bright spot. Her pay would only be for two days at the Fight and Flight workshop, but it was something. She hoped they hadn't deducted for the damaged poster sign.

"C'mon Girl," she clucked and O'Keeffe fell in step beside her.

Money. Just thinking about it made Amanda uncomfortable but it hadn't always been like that. She used to have a very healthy relationship with the stuff, until he-whose-name-shall-never-be-spoken bankrupted their business. The shock, the loss, the humiliation had been too much for her. Even now it still reverberated.

Worse yet, was her inability to use her mother's money. Technically it was hers now, but she couldn't bring herself to touch it. She'd tried once at the grocery store, pulling out the credit card emblazoned with 'Laura Sunderson', but it didn't feel right to use it. She'd ended up putting the groceries on her own credit card, which was approaching its limit.

A familiar pang of grief tore through her. She stopped and focused on taking a few deep breaths.

When would it get easier?

Joyce had said that the loss would always be with her, but one day she'd find that happy memories had become more prevalent than painful ones.

That day wasn't today.

When she was able to move again, they continued, walking among towering office buildings. O'Keeffe enjoyed the city sidewalks, which were rife with unfamiliar scents. She licked a few spots, until Amanda noticed and tugged her away in disgust. It was the end of the workday, and the streets were busy. A few pedestrians stopped to greet the dog, who drank in the adoration, her face stretched in a grin.

Moments later, they stepped into the office building, O'Keeffe skittering on the marble floor. Amanda didn't so much walk the dog here as slide her over the floor like a mop, to the delight of exiting employees.

Once inside the elevator, Amanda considered how to ask Jeremi why he had thought Oxana's death was a murder before it had been deemed one. He'd been quick to shut her down on the phone, calling her a suspicious Silly Billy. Sure, he could have taken a wild guess, wildness being one of Jeremi's top skills.

Maybe he had a connection at the Singing Swan Lodge, an aunt or uncle that he'd never mentioned. Or he might follow a news site that didn't show up in her internet search, the kind that promoted conspiracy theories, the kind that might promote a simple accident as a murder. Vancouver certainly had a lot of conspiracy theorists, people who followed counter-culture news sites that the average person would never stumble upon. By the time they arrived at the 12TH floor and stepped out onto plush carpet, Amanda had decided just one thing: that she would proceed with caution.

She opened the door to Timely Temps and they stepped into its small lobby. All was quiet. The late afternoon sun bounced off Coal Harbour and flooded the place with light.

"Hello?" Amanda called out but got no answer. She headed down the short hallway calling, "Jeremi?" His office door stood ajar. From within came a staccato of muffled voices. Was it a meeting? She tugged on O'Keeffe's leash, motioning for her to sit. No way Amanda was going to interrupt. She'd already caused enough trouble for Jeremi. O'Keeffe, however, had other ideas. The slightly open door was an invitation to the dog who wedged her snout in the crack, pushed it open and wrenched her leash out of Amanda's hand. When the door flew open, Amanda was surprised to find Jeremi alone, huddled in one corner, fussing with some sort of machine. His back was turned to them, obstructing the device from her view as she said, "Sorry to interrupt."

Jeremi whirled around, panic blistering his face. He raised both hands. Something tumbled from one and clunked on the floor. "Don't come in!" he yelled, fumbling to remove his cardigan and toss it over the machine.

O'Keeffe ignored the order, racing to him, her tail a whirligig at the wondrous scents and bric-a-brac that filled the room. She seemed undeterred by the cologne that assaulted Amanda's nostrils.

"Sorry!" Amanda yelped, sensing danger. What was he trying to hide? How could she get her nosy dog away from him? "O'Keeffe, get out!" Amanda stayed at the door, not daring to approach Jeremi. "O'Keeffe, come!" She yelled in a voice deep and loud enough to demand obedience. The dog peered at her from the far side of the room, panting in enjoyment, until something new caught her attention. Her eyes widened, snout quivering. A low growl began as she stretched her long neck toward the vintage cage holding Lola, the taxidermy cockatiel. Growls escalated into yelps as the dog lunged at the cage.

Amanda's alarm left her frozen in time and space.

Jeremi hunched in the corner, horror-struck, his hands covering his mouth.

O'Keeffe vaulted in the air, repeatedly, generating a breeze that ruffled the dead bird's yellow plume and seemed to breathe life into it. Amanda shuddered at the sight, yelling, "O'Keeffe, stop!" She sprang for the dog, who continued to leap, each time a little higher, like an over-achieving Mexican jumping bean, and making her impossible to catch.

"No!" Jeremi screamed, flinging himself across the room, toward Lola but he landed short and knocked over the cage. It sprang open with a rusty *hiss* and Lola flew through the air.

Amanda gaped at the arc of its flight until the bird hit her arm. "Gah!" she shrieked in disgust.

Lola ricocheted off Amanda's forearm and landed on the industrial carpet, where it rolled until coming to a full stop against the wall.

The cockatiel's glassy eyes stared into space, dots of orange on her white face like dollops of dollar store rouge.

O'Keeffe froze in place, staring at the now reachable Lola, as if she couldn't believe her luck.

Amanda needed to act fast, before the dog pounced and tore the foul fowl to smithereens. "O'Keeffe, want a *biscuit*?"

The magic word got the dog's attention. Amanda fumbled in her jean's pocket praying for the liver treats that she now swore by. "Look! Come get a biscuit!" She held out an ancient and fuzzy bit of dried liver, which transfixed O'Keeffe. Amanda backed out of the office, dog in tow, until they were safely in the hallway.

Her heart was racing—what in hell had just happened? O'Keeffe sat, polite and obedient, limpid eyes focused on the treat in Amanda's hand. "Right, here you go. Good Girl." The dog hoovered the treat then put on her best pleading face, as if hoping to manifest another one.

Jeremi emerged from his office, shutting the door behind him. "I have restored Lola's dignity." He smoothed his hair and straightened his bolero tie, his expression reverent.

"I'm so sorry about that," Amanda said, imagining Lola soothed and combed and returned to her final resting place.

He waved his hand toward his office. "What you walked into. . . Please put that out of your mind." He stroked his greying goatee. "You're both naughty girls for seeing that." He smiled. Half devil, half angel.

O'Keeffe snuffled in Jeremi's direction but Amanda tugged her away, taking a step back. Cautiously, she said, "I told you I was coming in to get my cheque."

Jeremi's face lifted, his voice brightening as he donned a new, friendly character. "Yes, of course!" He turned and ducked into his office, careful to shut the door behind him, leaving Amanda to puzzle over what had just happened.

She had distinctly heard voices coming from the office, but there had been nobody else in there. Jeremi hadn't been on the phone either—she'd seen it on his desk, handle nestled firmly in its cradle. What was going on? Was he schizophrenic?

Jeremi returned, holding a plain white envelope. "Here you go. Payment in full." He handed over the cheque, then bent down to pat O'Keeffe. "Hello you little monkey. You're a nosy girl, aren't you?"

Then, to Amanda's revulsion, he stood, opened his arms, and reached out to hug her. Internal alarm bells sounded, and her hand flew up to stop him. Realizing how obvious she must look and how that might trigger him, she faked a big fat sneeze.

The tactic worked. Jeremi took a step back, chuckled and said, "So lovely to see you and your little doggie too."

A chill seeped into Amanda as she turned and wobbled out of the office. O'Keeffe jounced alongside, oblivious to the crisis she'd caused. They landed at the safety of the elevator. She couldn't even remember if she'd said goodbye.

Thirty

Amanda squinted into the morning sun as she strode through the Downtown East Side, towards Police HQ. She was done with all the strange happenings in her life and the fear it created. Done with unanswered questions, with not knowing who to trust.

Jeremi's behaviour had been suspicious and needed to be reported. She'd be damned if she'd let the police eye her as a suspect when there were people far shadier. People with far bigger motives.

Besides Jeremi, there was Nurse Mary who had worked with Oxana, day in and day out. Mary, who had wielded the threatening letter. How did it get to her? She wasn't responsible for the mail. Had she devised that letter, cutting out the words from a magazine?

Amanda wanted answers. Sal had been right, if the police could question her, she could bloody well question them. She would pretend she was going to sign the waiver but needed some information before doing so.

As soon as she stepped inside Police HQ, the stench of urine and metal assaulted her. She put a hand over her nose and approached the weathered desk. There was no bullet-proof glass, no bars, only a wide laminate counter with a bored-looking uniform on the other side. She removed the odour-blocking hand to speak with the cop. "I need to see Officer Beaton." With those words, her feet grew cold, her face slackened. It surprised her to have such a visceral reaction to his name.

Bored cop checked a computer monitor then said, "He's off work." There was a pause as he stared at Amanda, but she didn't know what he expected of her, so she let him stare. Finally, he said, "I'll try his partner." He picked up his phone, punched in some numbers and started talking. Amanda remembered wide eyed McIver with her barely-there chin. She was so young and timid. How would she handle Amanda's demand for answers?

A minute later he told her to take a seat, motioning to the rows of welded plastic chairs in the far corner. She made her way to the waiting area, which had a luxury score of zero. She plucked up a tattered issue of *Time* magazine from a few years ago, which made it not so timely. A guy with a baseball cap pulled over his face slumped against the wall, snoring. A biker-chick glared—an arched scar carved above one eyebrow.

Amanda sat on a chair so uncomfortable it should be arrested, opened the copy of *Time,* and waited. After a few minutes, the din of the room faded as she tuned out the sounds of doors opening and closing, erratic voices and non-stop phone ringing. She was about a third of the way through an article on the disappearing polar ice cap when she sensed a presence. She lifted her gaze to see a middle-aged cop. He had a few pounds to lose but no hair to spare.

"Miss Sunderson," he said in a friendly voice as he extended a stubby hand. "I'm Officer McIver."

Amanda stood, saying, "No you're not." God, she needed a filter between her mind and her mouth.

He let out a laugh. "Actually, I am."

She took a second before saying, "Sorry. I mean, sure, if you say so. It's just that I was expecting, that is, I met a different Officer McIver," back when this whole nightmare began. She mimed a description. "Young woman, about this high. Quite shy."

The officer's face twitched, and he let out a snort. "You thought she was a cop?" His laughter exploded. "My daughter!" He raised his head to the ceiling, his body rocking. "Oh, that's the best thing I've heard all week."

Amanda failed to see the joke. Beaton had called her his *partner*. She remembered his derogatory tone and the pained look on his face. She opened her mouth to speak but realized that this Officer McIver, the *real Officer McIver*, wouldn't be able to hear her. He was rolling with laughter, waving his arms, and stomping his feet. Amanda feared for his health, that his laugh attack might bring on a heart attack. She checked out the reactions of the others in the waiting area. Suspicious chick glared at them. Baseball cap awoke with a grunt.

Finally, McIver straightened, pulled a hankie from his pant pocket, and wiped his eyes. "Oh, thank you Miss, I needed a good belly laugh." He folded his hankie, tapped Amanda's elbow, and led her a few steps away from the waiting area before saying, "Jessica. Hah. Just finished high school. Nutty dream to follow in her old man's shoes. No knack for police work." He pocketed the hankie and folded his arms, continuing, "I mean none. Zilch. She'd be terrible." He rocked on the soles of his feet. “I’d be afraid she’d get shot because she strolled into a gang war or pissed off the wrong guy. No, she’s no officer, and if I have anything to say about it, she won’t go anywhere near the Academy.”

“But she was with Officer Beaton at the Singing Swans Lodge, investigating the . . . “ She couldn’t say the *m* word, so searched around before choosing, “incident.”

“Beaton’s my partner. Watched Jess grow up. Did me a favor, see, took her on a few ride-alongs. Jess borrowed my uniform, it hung off her, looked bloody ridiculous,” McIver said with another chuckle. “But I needed someone to shatter the illusion that cop life is glamorous, cause it sure as hell ain’t.” He dropped the g’s at the end of his words. “Yeah, I owe him a bottle of scotch, the good stuff. Jessica was all starry eyed, and he was, well let’s just say he was in enough pain to turn him into his evil twin.” He couldn’t stifle another snort.

Good God, Amanda was swimming in fresh information. “Pain?”

“Poor guy’s been trying to recover from ACL surgery.”

She must have appeared puzzled because he explained, “He had a bum knee needed fixing. I hear a torn ACL hurts like a bugger.”

Amanda tried to process his words, her face contorting to help her mental acuity.

McIver continued, “But apparently it hurts like hell after the surgery too.” He raised both chubby hands in the air. “And we can’t take any painkillers when we’re on duty.” He shook his head, saying, “The guy’s been a bear to work with. Finally convinced him to use some banked time to stay home and recover. I want to work with Jekyll, not Hyde." He looked around, as if realizing he was still on the clock and not here to discuss his daughter's career path or his partner's injuries.

"So, when he suggested I was the prime suspect—," Amanda said.

McIver swished his hand in the air, "Technically everyone is a suspect, but Beaton has a gift for making everyone think they're about to be indicted."

She thought back to Beaton's interrogation, his pen clicking and table thumping. Had they been intimidation tactics, or outlets for his knee pain?

"He's kept me informed of the case. How can I help, *Miss* Sunderson?" he said, punching the salutation.

Amanda imagined Beaton telling his partner how bent out of shape the word *Ma'am* made her. A flush penetrated her face as she got down to business, launching into the story of her recent encounter with Jeremi and his suspicious activities. How he'd labeled Oxana's death a murder before the fact hit the news. How he had something in his office that he was desperate to hide.

McIver took down her details, saying that he'd explore the lead. He added, "Anything else?"

"I need some information." Amanda held her breath.

McIver squinted.

"Before signing the waiver about certain evidence and its chain of custody," she clarified.

His face relaxed and he said, "Okay. Only fair."

She considered her questions. Based on this conversation, she now knew that her smock and t-shirt hadn't been collected because Beaton's crime scene companion wasn't a cop. Beaton would have sweated about the broken chain of custody and how that could quash any case against Amanda, so he asked her to sign a waiver to get the cops off the hook. But she still wanted to understand about the release of Oxana's body and the time pressure that had created. "Officer Beaton said that Oxana's family is coming to collect the body, but how can they do that when her death is still under investigation?"

A group of cops entered the building, headed to the security door. McIver offered a salute in their direction, shouting, "Howdy Marty! Yo, O'Neil you slacker!" The cops waved back at him, one whistling, "That your girlfriend McIver?" which tickled McIver's funny bone and doubled him over again.

Once he collected himself, he turned back to Amanda, asking, "Where were we? Right—the release of the body. Up to the coroner." He shrugged. "Family can come to town whenever they want, but Jack decides when they take their loved one home." He checked his watch, and Amanda realized how long their talk had grown.

"One more item," she said. "Officer Beaton requested a photo and measurement of my right hand, but never explained why."

McIver said, "Had to do with a question from the coroner."

She raised her hand toward his face. "Does this one fit the bill?"

He rocked back on his feet, let out a laugh, then steadied himself and put on a poker face. "Can't say one way or t'other." McIver checked his watch, adding, "I'd best get back to work Miss, if you want to leave the waiver with me." He reached out a hand.

Amanda unzipped her knapsack and pretended to rummage through it before saying, "Hmm. Musta put it in my other bag." She made an exaggerated shrug. "Thank you for your time, Officer." She shook his outstretched hand then walked to the exit, smiling to herself at how much new information she had.

Turns out that sometimes lying pays.

Thirty-One

Visiting the jovial Officer McIver had slimmed Amanda's anxiety about being a murder suspect. Besides that, the successful reconnaissance mission to police HQ had empowered her. She felt strong enough to tackle some executor duties that afternoon, returning to the cancellation of her mother's Old Age Security.

This time she was prepared, having taken notes during her last odyssey through the government's telephone system. This time, she punched through to the correct extension for Old Age Security on her first try while wielding a duster so she could clean the flat while on the interminable hold she anticipated. She perched on a work stool, stretching the fluffy wand toward the blades of the ceiling fan when a civil servant picked up.

Before he could launch into his speech, Amanda said, "This call is important to me, but I'm currently tottering on a work stool so please hold for one moment."

The clerk, sounding surprised at being the one put on hold for a change, stammered, "Um, Okay, yeah I guess."

Amanda disembarked the stool and returned to her notes in the kitchen. She verbally confirmed all the details she needed for the cancellation, got the correct fax number, and told the clerk that she'd send the copies that afternoon.

The next call was to the Canada Pension Plan, and she got through the sad hits of that hold by dusting the rest of the flat. When her important call was finally answered, she recited all pertinent details needed to cancel her mother's government pension, promising them a fax too.

She packed up her notes, a copy of the will and death certificate, then hopped on her bike to cycle to the local copy shop where she got all the information faxed off in record time.

It was a huge victory. When she returned home a half hour later, she took immense satisfaction in the action of crossing those two items off her list of executor tasks. Mount Executor didn't look any shorter, but Amanda finally held some optimism that she could knock more items off with ease and speed.

She celebrated by taking O'Keeffe for a leisurely stroll around the neighbourhood, enjoying the warm fragrant air, the beauty of nature and a strange new sensation that was something akin to a sense of peace.

~~~

Early that evening, she met Toni and Keira at Spanish Banks Park, an expanse bordered by a tree-studded cliff on one side and beach along the other. On the grassy stretch between, every picnic table was occupied, so they continued to a stretch of beach, where they spread blankets on the sand. Amanda watched a dozen dogs running around the park, and even more on the beach. For an instant, she regretted not bringing O'Keeffe, but if the smell of meat searing on portable barbeques
~~~

made her own mouth water, it would have made that dog a holy terror. She imagined the dog terrorizing every group of picnickers. *Hi, it's O'Keeffe. Aren't I cute? How about some hamburger for all this cute?* Amanda wasn't up for chasing the dog and apologizing for her scavenging ways. Tonight, she wanted to relax and catch up with her girlfriends.

The sky was powder blue with Creamsickle swirls, holding the promise of a gorgeous sunset over the Georgia Strait. Across the calm waters of the harbour, West Vancouver rose, its wealthy estates dotting the lush mountainside. Toni popped open a craft beer and hoisted a tub of fried chicken onto the blanket as Amanda recapped her visit to police HQ.

"McIver and McIver. Sounds like a cop show," Toni said, taking a slug of beer then affecting a tv broadcaster voice. "Coming soon. He's an aging beat cop who's seen it all. She's a rookie, without a clue. Why does he keep her as his partner? Simple. She's his daughter." She drummed her hands on her knees, saying, "*da da da da,*" then swished her head around as if to be caught from another camera angle. "McIver and McIver. Tune in Thursday at 9."

"You gave them a good time-slot," Amanda said, pulling paper napkins, plastic plates and cutlery from her backpack. She felt the nip of a sand flea, so pulled the edges of the blanket to widen their domain.

Keira wielded a bottle of wine, the golden glow from the sinking sun highlighting her pretty features. She poured a healthy glug into Amanda's cup, returned the bottle to a cooler and pulled out containers filled with sliced raw veggies and a Caesar salad. "Well, that's quite the news flash about Officer

Beaton."

"He might not be a total douche after all," Toni said, tracing her fingers over a necklace that resembled a studded collar.

Keira bucked at the description. "He was in pain." It came out sounding like *payen.*

Amanda dug into her pack for the tub of potato salad she'd made, but her hand stopped short. "I guess I was quick to judge the guy, but—" She willed her thoughts to congeal, sitting back on her heels, "how could I not? There were so many red flags."

"I reckon you should go for it," Keira said. "Let him fill the hole in your heart."

"He can fill other holes too," Toni snorted, then began a fit of coughing. "Beer went down wrong."

"Eew," Amanda said. Sure, the man had some appeal, she couldn't deny, but Amanda with a cop? It just didn't feel like a good fit. She tilted her face toward the breeze.

"Time to step out of your comfort zone, Gurl. Live your life," Toni said with a wink and a smug grin. Behind her, the golden orb of sun kissed the horizon, and a halo of deep orange spread around it.

"He's turned out to be a good man, just one who's hurting," Keira said. "Heavens above, last year when Liam had to pass a kidney stone it was like living with Satan himself." She shuddered at the memory.

Amanda stared at the lapping surf, which reflected an increasingly vivid lemon and tangerine sky. She loved the beach. It was peaceful. Too peaceful to ruin with thoughts of a romance with Beaton.

Keira started loading a plate of food, asking, "And by the by, when Officer McIver laughed at your hand, did he mean it wasn't a match for the handprint on the dead nurse?"

"Guess so." Amanda grabbed a plate and leaned in to examine the buffet.

"So, you're off the hook," Keira said, deliberating over the perfect piece of fried chicken and saying for the record, "I'll just have one piece."

"Not exactly off the hook." Amanda piled Caesar and potato salads onto her plate, continuing, "He said that *everyone* is a suspect, even if Beaton scares us into thinking we're Numero Uno."

"Classic cop strategy." Toni screwed up her face, sipping the final dregs of her beer.

Amanda noticed Toni giving her crotch a scratch, so asked, "Everything okay?"

"Sorry, it's hard to be discrete with an itch down there," Toni said, blushing before busting into a wide grin. "Everything is better than okay with my gazillionaire."

"Good to hear," Amanda said, adding, "Gazillionaire is kinda long. Can we call him Gaz?"

Toni nodded enthusiastically but didn't say more. Unusual, that. She must have wondered why her friends were staring at her with anticipation. She lowered both her chin and her voice saying, "I don't want to jinx it."

Keira gave a look of surprise to Amanda, then returned to the previous subject. "Is it classic cop strategy to whisk you away from Singing Swans and have you delivered to the precinct?" She tucked into the fried chicken, her eyes glazing over in delight.

"Maybe he knows you don't have a car?" Toni reached into the chicken bucket, adding, "Or because parking is a bitch around the station?" She pulled out a chicken leg and sunk her teeth in it before noticing the others looking at her quizzically. "What? He couldn't be considerate?"

"Who do the police think committed the murder?" Keira asked.

"My money is on Jeremi. He's suspicious," Toni mumbled. Behind her, the sky dimmed to blood orange.

The sound of the surf had grown louder, and Amanda admired its coppery sheen. "You have no idea how suspicious he is." She recapped the escapade of the flying taxidermy cockatiel, adding, "He definitely has something to hide."

"The good news," Keira said, raising her glass in salute, "Is that you're not about to be arrested."

Amanda's brief respite from anxiety juddered to a stop with an image of the threatening letter. Just her luck that when the cops eased up, the killer moved in. Fear must have shown on her face because Keira asked what was wrong. Amanda took a ragged breath then told her friends about the threat against her and Sal.

"What!?" Keira's eyes were big as moons.

Toni said, "Cripes, Mand. You've got to back off from the snooping." Her nerves seemed to need a hit of carbs, and she slapped a massive mound of potato salad onto her plate. "The killer is *watching* you," she said, with more than enough volume to override the surf. "This guy's gonna turn you into a vegetable." She wasn't even trying to hide her worry.

Amanda nodded her head.

"How did anyone know you'd been asking around?" Toni asked.

"Dunno, but it's a good question." Amanda put down her plate, her appetite vanishing more quickly than the setting sun. "Maybe there's a rat at The Singing Swans."

"I certainly hope not—with all those elderly folks! The health department would be all over that," Keira said, without a hint of irony.

Toni and Amanda exchanged glances, before Toni said, "Promise me you'll stop snooping."

Amanda nodded until she felt like a bobble doll.

Keira extended her hand. "Pinkie swear, Mands."

"Guys, quit worrying." Amanda stabbed her hands in the air. "I'll stop." She felt her skin prickle, as if she was breaking out in hives. *Liar liar skin on fire.* Good thing she left out the bit about her trip to the morgue. A pang of remorse hit her.

Keira reached for her second piece of chicken, asking, "How did Sal react to the letter?"

"Calm as a still pond." Amanda smiled, a blush of relief filling her at the thought of being back on track with Sal.

"Glad that you two got it sorted," Keira said, "Craicing." Then she dug her arms deep into her bag, searching for God-knew-what. "I'm impressed by Sal. He—I mean she—is finally able to live out her life the way she wants." She pulled out a rainbow pack of crayons.

"Besides, this situation has lots of advantages." Toni fingered the silver studs at her neck.

Keira pulled a jar of moldy applesauce from her bag. "Like, if you need a jar opened."

"Or needed to reach something on a high shelf," Toni added.

Keira held up a toy truck, saying, "Or need a tire changed." She dug in again, coming up with a package of wipes, tore one off and got to work on her greasy fingers.

"Funny," Amanda said as the sunset flared red. "Sal said she used to be a trucker. I thought she was kidding." She took a sip of wine. "But maybe she wasn't."

Thirty-Two

The drive to Singing Swans Lodge was smooth as Amanda wound her way through the pretty suburban area bordering it. Greenery shimmered in the summer sun. Post-war brick houses reflected a character and solidity that spoke of a bygone era, long before the advent of the monster house. Traffic lights seemed to be on her side today, all of them lining up green along the route. She found a place for the share-car a block away from the retirement home, unloaded and fobbed out. "C'mon Girl." Amanda tugged on the dog's leash, pulling her away from some fascinating shrubbery.

As they approached the driveway to Singing Swans, the ever-curious O'Keeffe strode directly to a parked black Range Rover. It made Amanda smile that the dog could never get enough of sniffing, even if cars must collect some delicious scents. She'd have to find a dog sweater that said, 'Born to Sniff.' She jounced along behind the dog, half-expecting the SUV passenger door to pop open and a resident to totter out. So, she was startled when the engine leapt to life with a roar and the Range Rover took off at top speed. The squealing tires sent the dog into a frenzy of barking. Amanda raised her fist and muttered, "Jackass." But he'd already sped off, turning onto a side street and out of their view.

Jeez, why was everybody in such a rush?

Maybe because most people had jobs and families and things to do. The thought immediately depressed her, and she sighed as they entered the home. They walked to the reception desk, where she reached for the Visitor Log. Mai was on a call but waved a silent hello. The notation above Amanda's signature was little more than a line, as if someone had given up halfway through the attempt. She noticed how sloppy her own handwriting had become, saying, "Hope that's legible," as she pushed the book towards Mai, who hung up the phone and slumped into a stack of mail.

Amanda thought of the threatening letter. Who better to create that than the person in charge of the mail? Maybe Mai had a grudge against Oxana. She assessed the petite, sweet woman. Was it all a fake front? Did she have an alter-ego? Maybe she stepped into the mailroom as Mai but emerged as a Samurai warrior, hell-bent on avenging injustices.

Why not? Lately, everybody seemed to have a secret.

"Amanda, are you listening?" Mai had stood and was shaking her sleek hair. When she got a nod of affirmation from Amanda, she continued, "Some signatures, very bad. One of them looks like 'Road Runner'." She giggled, flipped the page, and pointed a delicate finger at a scrawl that did indeed appear to say that. "You and O'Keeffe doing your visits?"

"We're going to try." O'Keeffe was snuffling the nook where the desk met the carpet. A wave of guilt washed over Amanda at the thought of how little work they had done so far. Her intentions had been good, she'd tried to give of herself, to help others, but life—and death—had gotten in the way. Their first certified visit hadn't gone so well, what with confronting Sal then getting a letter threatening to turn them into vegetables if they didn't stop snooping. She imagined her and Sal side by side in hospital beds, hooked up to ventilators and the chokehold in her throat grew tight as a vice grip.

"Sorry Amanda. I said the wrong thing?" Mai gaped at her.

"Not at all." Amanda donned a bright expression, rejoining the land of the living.

Mai smiled in relief, saying, "Good. Would you mind giving this to Sal, please?" She held out a ceramic pot containing a cactus and a mini gnome. A plastic spear held a gift card. Amanda took the plant just as she heard an exaggerated cough nearby. Scanning the lobby, she saw someone in the corner, hiding behind a newspaper. A face peeked around *The Daily Mail* and Sal stood to her impressive height, clad in a trench coat.

Amanda said goodbye to Mai then let O'Keeffe pull them to Sal. "Going somewhere?" Amanda asked, "Or are you trying to crack the case?"

"Exactly my Dear. This has gone on too long," she said, tightening the trench belt. It was an unflattering look. "This was the best private eye costume I had. She pointed at the cactus, saying, "Thank you, Amanda. Very kind of you."

"Oh, it's not from me. Mai had it."

Sal retrieved the card and read it aloud, "From your favourite person." She shrugged.

"Seems I have some competition," Amanda said. "It's pretty, but careful of the prickles."

Sal approached Mai and asked who had delivered the plant. Mai made an apologetic shrug, saying that she'd gone off to collect the mail and the cactus was sitting on the desk when she returned. Looking quite pleased with herself, Sal said, "Well I do have quite a broad fanbase, so this could be from any number of people." She shook her head, and her jowls swung gently with the motion. "But we don't have time for another case. We need to get *The Case of the Murdered Nurse who Everyone Hated* done and dusted first." She folded the newspaper, tucked it into her coat pocket and pulled out a notebook. "Let's sort this out." She sat and cracked open her notes.

"There have been two interesting developments," Amanda said, taking a seat and briefing Sal on her visit with Officer McIver.

"I'm supposed to believe that smug beast of a Beaston is acting out of pain?" Sal harrumphed. "Pain, my ass." She mumbled, "More like a pain *in* my ass."

Amanda continued, recounting Jeremi's phone proclamation that Oxana's death was a murder, plus his suspicious behaviour when she visited Timely Temps. She left out the part about the flying taxidermy bird, shuddering at the memory of the dead claws scraping along her bare arm.

"Shady one, that Jeremi," Sal said, adding, "How the blazes could he have known the death was a murder?" She squinted. "And what could he be hiding in his office?"

Amanda scrunched her face, saying, "A laptop full of porn?" She winced at the thought.

"That's an option. But you mentioned machinery," Sal said, unbuttoning her trench coat then peeling it off. She wore a tunic with a complicated tribal pattern on it. "Maybe he's printing money."

"Well, I can't see that." Amanda squinted.

"You have commented on his beautiful office, Italian leather sofa, pricey paintings." Sal tossed the trench coat over the back of her chair. "That view alone is worth a fortune. Aha—he could be a counterfeiter!"

It was true that Amanda had long wondered how Jeremi could afford such a space. But it wasn't her place to ask. And good God, she couldn't buy an idea as implausible as him being a counterfeiter. "That seems hard to believe," she said, "Besides, I heard voices. They were muffled, but still—."

"How many voices?" Sal was making notes. O'Keeffe lay at her feet.

"Hard to tell, but at least two others."

"Might be a Help Line."

Amanda scowled. "So, you're suggesting that Jeremi's money printing machine needed a software update, so he called the counterfeiter's IT department for tech support?" She raised her hands in the air then brought them down on her thighs with a slap, making O'Keeffe leap to attention.

Sal was rolling up the sleeves of her dress, her coarse arm hair springing into view. "It's so warm in here!" she said and Amanda felt a wave of empathy for her. "Clearly the lad is up to some kind of monkey business, something big." Sal fanned herself. "From what you've said about him, he sounds like a criminal, or at least a nut job. Maybe both." O'Keeffe stared between Sal and Amanda, growling to get some attention. "Good thing you had O'Keeffe to protect you." Sal petted her.

"Yes. You're a guard dog, aren't you?" The dog lolled onto her back, exposing the blond fuzz along her belly. "What a vicious hound." The dog let her legs flop open, a smile creeping onto her brown lips.

Amanda sighed, saying, "Vicious. Codename Killer. Right, Girl?" O'Keeffe rolled back and forth before letting out a sneeze of delight. "Speaking of killers," Amanda continued, "I had a crazy idea." She wondered if Nurse Mary might have done more than simply hand over the threatening letter. But she barely got her suspicions out when Sal shook her head so hard Amanda feared it might fall off.

"That is a firm no, Amanda." Sal leaned forward, levelling her gaze. "I have known that woman for years. I trust her thoroughly. She has nursed me to health many times. Knows all my secrets. She is not capable of treachery."

Amanda nodded, then turned her focus to Mai. She tilted her head towards Reception with a quizzical expression.

"My Dear, do you have a kink in your neck?"

Amanda shook her head, trying to point her eyes towards Reception.

"Do you have water in your ear?"

"No!" Amanda widened her eyes, muttering, "What about Mai?"

"Mai!" Sal squealed, causing the half dozen people in the lobby to turn and stare. Mai stood, peering over the desk, a tender smile on her face, offering a double-handed wave to them. Sal began a titter that expanded like a mushroom cloud from a nuclear explosion. "That is the funniest—" Her laughter accelerated until it became hysteria and a tear rambled down her face. "Oh, Amanda, you do keep me young!" She doubled over so quickly that another resident asked if she needed medical attention.

"She's fine." Amanda assured the resident. "Just a laughing fit." Because she doesn't take me seriously.

The elevator doors opened, spitting Elaine into the lobby. She pulled some letters from a clipboard and dropped them at the reception desk. Her dark hair was a mess, and her tan dress made her skin look waxy. Amanda muttered to Sal, "That is not the woman I met a few weeks ago."

Having calmed from her fit of hysteria, Sal said, "Healthcare administrators. Tough job." She pulled a tissue from her coat and wiped her nose. "Her frock is hanging off her like a fashion mannequin draped in a size 12." She smoothed the front of her tunic, saying, "Not that I wouldn't love to squeeze into a size 12. Those were the days my friend." She let out a heavy sigh.

Why had Elaine become a ghost of her former self? Amanda recalled the barrister's letter on the manager's desk. Was Elaine, or The Singing Swans Lodge, in legal trouble? At the sight of O'Keeffe, Elaine visibly perked up and headed towards them. It was only a matter of seconds before she was on the floor with the dog in an unabashed public display of affection.

"How are you?" Amanda asked.

"It's been awful. The fallout since the. . ." Elaine looked up at Sal and Amanda, whispering, "since the *incident* with Nurse Oxana." Her hands didn't stop stroking the dog that wriggled around her.

"She got snuffed, you can say it." Sal shrugged. "But don't worry, we're on the case."

"Hence the private eye trench coat." Amanda pointed a thumb at Sal. "So, what's been the fallout from the murder?" Her skin crawled at the word.

Elaine sat on the floor and O'Keeffe settled into her lap. "Things are worse than I last reported to you, Amanda. A total of three prospective residents have withdrawn their applications and the money that went along with them." She sighed. O'Keeffe stretched up and started licking her face. Elaine reveled in the affection.

"Don't you fret," Sal said. "On the upside, Mr. Galloway and Mrs. Finch admitted that the," She lowered her husky voice to a whisper, "*murder* had been more exciting than Christmas. We'll be drawing a crowd in two shakes of a lamb's tail."

"Here's to hoping," Elaine said, and gave O'Keeffe another cuddle before rising to her feet. "Must get back to my task." She pointed at the women. "Wouldn't mind some company."

~~~

The group rode the elevator to the second floor, where Elaine led them past her office, around a corner and into the Ladies Staff Room, a drab but clean room with benches in the middle and a separate bathroom to one side. A row of lockers lined one wall, and that's where Elaine aimed her focus, saying, "Need a free locker. New nurse starting next week."

Sal rolled her eyes, saying, "Another one? I'm just getting used to Nervous Nelly."

Elaine fumbled, dropping her clipboard, which skittered across the laminate. "Nelly, yes. . ."
~~~

Amanda and Sal exchanged glances.

Once she'd regained her composure, Elaine said, "I've had to cut Mary down to part time."

"Oh, I do hope she's not retiring," Sal said.

Amanda couldn't shake the image of Mary with the threatening letter in her hand.

Elaine checked lockers against a chart on her clipboard. "Mary has just been a bit, um, how do I say this diplomatically, distracted lately. I thought a lighter workload would do her good." She stopped her task, frowning, then turned to the others. "Sometimes I think this place is killing us all, Oxana was simply the first."

Noticing Sal and Amanda cringing at her comment, Elaine added, "Sorry, that was indelicate." She returned to scanning the rows of lockers and comparing them to the chart. "Something doesn't add up." She double-checked her notes. "That's so odd. I have no record of who this one belongs to." She tapped one locker with her pen.

O'Keeffe had pushed through into the bathroom and emerged with a stream of toilet paper stuck to her snout. Amanda bent down to her, asking, "Why can't you sniff out clues instead of toilet paper? You're a dog, you're supposed to be nosy." She pulled tissue off the dog's snout, adding, "Fine, I'll play detective." She shook the damp toilet paper off her hand and turned to Elaine. "Maybe that was Oxana's locker?"

"Nope." Elaine shook her head. "Officer Beaton already got into her locker." She scribbled a note asking who used the locker, reached into her pocket for a roll of tape and stuck it to the locker. "If nobody responds, I'll have to get maintenance to cut the lock."

Thirty-Three

Ten minutes later, Amanda sipped a coffee and pored over her notes at the corner table in the Oak Lounge. Sal had taken the dog for a much-needed walkies. At the sound of the door, Amanda looked up to wave Sal over to the table. But it wasn't Sal.

It was Beaton.

Gone were the cane and the pinched expression Amanda associated with him. He spotted her and did something with his face that was close to a smile.

She was acutely aware of the jolt that shot through her.

The man looked five years younger, five times friendlier and damn handsome. It was amazing how much a release from pain can change a person. This wasn't the caustic cop who had made Amanda cry and Sal fume. This wasn't the pompous policeman who'd rolled his eyes at McIver junior.

This was Beaton 2.0. And he was striding towards her, all muscle and confidence.

"Miss Sunderson. Just the woman I was seeking."

She liked 2.0.

He slung a camera case over one shoulder, pulled out his notepad and launched into a story about Coroner Jackson telling him that some woman had been sniffing around the morgue. Beaton quoted from his notes, "Said woman was caught on security tape, waiting in the reception office before being spooked by something off-camera and running away." A smirk spread across his lips as his story continued. The footage had been a random finding by hospital security but one they thought Dr. Jackson should know about. The kicker was, Jack said, when she saw the footage, she recognized *the skinny bitch* who had locked her out of the building when she'd gone for a smoke.

Beaton stopped the tale there, the smirk on his freshly shaved face now full-fledged.

Amanda raised her chin, saying, "Not very professional words for a coroner to use."

"Her clients are dead bodies, what do you expect?" Beaton towered over her. "When Jack described the woman, I had a pretty strong feeling I knew who it was. Told her I'd ask around."

Amanda felt herself flush with embarrassment. "Hmm."

"Miss Sunderson, was that by any chance, you?"

"Let me think." Amanda's fingers tapped across the marble table she was studying. "What day was that?"

"I think you'd remember the day you went to the morgue."

She was running out of ways to stall.

"Listen, it's no use, I saw the footage. Made a clear ID," Beaton barked. "Would you like to explain yourself?"

Amanda took a deep breath, then slowly blew it out of puffed cheeks. "No. No, but thank you for offering."

"Miss Sunderson!"

Her pulse raced. Oh God, she was so busted. She held up her hands, saying, "Okay, I just wanted to ask a few questions. I thought I was Suspect Number One!"

Beaton paused, moving his head up and down as if he already knew the answer to his own question. "Well, here's your chance to ask. Maybe apologize for locking her out. I'm going to take you to the morgue."

"What's that now?" Amanda asked.

"Yup. Tomorrow is wide open for me and Coroner Jackson. What time works for you?" Beaton stared at her with a poker face then added, "Maybe you could bring that waiver that you offered my partner but accidentally 'left in your other bag.'" His use of air quotes irritated Amanda, as did the thought of an excursion to the morgue with him. She was relieved when Sal showed up, O'Keeffe in tow.

"Is this more questioning, Mr. Beaton?" Sal said, her tone challenging.

"Ah, Ms. Falconetti." A fresh glint twinkled in the cop's eyes as he flipped through his notepad to another page. "It has come to my attention that you've been asking multiple residents multiple questions."

"And you fear multiplicity, Sir Beaton?" Sal snapped.

He took a second, let a smile flicker in acknowledgement that she was having fun at his expense. The fact that she refused to address him as Officer must have bugged him, but he didn't let on. "Let me rephrase. Many residents have expressed concern that you've been out of line in asking them for detailed information."

Sal took a step closer to the cop, her impressive height

matching his. She practically purred her words, "I'm investigating a crime, Officer."

"No, we're the ones investigating a crime," he said, tapping a hand to the badge pinned on his manly chest. O'Keeffe took this as a call to attention. The dog raced over to him and stood on her hind legs, tail whirling like an outboard motor, stretching her extensive body up Beaton's sturdy thighs. He looked to Amanda, who called O'Keeffe off. The dog claimed a spot under the table, circling a few times before settling in.

Sal's face was smug as she nudged Amanda's arm. "We outnumber him, three to one."

Beaton cleared his throat, saying, "I repeat, your lines of questioning haven't gone over well with some residents."

"Who complained?" Amanda asked.

"That I can't disclose."

"Not this again," she yelped, rolling her eyes.

Sal took over, saying, "I was merely attempting to solve the broken telephone mystery, and believe I have."

Her comment met with a quizzical stare from Beaton.

"We have it all written down," Amanda said and looked to Sal to supply the proof. "Show him."

"It's in my suite, tacked onto the investigation board." Sal turned to Amanda, adding, "which is quite impressive since adding the recent notes and more coloured yarn to link—"

"Ms. Falconetti!"

Sal spoke directly to Amanda. "Tell him that I can get it for him but only if he asks nicely."

Beaton let out a heavy breath then said, "We've had access to your file Ms. Falconetti. We know that you have the—" He stopped, as if to search for the right words before continuing, "strength to break a neck. We know that you were with the Royal Canadian Marines."

First a trucker, now a Marine! Amanda couldn't keep up with Sal's resume.

Sal's expression had turned cold and her words were sharp when she said, "Yes, I was a Marine. Briefly."

Beaton said, "I hope you can understand, Ms. Falconetti, we are looking at everyone who had means, motive and opportunity. We know that you weren't fond of Nurse Oxana."

"Nobody was!" Sal's voice rose an octave, and she glared at Beaton. It was Amanda's turn to calm Sal, as she had done when their roles were reversed. She patted Sal's arm, then traced a slow circle on her back.

Beaton held up a hand. "Yes, we know." He clicked his pen, in that annoying habit that Amanda had witnessed during her detainment. He put a cautious look on his face and continued, "Fine. Please get me that breaking phone record."

"Broken telephone," Amanda corrected him. "The residents misheard things then passed along inaccurate gossip."

"Ah. Right." Beaton considered. "Let me see your notes on that. And should there be any developments, please let me know."

Sal narrowed her eyes and hissed in a disturbing treble, "Well I wouldn't just sit on my hands now, would I?"

Beaton nodded then slung the camera case off his shoulder. "About those hands." He unfolded a ruled sheet of plastic and smoothed it onto the table. "Your right hand please, Ms. Falconetti."

Thirty-Four

Amanda fumed the entire drive home, recalling how Sal had remained cool as Beaton measured and photographed her hands. She'd cooed to Amanda, "Let Officer Beaston do his job, my Dear." Beaton had ignored the malapropism. He left shortly after that task and Sal convinced her friend that they both needed to get some rest. Reluctantly, Amanda had headed home.

Piecing together a toasted peanut butter sandwich and getting O'Keeffe out for her evening walk zapped the rest of Amanda's energy. She couldn't wait to get to bed, but once there, all she could do was stare at the ceiling. When a vibration beneath her began, Amanda feared that the local Juan de Fuca tectonic plate had finally rumbled under the North American plate and that 'The Big One' was happening.

If the cops or the killer didn't get her, it would be a natural disaster. Just her luck.

After another vibration, she realized that her cell phone was underneath her, and ringing. She let out a massive exhale.

How could she be so wound up?

She answered the phone to hear Toni, calling to say that she was in *luuuv!* The gazillionaire and her had an *energy* between them. He was *so attentive and sweet.* It didn't seem to bother Toni that Gaz got her skunk drunk every time they went out for expensive dinners. "He insisted I order King Crab, and holy shit Amanda it was 99 bucks!" Toni tittered. "Although I haven't had this much sex since the last time I had this much sex. My tender vittles are on fire!"

Amanda flipped on the bedside lamp. "Well, you're hot." O'Keeffe stirred from her nap at the foot of the bed.

"No, I mean really, they're burning me."

"Well, other than that, I'm glad it's working out," Amanda said. She really did hope for the best, but Toni's words got her Spidey- senses tingling. Was Gaz too good to be true? "Just be careful."

Toni sighed. "Oh don't be such an old woman. I'm having fun."

Fun, Amanda thought, when was the last time she'd done that? Surely, she couldn't deny it to her friend. "Right. Of course." Maybe she *was* turning into an old woman. O'Keeffe blinked lazy eyes at her, as if agreeing with the thought.

"Hey, why don't we go out one night, get caught up?" Toni said, "Oh, but not Saturday. Gaz is taking me to Cirque du Soleil." She giggled, "Then we might have a private circus of our own."

Yeesh.

Once the call wrapped up, Amanda found the dog staring at her. "What are you looking at?" O'Keeffe cocked her head and Amanda continued, "I don't want a man. I don't need a man." She tossed a giraffe stuffy at the judgmental dog. "Go back to your giraffe." She snapped off the light.

Wow, things were pretty bad when Amanda thought that Toni had her act together. She had a job, a man, and no crises. Amanda had been suspended from Timely Temps, and her dog visitations were a failure. Once Elaine got back to her old self, she'd probably fire them, despite her affection for O'Keeffe. Mount Executor was collecting dust on her kitchen table.

She tried to rest, but couldn't manage to keep her eyes closed, even though she knew she needed to sleep. Tomorrow would be a big day. Why the hell did the coroner want to see her? She shuddered at the thought of going back to the morgue. And she double shuddered at the thought of having to confront Dr. Jackson. She remembered the sarcastic pasty-faced woman turning her fury on Amanda, whose only crime had been accidentally kicking a doorstopper out of place.

And to be escorted by Officer Beaton on the gruesome mission—*yech*. The man was becoming her nemesis. He was always full of surprises, and none of them had been good. Who knew what he had planned for her in the bowels of Vancouver General Hospital?

She sat up with a jolt.

What if there was an arrangement between the cops and the coroner? Maybe they conspired to silence her, get her out of the way once and for all. What if they locked her in one of those body drawers? One of the tiny, airless, dark as death refrigerated drawers? Good God, nobody would ever think to look for her in there. And nobody would be able to hear her from the stainless-steel coffin—her screams wouldn't even reach the nearby Janitorial offices.

Her heartbeat sped into the danger zone. She flicked on the

bedside light, but the wattage couldn't illuminate the darkness of her psyche. She put her head in her hands.

She was embroiled in a murder investigation. Murder, with a capital *M*. And it wasn't just Amanda's freedom at stake anymore—now Sal was a suspect. Things had become too real. So real that the actual killer had threatened her and Sal's very vertebrae.

What had they been doing? Cavorting about like a couple of Miss Marples in the seniors' lodge. What a joke. She felt the heat rise on her face and the tears advance. It was ridiculous to imagine their limp investigation skills would ever be enough to clear either of their names. She clasped her hands around her knees, starting a rocking motion.

Amanda longed to turn to someone now, but who? She'd grown suspicious of everyone. And who could blame her? Nobody was who they seemed to be: Sal, Jeremi, Officer McIver and both versions of Beaton.

And of course, there was a killer who had her in his sights.

O'Keeffe roused from sleep, lifted her tousled head then gave Amanda's feet a good licking. "At least I have you, Girl." The dog stood and yawned, then jumped off the bed and exited the bedroom. "Et tu, O'Keeffe?" Amanda asked in amazement.

Amanda leapt from her bed and sprinted around the flat, re-checking that all the doors and windows were secure. She was aware of a coldness settle in as she made her security check. The place would be so easy to break into. Front door, back door, windows on all sides.

All it would take was a stepladder and a screwdriver.

And the killer would be inside.

~~~

A half-hour of pacing, checking the windows and doors, finally led to fatigue. She left a few lights on before returning to her bedroom, setting the door ajar then slipping into bed. O'Keeffe nuzzled alongside her, but there was just one person Amanda wanted right now.

"I wish you were here to tell me that everything will be okay." She sent her words up to the ceiling, but they must have evaporated in the darkness because there was no bolt of lightning, no sign from the beyond, not even another phone call. "But you're not here."

If heaven could be anything we want it to be, Amanda imagined that her Mum's version would be a tropical vacation.

A memory of their last vacation together, to Cuba, floated into her mind.

They'd both been so happy. Days in Havana, touring the neoclassical buildings with their elegant pastel facades. Everywhere the earthy scent of cigars. An outing to Rick's Café, where they stripped down to their underwear and jumped into the grotto. Perfect days on the dazzling Varadero beach, the air salty and warm, the turquoise water blissful. Visiting dragonflies, green and iridescent, hovering in the breeze. All was right in the world. They had such fun jumping waves. Amanda imagined diving into those ocean swells now, into wave after wave, joining her mother again. The images mixed with O'Keeffe's rhythmic snoring and lulled her into sleep.

Hours later, she woke briefly.
~~~

A sliver of moonlight streamed through a crack where the curtains met.

~~~

The aroma of coffee infused Amanda's senses and kitchen, as she shaved a long curl from a dark chocolate bar, for her morning mocha. Her mother had always said, "You never know what the day will bring, so get your chocolate in the morning." She sipped her mocha and smiled. The mother she had seen last night was in her prime. Fit and healthy. Full of life. "I hope she really is spending the afterlife in the Caribbean, O'Keeffe," she said, and stroked the dog's back. Her thoughts turned to the day ahead and all the tasks she'd put off. She reached for the stack of executor duties. Time to get things done.

She had just settled at the kitchen table when her phone rang.

It was a breathless Sal. "I need you to get over here, *now*."

"Slow down Sal—"

"Remember the mystery locker? How Elaine was going to hack off the lock?" Sal was racing.

Amanda did remember but she couldn't get a word in.

"They cut the lock. You'll never guess what they found in there." Sal's voice quivered. "Oxana had a secret life." She took a moment, as if struggling to get the next words out. "And I think we're in huge trouble."
~~~

Thirty-Five

"We must crack the case, Amanda! I dreamt they locked me in the slammer and made me back into a man." Sal panted, pacing in front of the Singing Swans' reception desk. "It was horrible. Orange is not my colour." Her wig stuck out at odd angles, and there was a wildness in her eyes.

Mai adjusted her headset with a twirl of her finger that said, *this is a crazy woman here.*

O'Keeffe stood on her hind legs and put her paws on Sal's thighs but fell back when she got no response. "Imagine me, fresh meat for who knows what kind of Cellie. I'd go mad." Sal's jaw dropped and her lips stretched back. "Crimini— they'll put me in the Ding Wing!"

"Whoa, slow down there Big Sal." Amanda could see the whites above Sal's irises, and it made her own anxiety ratchet up. "What did they find in the locker?"

It was just then Sal spotted the dog. "Poor Sausage Roll!" She gasped, "I've ignored you." She kneeled to pet O'Keeffe, before looking at Amanda with wet eyes. "Do they allow dogs to visit prison?"

Amanda sighed. "You're not going to prison." She led Sal to a chair and eased her into it. "What's this about Oxana's secret life?" Amanda asked as O'Keeffe nestled onto Sal's slippers.

"Beaston seemed to suggest prison," Sal said, her voice dripping with mockery. *We are aware that you were a Marine and have the strength to snap a neck.* Her thick features clouded over, and she raised her hands. "Crikey Amanda, he measured these ham hocks." She buried her face in them and blubbered.

"Oh, Sal. It'll be okay. I promise." Amanda rubbed Sal's back.

Finally, Sal's shoulders stopped quaking. She reached one hand into her cleavage and pulled out a tissue. "Thank you, my Dear." Sal blew her nose and returned the used tissue to her bosom. She rose with all the elegance of a water buffalo, an exhausted one, and said, "Come with me."

~~~

The trio entered the Ladies Staff Room to find a catatonic Elaine slumped on the bench. Sal whispered, "The chief was in the same position, staring at the locker, cell phone in her lap, when I left an hour ago." The maintenance man and his bolt cutter were long gone, leaving an open locker with a dangling padlock.

Amanda kept her movements slow as she eased herself beside Elaine. "Hi there. You doing okay?" She touched Elaine's hand, asking, "Did you call the police yet?"

"Just going to." Elaine's tone was robotic, and Amanda got a whiff of body odour, which suggested that the manager hadn't bathed recently. The scent didn't seem to bother O'Keeffe, who gave the manager a good once over. It was the first time that Amanda ever saw her ignore the dog.
~~~

"Said that same thing an hour ago, when we found the stash," Sal said, not bothering to whisper as she strode to the open locker. She reached in, her big hands sweeping up a bikini so skimpy it appeared to be held together with dental floss. Next came a shimmery bustier complete with garters.

"Oh my." Amanda narrowed her eyes. "I'd like to suggest that Oxana was a lingerie model, but judging from the look on your face, I'm going to say that it's something a bit more nefarious."

"There's more." Sal arched her brows as she reached back into the locker and pulled out a wig; its hair long and red. Amanda sucked in her breath. It was the same hair as the blood-spattered strand that had clung to her t-shirt. The one she'd washed three times to purge any possible remnants from the dead body it had landed on. The one she had ultimately pitched into the Goodwill donation box.

When Sal shook the wig, something fell from it, a cardboard disk. O'Keeffe rushed to snuffle the discovery as Sal bent to retrieve it, saying, "What do we have here?" She groaned herself back into a standing position and examined what turned out to be a coaster. "Aha." She wagged her silver eyebrows. "I see that our nurse wasn't just nasty to the Singing Swans' residents. She got nasty at The Jewell."

Amanda recognized the logo emblazoned on the coaster, curvaceous legs caught in mid-kick, and she felt her eyes widen. "Oxana was a stripper?"

Sal held up one fleshy hand. "I believe that the politically correct term is *exotic engineer.*"

Elaine, who still hadn't moved a muscle, whimpered.

Amanda raised an eyebrow at Sal, who responded with a mighty shrug. Whatever was going on with Elaine, surely, she wasn't involved with Oxana's death. But one look at the manager and Amanda knew it would be futile to question her right now—her expression was as glazed as a maple donut.

"Wait. What is this?" Sal had flipped the coaster over and was performing an optical dance, glasses on or glasses off, before saying, "It's a drawing, but of what?"

Amanda reached out for the coaster and examined it. Her fingers traced the childish drawing of a rectangle with rounded edges, a circle on one end, two smaller circles below, and a squiggle at the other end. "Is it a Lego piece?"

"The doodle on the left could be an eye. That mark on the right a tail. Might be a turtle?" Sal said.

"The body is too square for a turtle, or any animal really." Amanda frowned. "Looks like a kid's drawing." She pulled out her phone and took a photo, saying, "Might as well chronicle all of this." She pointed at the contents of the locker. "The cops will have their hands on it soon enough."

Sal flashed a glance at Elaine, who remained unresponsive. "Not as long as she's in charge of calling them."

"That'll work to our advantage." Amanda checked the time, then put away her phone. "Look Sal, I hate to run, but I have an appointment I can't miss." Amanda nudged Elaine but got no response. "This is worrisome. Like she ran outta gas and left the car in neutral. I'll report it to the Nursing Station on my way out."

"One more thing before you abandon us," Sal said, holding up another item. "Here is the pièce de résistance, the object of my doom." It was a cell phone, with a torn coaster stuck to the back. A note scrawled on the coaster read, 'If anything happens to me, talk to Sal Falconetti.' It was signed, 'Oxana.'

Sal bit her quivering lip. "That just about seals my conviction, doesn't it?"

All Amanda could do was give her friend a hug. Then find a way to clear her name.

Thirty-Six

After rushing home, dropping off O'Keeffe, and gnawing on a stale slice of multi-grain bread, Amanda still managed to arrive at Vancouver General Hospital on time for her meeting with Beaton.

Despite her friends urging toward romance, her awful first impressions of him clung, and version 2.0 hadn't proven himself. Yet, as soon as the lobby doors parted, and he strode in, she had to admit he looked good in his snug jeans and t-shirt, even if he did still hobble. She stood, offering a small wave. He tilted his manly chin toward the elevator.

More awkward than the preliminary small talk—*nice day out there. Sure is* —was being together in a confined space. The first thing she noticed was his citrus and leather scent, one that increased her temperature in the already warm enclosure. The second was her regret that she hadn't put more effort into looking good today, having opted for comfortable shorts and a tee, with her hair in a ponytail. Worse yet was the fact that she'd run out of things to say, so offered a gummy smile that must have made her look like a maniac. Beaton, on the other hand, rested against the Otis wall, thumbs hooked in his jeans, body as relaxed as a puma. He didn't seem to mind the silence and didn't react to Amanda's bizarre grin.

When they reached the City Morgue, he opened the door, a hint of a smile as he held it and angled his head toward the reception area. There was something in his eyes—was it a dare? She raised her chin and squeezed past him. Her arm brushed along his and sent a shiver through her. Probably her fear at stepping into the offices of the morgue.

A receptionist sat at the front desk, sporting frosted hair and a fuzzy cardigan draped over her shoulder. She held a coffee mug, this one with the outline of a body holding another mug. Who knew there'd be so many crime scene niche mugs? "You must be Miss Sunderson?"

Amanda nodded, "Un huh." Her brush against Beaton had left her short on language.

"Go right in." The receptionist pointed to the interior door, which stood ajar, then took a sip from the mug. She arched her brows when Amanda didn't budge. "Go on. She's expecting you."

Beaton turned to go. "Gonna head up to ER, say hi to the guys. I'll leave you alone with Jack." Was that a wink?

He was leaving her?

Worse than going to the morgue with Beaton was having to go there alone.

Oh God, she was heading into the inner sanctum of death. She bristled as she pushed open the door and took a step into who-knew-what horrors. The next thing she knew, she tripped on something that sent her stumbling into the room. Wriggling to keep her balance, she heard something skid ahead of her then scanned the speckled linoleum for the culprit.

It was the bloody stump of a foot.

Her scream was loud enough to vibrate the third ring of Saturn.

The receptionist, hovering at the door, doubled over in laughter. Dr. Jackson got up from her massive oak desk, a blush of colour in her otherwise grey face. "Oh, there's the other foot!" She spoke in a husky voice as she retrieved the severed body part and waved it under Amanda's nose.

"Gah!" Amanda leapt, bumping into the receptionist, and setting off a fresh wave of laughter from the colleagues.

"Door stopper, Miss Sunderson." Dr. Jackson held it up, allowing Amanda to see that it was nothing more than a carved block of wood with a gory paint job. "A little gallows humour," the coroner said, wedging the stopper against the door.

Apparently, the swag market included a lot more than mugs, Amanda thought, her heart racing at Mach speed. She rested a hand on her chest and took a moment to catch her breath. Her throat was sore. She silently berated herself for screaming. Dr. Jackson returned to her desk, which was cluttered with files, dirty coffee mugs and an open banker's box.

Amanda saw that the room was ringed with stainless steel stations, sinks and tables with creepy paraphernalia. The air held a chill and a thousand secrets. At the far end was another door, probably leading to the autopsy room or whatever other hellish things went on here. Oh God, that must be the place with the refrigerated drawers! Amanda took a step back, closer to the reception door and bloody stump of a foot. "Sorry to bother you," Amanda stuttered. "I'm sure you're super busy."

"Busy place," Dr. Jackson said, keeping a stone face. "People are dying to get in."

Amanda manufactured a laugh that made her sound like a squealing rat. "Well, Officer Beaton suggested I come here to apologize—"

"What in the seven circles of hell are you talking about?"

"Um. The last time I came here, well, nobody was in the reception room. I waited but. . ." Amanda pointed to the front door then cocked her finger toward the exit. "Then I used the emergency exit and locked you out." She threw her hands up. "It was an accident. I didn't know you had propped the door open."

"Christ in a kayak, stop your blathering, woman," Dr. Jackson barked. "Officer Beaton told you to come here because *I asked you to,* not because you needed to bloody apologize."

"You asked me to come here?" Did the woman want to be friends?

"Yes." The coroner fished around in the banker's box, then held up an official-looking plastic bag labeled, *Evidence*. The bag held about a dozen white tablets. She locked eyes with Amanda, asking, "Were these Vicodin yours?"

Was Amanda being accused of using drugs? "Say what now?"

Dr. Jackson took a sharp inhale, then slowly exhaled in an unabashed sign of impatience. "These were found scattered on the floor around the DB." She furrowed her brow. "Remember the dead body you found?"

"Yes, yes, I remember." Sheesh. Amanda restrained herself from rolling her eyes. "What's Vidocin for?"

"Vi-co-din." Dr. Jackson pronounced the word with the

sharpness of a razor blade slicing three clean incisions. "Well, if you took them, you'd bloody know." She leaned across her desk and her hazel eyes reduced to cat-like slits.

Amanda wished she could control the twitch in her left cheek. "I don't take drugs. None of them." Another twitch. "Except wine, which I suppose is technically a drug."

The feline eyes narrowed again and held for a moment. "Fine." Dr. Jackson retrieved a clipboard and silver monogrammed pen. "Police report says you're right-handed." She barely waited for Amanda's nod of affirmation. "Hold up your hands."

Amanda snapped her hands in the air, making a stop sign.

"The other way." Dr. Jackson sighed as Amanda corrected her pose. "Wear any large rings on either hand? Signets, high school, Super Bowl, that type of thing."

As if she'd have a Super Bowl ring, Amanda snickered.

Dr. Jackson didn't join in the laugh.

Amanda cleared her throat. "No."

The coroner pressed pen to paper, scratching out some notes.

Geez, they really weren't connecting, were they? Amanda ventured a few steps forward and leaned one butt cheek onto the edge of the doctor's desk. "What's your theory?" She was hungry for answers.

Dr. Jackson's gaze snapped to the corner of the desk that Amanda was sullying. "You can read it in the cops' report." She sat at her desk, turning her attention to her work.

Amanda realized that she had been dismissed.

~~~

She found Beaton back in the main lobby, slumped in a chair, a sports magazine in his hands. "Why did you tell me I had to apologize to the coroner? That's not what she wanted," Amanda said, with a bit too much volume. Dr. Jackson had made her feel like an ass.

Beaton closed the magazine, tossed it on a table and stood. "I only made the vague suggestion. Knew she wanted to look you in the eye. We suspected you wouldn't come into the morgue if she just had a question. You'd have asked to do it on the phone."

The nerve, thinking he knew her mind. She made for the exit. He caught up, saying, "Wouldn't you?" They walked out of the main doors, to the covered carpark, which was quiet. A row of ambulances sat empty. A sign on a concrete parking pillar reminded them, 'Emergency Parking Only!'

Amanda stopped when his hand grabbed her arm. "Okay, yes I suppose I would have." She sighed.

Beaton shook his head, saying, "Jack doesn't work that way." He sounded like such a cop. "Besides, I wanted to collect that waiver you said you were going to sign."

Amanda tilted her chin high as she strode away and said, "Change of plan. I won't be signing the waiver." Plus, I'm not going to tell you about Oxana's secret locker or cell phone either, so there. *Na na na na na.* She felt quite good about herself, as her peripheral vision caught his mouth curl. She turned to look at him. It was a nice smile, Amanda thought, until her face collided with a concrete pillar.
~~~

Thirty-Seven

In lieu of turning around and going straight to ER, Amanda promised Beaton she would go home to ibuprofen and an ice pack. He warned her to watch for signs of concussion. She laughed that comment off, despite her dizziness. "It was just a gentle bump!" A gentle bump that stung like hell and embarrassed her so much that she almost ended up back in the morgue, this time under a sheet. She was desperate to cry and couldn't wait to get away from Beaton. He put her in a taxi where she shed a hurricane of tears as shock thrummed its way through her body.

Once home, she popped a painkiller and pressed an icepack to her cheekbone then settled into the sofa to make a call. Sal was aquiver at Amanda's report. *A new clue: a big ugly ring! Vicodin: pain reliever, narcotic, highly addictive.*

Amanda patted herself on the back for doing some decent detective work. Then she asked, "Any chance you looked through Oxana's phone?"

"I tried but it kept asking for a passcode."

"It's locked. Of course. Shite." Amanda flipped over the ice pack, searching her brain for an idea. "When are the cops coming?"

"Nurse Nelly came and checked Elaine over, insisted she go for a lie down. The two of them certainly do get on." Sal paused a moment before adding, "Short story long, Elaine never called the police."

"Good. Tell her to hold off. Cops don't need to know *when* we found the secret locker."

"Listen to you lying." Sal sounded pleased.

"As for the locked phone. . . Pish. Surely we can hack into it." She got up and opened her computer.

"Stellar plan. Look at you hacking into private property." Sal had a catch in her voice. "I'm so proud."

"Googling it now. Stand by."

"Ten-four that."

It took about fifteen minutes for Amanda to watch two instructional videos and cross-check details on a techie chat forum. Sal followed her instructions, frustrated with the more technical steps and that her fingers were too big for the cell phone buttons. Finally, she shouted, "Glory be, we're in!" She added, "Wow, there are a lot of colourful squares. What are they?"

"Those are called apps. Maybe ask Mai to explain." As good as their achievement felt, Amanda's energy was bottoming out.

"Implicate that sweet girl?"

"Good point." Amanda had a twinge of guilt. It was bad enough hacking into private property but now she was implicating someone else in the criminal offence. "I dunno, Sal," she said, too tired to think.

She realized that she'd neglected to mention the phone find to Beaton today, but since he'd been off duty that probably didn't count as withholding evidence from the cops. Her head shook at her convenient rationalizations. Geez, what kind of a person had she become? "We'll tell Beaton all about this soon, right?"

"That's a definite maybe, my Dear." Sal sounded distracted. "Heavens to Murgatroyd, Amanda, this thing can tell me the weather forecast! Did you know that?"

"I'm sure it's going to tell us a lot more about the past than the future." Amanda couldn't resist her fatigue any longer. The hand of God was pushing her towards sleep. "I'm gonna go. I need a nap."

"In the middle of an investigation?"

"Long story." Amanda touched her cheek and winced. It was burning, a headache had bloomed, and the room was spinning. This was not the time to recap her embrace with the concrete pillar. "Got to go."

"Good job, Partner. I'll poke around the phone, see what I can find."

~~~

The world was clearer when Amanda woke from her nap. It was after 3 pm and she was ravenous. Too bad the fridge was so bare. "O'Keeffe, we need groceries." She settled for toasting two slices of frozen bread and topping them with Cheddar that was so old she had to trim green fuzz off it. While crunching on the mediocre meal she put in another call to Sal, only to get the answering machine. Her message was bland, her brain still too fuzzy for wit. At the sunny kitchen table, she scrolled through
~~~

recent photos on her cell phone. The scribbles on the Jewell's coaster continued to confound her. She might not be able to decipher them, but knew someone who could, and punched in a phone number.

Keira answered on the fourth ring, listened to Amanda's question then said, "We're at the shops around the corner, if you want to consult with Essie in person."

"Some fresh air sounds good. See you soon." Amanda put away her plate and went to the bathroom to fix herself up. The reflection in the mirror was startling. A halo of red bruises surrounded the cut on her cheekbone. She opened a pack of Band-Aids. Although the rectangular shape didn't cover the round bruising, it was the best she could do.

The walk to the shops was long enough to pique some perspiration, but short enough that it didn't fatigue her. She found Keira staring into the window of a designer boutique. Her curls were a soggy mess in the afternoon heat, her sloppy t-shirt damp with sweat. She rocked the stroller with one hand and clasped Essie's hand with the other. Amanda sidled up beside them, gesturing to the mannequins in the display window, who were styled in an elegant throw-back to the disco era. "Nice dress. I'm guessing $1000?"

"Aye, it'd be gauche to let the price tag show." Keira leaned in to hug her friend but stopped when she saw Amanda's face. She blinked round eyes and shook her wilted curls. "What happened?"

Essie twirled once to show off her frilly cotton dress. Then she pointed at Amanda's face. "Auntie Mands, what's that boo-boo on your face?"

"I wasn't watching where I was going and walked into something."

Essie sidestepped a sapling that was intended to offer a tidbit of nature on the urban strip. "Was it a tree?"

"No. It was a concrete post." Amanda welcomed a pat of sympathy from Keira.

"Is concrete hard?" Essie asked.

"Yes, very hard." Amanda patted her cheek but even that light pressure made her wince.

Essie cocked her head. "Did it hurt?"

"A lot. Still does." Amanda's pride still hurt too. Beaton must have thought she was a complete idiot.

"This will make it better," the little girl said, digging stubby hands into the pocket of her dress and pulling out a fistful of stick-on tattoos, in the shapes of stars and moons.

"Thank you, Princess. I feel better already. Can I ask for another favour?" When Essie nodded in agreement, Amanda pulled out her cell phone and scrolled to the photo of the drawing on the Jewell's coaster. "I found this drawing, but I can't tell what it is. I think it might be Lego or a turtle."

Essie took the phone, examined the image, and giggled. "It's not a piece of Lego." She looked again, put her small hand on the screen and spread out her fingers to enlarge the image, like she was four going on forty. "You think it's a turtle? That's just silly." She shook her head as if she pitied Amanda, saying, "It's a truck."

Amanda leaned in to assess the stretched image. "Hmm. Could be."

"If I add a ladder and hoses then colour it red it could be

the fire truck from Paw Patrol. Or you could paint it blue and make it a garbage truck. See what I mean? A truck." Essie returned the phone to Amanda and started kicking pebbles on the sidewalk.

"Thanks Princess." Amanda contemplated Essie's verdict as she put her phone away, following Keira past shops no mere mortal could possibly afford.

"Ach, this stretch is too expensive for anything other than window shopping," Keira said, turning to Amanda. "Have you heard Toni's news?"

"Yup. She's in luuuv."

"The other news." Keira looked at Amanda, whose face must have been blank. "Gaz gave her gonorrhea. Probably too embarrassed to call you."

"Gonorrhea!?" Amanda yelped.

Essie stopped kicking pebbles and looked at Amanda. "What's gonorrhea?"

Keira froze for a moment then her eyes shifted right to left. She put an arm behind her back, crossing two fingers. "It's a town in Kilkenny. Graiguenamanagh." She ruffled Essie's hair. "One day we'll take you to Ireland."

Amanda mouthed an apology to Keira, then continued, "I thought that disease died out with scurvy."

"Apparently it's making a comeback."

"But how did he? When did he?"

Keira whispered, "He's been sleeping around."

"Damn it." Amanda stamped her feet on the ground. She knew he was too good to be true. "How's Toni coping?

"Angry. Hurt."

Squeaks escaped from the depths of the stroller, whimpers from the baby. At the same time, Essie noticed something across the street and asked, "Mama, can I have ice cream?"

Keira flapped her arms in frustration. "We just had lunch!"

"But I'm hungry." Essie screwed up her face, a threat to cry, just as the baby was doing.

Keira slumped against the stroller. Fatigue was etched on her face. "Amanda this is my life. Crying. Eating. Crying. It's tough having three kids."

"You have two."

"I was including Liam."

"Your husband doesn't count," Amanda said.

"Spoken like someone who doesn't have a husband." Keira threw her hands in the air.

"Okay, what do you need?" Amanda asked.

Keira pointed to the plastic containers lining the bottom of the stroller, "I'm loaded up with cereal, string cheese," She tugged on her t-shirt, "And breast milk." She wheeled the stroller out of the way of a happy young couple and readjusted the massive bag hanging off her shoulder. "I need a place to sit down," she said, looking ready to fall over.

Amanda pointed across the street. "There's a coffee shop." No surprise since Vancouver had a coffee shop on every corner. "Let's get you settled."

"Grand plan. You can wander around the bookshop next door," Keira said, "We can drive you home after."

By now the kids were in full-blown melt-down. "I hate my life," Keira whined over the crying. She looked up to the clear blue sky. "Lord don't smite me." She made the sign of the cross then said, "Amanda I'm a terrible person."

"No, you're just a tired person, with very tiny demanding persons to take care of." Amanda folded her in a hug. "Come on let's get these kids fed."

~~~

They settled into a nook in the coffee shop, Essie content with her ice-cream cone, the baby breastfeeding. Amanda left them to their snacking and ventured into the adjoining bookstore. She wandered past the 'Featured Books' tables, which spilled over with dystopian tales of the world's end, memoirs of trauma and misery, real-life crime, and bone-chilling thrillers. Didn't people want to read cheerful books anymore? Have a laugh, enjoy a few hours of escape? Amanda sure wanted that. She reflected on events of the past three weeks—*had it only been three weeks*—and how her life had become a tale dark enough to rival any of these best-sellers.

Stumbling into a murder had upended her life. The case had consumed her and obscured everything else, most importantly her grieving process and executor duties. All that had faded to the background of her everyday life, to the background of her psyche. How long would it stay recessed?

What would the consequences be?

A table laden with shiny cookbooks was the perfect distraction. She grabbed one, heavy and thick, named *Brutes Bites*. Its pages were glossy, full of photos of muscular arms and necks covered in tattoos and gangster jewelry. This would be a great escape, she thought, as she paged to the table of contents.
~~~

The first section was titled, 'Wake Up to a new kind of Bake Up! Breakfast.' The pun on the wake and bake culture was cute, but it made something scratch at the back of her brain. The next section was called, 'Vegetables - Don't become fucking vegetarians, just make 'em taste good.' Bells started ringing in her head as she read on. 'Save Yourself Bucks – Cheap meat ain't for losers! It can take some pounding.' The next section was, 'STOP the Salt Now.'

Why did it all look so familiar? She flipped to the first recipe and found it had a background covered with bold splashes of red, as if someone had thrown blood against a white wall. The penny dropped in Amanda's brain, then spun around as she re-jigged clusters of words to form:

'Wake Up losers!

Don't become fucking Vegetables

Save Yourself or take some pounding

STOP Now'

All someone had to do was cut out a few titles or recipe snippets, glue them to a blank sheet of paper and—voila, they had one threatening letter.

Coldness settled into her hands and feet as she grabbed her cell phone and snapped pictures of the book.

Now she knew who was on her tail: a thug who knew his way around flames and knives.

Thirty-Eight

Keira flew into a tizzy when she found Amanda with both the cookbook and her jaw wide open in the bookstore. "You look set to faint! Mother Mary help us!" She set Amanda on a bench, scooped up the kids, retrieved the car, doubled back, whisked Amanda home, then walked O'Keeffe in a well-executed set of tactics that only a military general or mother could manage.

Once home, Amanda wanted to call Sal and tell her what she found. Time was critical, but when she saw her bed, she collapsed onto it and didn't rise until morning. Her dreams featured street gangs throwing flaming knives at her as she stood against a massive dartboard, wearing a sequined string bikini.

Waking to a sunny morning was a welcomed relief. Her headache had disappeared. Much to her surprise, she found no sensitivity to light or sound, or any other concussion-like symptoms. Unfortunately, the bruising on her face had widened and featured variegated hues of blue and purple. The wound remained painful to the touch. After getting O'Keeffe out for her morning pee, Amanda put on some coffee and oatmeal then called Sal to detail what she'd found at the bookstore.

"Christopher Columbus!" Sal yelled, "Why did you wait to tell me? We're on the clock, you know."

"I know that!" As if she could forget.

Sal cut in, saying, "Hang on, I need to make a new card for the investigation board, a drawing of the book."

"What happened to being on the clock?"

"It's a quick sketch, you know the wild outline ones—"

"Gestural drawing," Amanda said. She'd picked up a few things from her mother's art career.

"That's it. Done. I'm using blue yarn for this one. Well, ding dong, here's an obvious connection."

"Tell me," Amanda said, imagining Sal crisscrossing lengths of yarn.

"Your cookbook was geared towards thugs. The local ones all frequent The Jewell."

"How do you know that?"

"Told you, I was a trucker, we spent time there too, although it was never my cup of Oolong," Sal mumbled. "Let's line up the clues."

Amanda envisioned Sal pacing before the homemade investigation station.

"The coaster is from The Jewell," Sal said, her tone clipped, procedural. "Oxana was a stripper, excuse me, an exotic engineer, so I'm guessing that she worked there. Come to think of it, when I saw the photos on her phone, some of them looked like they were taken behind the club."

"You're sure?"

"My Dear, the things that went on in the back parking lot of that place have left an indelible imprint on my brain. There's a reason they called it *the rear lot*." She snorted a laugh. "Yes, I'm sure." Her voice held a hint of pride even as it whispered of scandal. "I'd best make another gestural drawing."

"You don't need to sketch the rear lot!" Amanda was ready to make a gesture of her own. "Tell me about the photos you found on Oxana's phone."

"I'm spooling now."

"Scrolling."

"That's what I said. Okay, there are pictures of Oxana with a young pretty woman. Oxana looks funny. Oh wait, it's a smile. Huh, never saw her wearing one of those. They are looking quite glamorous, like they're out somewhere special." Sal continued, "Then there are some photos of local scenery: the beach, Pacific Spirit Park, Gastown." Sal sighed, adding, "You know, my Dear, I haven't been to any of these places in absolute Yonks."

"We'll get you out soon, Sal. Sounds like touristy places, the kind you'd send your family to show them your new home."

"Perhaps. Aha, like I said, here are photos of a redhead in Jewell's rear lot," Sal said. "I think it's Oxana made up in the red wig. Kinda cheap looking, although the dress is tasteful. My goodness, someone likes to look at herself." Sal sucked in a breath, adding, "Then there are shots of the building across the alley, but these are blurry. Hmm. Her photography skills declined as the photo shoot went on."

"When were those taken?" Amanda asked, then realized Sal wouldn't know where to look. "Should be a date above the photo."

Sal gasped in delight. "Oh, there is! I tell you Amanda you're quite good at all this. Oh look, there's even a time there, what a marvelous feature. August 13, 3 pm."

"The day she died." A day that was forever seared on

Amanda's psyche. You never forget the first time you land on a dead body. "She must have snapped those an hour or so before her death."

"The D-O-D! That's investigator-speak for the day of death. That cannot be a coincidence," Sal said, "But what does it mean?"

"Was she spying?" Amanda asked. "Or maybe she was planning on buying a condo, and liked the architecture?"

"If I remember correctly, it's an industrial building," Sal said.

"Can you send the photos to me? Maybe ask Mai to download them and email them?"

"I suppose. Let me find a pen," Sal said. "I'm writing that down now. Enlist Mai's help to get the photos off-loaded and into your email."

"I think you mean downloaded and onto my email."

"That's what I said." Sal's voice held a tinge of annoyance. "You're not listening well today."

"Get her to download the texts and emails too," Amanda said, "Then call Officer Beaton. Say you just found the phone this morning. Don't know what it contains."

"Lying, are we?" Sal's voice was tinged with delight.

"Well, technically the phone is police property, but it's property that had your name written on it," Amanda said, "So, it's more of a grey area." She almost believed it.

"The next thing we must do is go to The Jewell," Sal said. "Pick me up in an hour."

"Agreed—wait, it's still morning."

"Of course. Make it two hours. They open at noon.

Lunchtime buffet," Sal said. "Not a bad spread. Lots of sausages."

"Yech." Amanda cringed at the sanitary implications of a buffet in a room full of naked women.

"Wear a disguise," Sal said, "If someone at The Jewell knows about the murder, they might know something about *us*." Her voice twitched with excitement. "Oh Goodie, a field trip. If I had to sit through one more lunchtime sing-along here, I'd go nutty as a caged monkey."

~ ~ ~

When she pulled up to the foot of The Singing Swans' drive, Amanda didn't recognize the man standing there. After all, she'd never seen Sal as a man. Gone were the dowdy house dress, pancake makeup and wig. She had gelled her hair back and wore a suit, complete with vest and pocket handkerchief. She held a fedora. It looked like she'd stepped out of a gangster film noir.

Sal climbed into the car and lowered the timber of her voice. "Hey beautiful."

"Eew, don't flirt with me! That's creepy." Amanda pointed at Sal's outfit. "You look like a mafia hitman."

"I'll take that as a compliment." Sal looked her over. "I said you needed a disguise, not a Halloween costume." She noticed Amanda's facial bruising. "Did someone beat you up?"

"Yes, a concrete post." Amanda gave up the *Reader's Digest* version of the story.

"Curse that Beaston. He's such a troublemaker. I'm sorry to hear that, my Dear." Sal sighed. "And that gash certainly compromises the look." She swept a hand over Amanda's tattered sequined dress, long feathered lashes, and brittle platinum wig. "You look like Dolly Parton, minus the big bazingas."

Sal took a minute to ponder, then said, "Let's tone it down a bit, shall we?" She spent the next five minutes styling Amanda, who had to squeeze out of the yard-sale dress, tear off a set of cheap lashes and doff the wig she'd bought years ago for an eighties tribute night. It took a bit of maneuvering, behind the wheel of the car, but soon Amanda's outfit was pared down to workout tights and a tank top.

Something in the back seat caught Sal's attention. "What's the pink creature in your bag?"

Amanda pulled out a fluffy sweater, which had been part of the ensemble but had proven too warm.

"Yes," Sal said, making her put it on and button it so tightly it drew attention to her boobs. "Now you have the best part of Parton." Sal handed her the fedora. "Stuff your hair into this and pull it down low."

Amanda complied, and Sal nodded her approval, adding, "Spiffing. Early Madonna meets Dolly. Now, how can we cover that travesty on your cheekbone?"

"It's too fresh to put makeup on. There's not much I can do." Amanda shrugged and then had an idea. She dug around in her bag for Essie's stick-on tattoos then showed Sal. "Stars or moons?"

Sal thought for a minute. "Let's go with the star." She peeled it off the strip and gingerly pressed it onto Amanda's cheek. "Wearing a moon on your face in a strip club might send the wrong message."

~ ~ ~

As they approached the front doors of The Jewell, Amanda grabbed Sal's arm. "Tell me you have a plan."

"Yes. We go inside and snoop." Sal pulled the door handle. "Try to be inconspicuous." She marched inside, sure-footed.

Even before her eyes adjusted, Amanda felt the ick factor and was reminded of why she'd turned and run out of there on her first visit. Sal, however, seemed to revel in it. "Ah, this place brings back memories." She took a deep inhale and looked around.

Amanda watched her friend, wondering if it was the odour of stale beer or scuff marks on the antique paneled walls that were enchanting her. She spotted a display case that she'd missed on that first visit. "Check this out." The display held a row of stripper's publicity photos, one of them a lanky redhead who went by the name *Volga*.

"Well, well," Sal said as she studied the photo. "Nurse Oxana certainly did clean up well."

That was an understatement, Amanda thought, gazing at the photo. Volga looked downright beautiful. Soft and feminine. The red wig flattered the skin tone that Oxana's muddy brown hair had left dull. A whisper of a smile pulled at her lips. Then there were her eyes. The last time Amanda had seen them was up close and lifeless. Even now the thought made her tremble. But these eyes shone with light, with something else—was it hope? Amanda wanted to cry at that light being snuffed out.

Sal pointed to the bar at the far end of the room, and they made their way over a carpet that could best be described as crunchy. Amanda pointed to a $20 bill laying on the floor. Sal grabbed her arm to stop her picking it up. "Don't do it. Never know who's watching." Sal barely moved her lips as she spoke, coming off like a gangster ventriloquist. "Don't want to piss anyone off."

"Right," Amanda muttered through closed lips, leaving the money where it lay.

They took seats at the bar when a young woman tottered out of the DJ booth, wearing sky-high heels, big hair and a skimpy underwear set. She smiled at them, using her lips, eyes and, somehow, the rest of her body too. She approached Sal. "Lap dance, Honey?" The voice was fake-sexy, as though she'd learned it from porn films. When Sal shook her head, the dancer turned to Amanda, asking, "You here for an audition?"

Amanda bit back her laugh as Sal took over, saying, "Actually, we're hoping for some information." Sal offered a manly look as she pulled a tenner from her vest pocket.

The private dancer accepted the cash and planted her tiny rear end on a barstool. "Ok, mister. You can buy me a drink too if Luis ever finishes his break." Her voice had abandoned the fake sexy now that her earning opportunity had declined. She sounded young and Amanda studied her face, deciding that she couldn't be more than 20 years old. She smelled like cheap coconut suntan lotion.

Sal said, "It's about Volga, Miss—"

"Twin Peaks," The dancer said, slumping when Sal mentioned Oxana's alter-ego. "Ain't seen Volga in weeks.

Nobody has." She tapped orange acrylic nails against the bar. "I'm pretty mad, you know, 'cause I thought we were friends." She narrowed her eyes, her glittery eyeshadow sparkling under what Amanda realized was blue light. "Hey, who's askin'?"

Sal wore a poker face. "I'm her uncle and haven't been able to reach her lately."

Liar liar, man pants on fire.

"Her uncle?" Twin Peaks said, her nose crinkling. "Thought everybody was in Russia, or Ukraine. Someplace cold. Volga has a sister there. They Skype a lot."

"Yes, most of them are there," Sal said, nodding in a knowing way. "I'm one of the few living here." Amanda was impressed by how smooth Sal's lies were and how easily her questions flowed. Sal pressed on with, "Can you tell me about the last time you saw her?"

"Fer sure," Twin Peaks leaned her elbows on the bar, causing her breasts to spill halfway out of her bra. "We both did the lunch shift that day. Sometimes you get a lot of lap dances at lunch, since there ain't many performers here during the day, like you can see." She tilted her dainty chin toward the empty stage that rose from the centre of the room. "So, I remember she'd had a really good shift then she changed clothes but kept her wig and makeup on. Always did, right until she left the club. Like she didn't want nobody to know what she looked like in real life. Me, I don't care." She inspected her fingernails as if she needed a break from remembering. A minute later she continued, "Anyways, she went out back to have a smoke—everybody in Ukraine smokes, right? When she came back inside, she looked real funny."

"Funny how?" Amanda asked.

"Freaked out. In a hurry. I was out on the floor, trying to sell lap dances, see, so I didn't get a chance to talk to her. She grabbed her purse, a couple coasters then a-scrammed out the front." Twin Peaks blinked slowly, her fake lashes accentuating the movement.

Amanda sensed the dancer's sadness. She never got to say goodbye to her friend. Didn't even know she was gone. As much as Amanda wanted to tell her that Volga had died, that would only compromise their investigation, so she added, "Anything else?"

Twin Peaks ran her hands over her arms as if trying to warm herself. "She was pale. It's super noticeable under these blue lights. They're killer."

Amanda's guilt surged at the word, but her focus was drawn to the slim and oily guy who appeared behind the bar. She recognized him as the one who'd been wiping down tables her first visit.

He yelled, "Yo Twinnie, you workin' or talkin'?"

"Yeah yeah, Luis. Gimme a vodka and Red Bull, on this guy here." She pointed at Sal, got up from her stool, and whispered, "Be careful with Luis. He's super pissed that Volga disappeared." She tottered away, then grabbed her drink from Luis who strutted over to Sal and Amanda. He walked in time to the beat of the current song, *Stayin' Alive*. His smile revealed two gold capped teeth. "What can I get you?"

"Actually, we're not here for drinks," Sal said, pulling another tenner out from her—his?—vest. "But that's for Twin Peaks' drink."

Amanda worried how Luis would react, so she put on a bright smile, one that wasn't lost on him. His gaze moved slowly over Amanda's body like a snake slithering down a tree. "I get it, Mamacita." He gave her the creeps. "A bit on the old side, but a lot of guys like that. Young guy - older woman fantasy." One of his gold teeth caught a glimmer off the disco ball as he nodded. "So, you're lookin' for work."

Insulted, Amanda spit out her words, "I am not!" Sal elbowed her in the ribcage, making her jump to her feet. "I am not," Amanda squeezed her eyes in an attempt to appear sexy, "leaving here until I book an audition." She offered what she hoped passed for a sultry smile. Was that a muffled snort from Sal? Within a second, Amanda sensed the heat of embarrassment on her face.

"That's the 'tude Mamacita!" Luis' laugh was hoarse and full of phlegm, like he smoked a pack a day. "I like that." He fondled a dab of hair that grew from the base of his chin. "Gimme a full 360."

Amanda rotated, slowly, struggling to keep down her breakfast. When she'd done a circle of humiliation, she faced him again. She angled her head and tipped the cap of her fedora. Surely that was sexy.

"Okay Mamacita! You come back on Friday afternoon for your audition. Bring two songs and two outfits. Keep 'em both short."

Amanda smiled, fighting the bile in the back of her throat. "Thanks." She extended a limp, girly hand.

"Luis." He squeezed her hand and a chill traveled up her arm then down her spine. "What's your name Sweetheart?"

"Am-" She stopped herself, knowing she couldn't very well use her real name. Her slow smile bought her some time to think. An image of the tattoo stuck on her cheek sprang to mind and she blurted, "Star."

"Am-star?" Luis asked. "Like Amtrak?"

"Exactly," Amanda practically moaned the word. Sweet Jesus, what was happening to her?

Luis' laugh rattled. "Nice." His gaze slithered again. "I bet lotsa guys would love to pull their train along your track."

"Eew –" another stab in the ribs from Sal. "I mean eew that sounds great," she squealed.

"One more thing," Sal said to Luis, "I was hoping to see Volga today. Know when she'll be here next?"

Luis's friendly mood took a turn. "Don't know nothin'." He squinted his dark eyes and pursed his lips as if trying to trap more words from escaping.

The back door sprung open, flooding the bar area with sunlight. A burly guy in coveralls stood haloed in the light. He stepped into the bar, all spiky hair and bad attitude, shoving his sunglasses onto his head. Amanda made out the word *Trucking* stitched on his breast pocket. He called to Luis, who flew to his side. Amanda overheard the bragging tone, a snippet, "Nobody gonna mess with me." After a minute, he looked over in their direction, snapped his sunglasses down and vamoosed.

Luis yelled to Amanda, "See you Friday Am-Star." He pointed at Sal. "But leave Big Daddy at home."

"Get me out of here," Amanda said through gritted teeth. "I need a shower. Or maybe a fumigation."

Sal rose from her barstool, whispering, "Do the fumigation.

That man seems like poison."

They retraced their steps to the front door, where Sal looked behind her, confirming that Luis was watching them. She reached for the door handle, giving Amanda a once over. "I need a proper drink to get that image of your 360 out of my mind."

"I'll fix you one as soon as I get you home," Amanda said.

"You might want one too," Sal said, "Seeing as we just found the mystery woman from Oxana's photos." She pushed the door open, and the sound of traffic overtook *Don't Stop Believing.* "And because you just got ogled by the killer," Sal said as they stepped into the sun.

Thirty-Nine

On the drive back, Sal pulled down the passenger seat visor, mussed her gelled hair and dotted on some lipstick. "We are off to the races now, my Dear." She double checked in the mirror then slammed the visor back into place. "Shame that they no longer have the lunch buffet, though, I am quite peckish."

"So, if Luis is the killer, what's his motive?" Amanda asked, focused on driving out of the Downtown East Side.

Sal squeezed out of her suit jacket and unbuttoned its vest. "That's where our sharply-honed detective skills will come in." She buzzed with excitement. "So many new clues—I'll need more yarn!"

Amanda steered through the streets of the business district. "First, we need to find out if Luis owns the club, or if he's the manager, or just a bartender."

"And what his relationship was with Volga," Sal added, "Although I can't see her going for a slippery toad like him."

"You're sure it was Twin Peaks in the photos with Oxana?"

"Affirmative. Out on the town and dolled up like a couple of glamour-pusses."

Amanda was deep in thought as they headed towards the steel trusses of the Burrard Street Bridge." Could Oxana and

Twin Peaks be a couple? Maybe Luis was jealous?"

"Anything is possible, my Dear. Let's review our notes and work on the investigation board. It's become quite robust." Sal turned to Amanda. "And remember to give your email number to Mai." She clucked, "We might want to give her a cut of the action, seeing as she agreed to keep our phone hacking on the down-low."

Clearly Sal had been brushing up on her gangster speak, even if Amanda had no idea what *a cut of the action* would be. "Besides the photos, what else did you find on the phone?" Amanda asked, driving beneath the Art Deco arches of the bridge, the waters of False Creek sparkling below.

"Lots of texts and emails in Russian. We'll need to find a translator." Sal looked out the window. "Mai is asking around. She also commented on how many selfishies Oxana took in the parking lot."

"Selfies, not selfishies."

"Okay, *selfies*," Sal said. "Mai downloaded the photos onto email, no questions asked, before I called Beaston and told him we found the phone." She snorted. "He was his usual cheerful self. I left out the part about hacking it open."

"Thanks for calling him," Amanda said, and they sat in companionable silence until she pulled into the drive of The Singing Swans Lodge. There were no empty parking spots, so she dropped off Sal, then found street parking two blocks away. She took her time walking back. The sunny stroll lifted her spirits, along with the sense that they were closing in on the case, finally. She stopped to inhale the scent of a bush of monster white peonies.

Once back at the lodge, she signed in at the reception desk, an action that had become tedious. It must have shown in her expression because when Mai got off the phone, she said, "Thank you. Some people don't bother to always sign in and out. It can make things difficult for us." The receptionist was sweet, considerate. How could Amanda ever have suspected her of killing Oxana? She had to stop being so paranoid, seeing everyone as a potential killer.

The elevator doors opened, and Nurse Mary stepped into the lobby. When she spotted Amanda, her chubby face lost its usual cheer. One hand flew to her scrubs pocket then she marched towards Reception, saying, "Just the lass I was seeking." Was that a quiver in her voice?

Amanda made her greetings as Mary steered them down the corridor, away from the lobby. Whatever she had on her mind must be important. Amanda hoped that the nurse had another piece of the puzzle to offer, maybe some new discovery about that threatening letter she had passed along. They walked by the dining room, its doors closed for the break between lunch and dinner. Across the hall, the pub was also closed.

Mary glanced around, seeking something, and said, "Let's find a wee bit of privacy." The nurse took a few steps as she stuffed her files under one arm. Approaching the stairwell door, she grabbed her ID lanyard and snapped it against the keypad. The door opened with a *thunk,* and Mary stepped behind Amanda, whose unease swelled.

"No. I'd rather not go in there."

"Just a quick visit," Mary said, her stout body blocking the escape route. She took a step, backing Amanda into the stairwell.

Amanda's feet were like lead. She tripped over the floor plate, stumbled backwards, and landed on the bottom step, the one on which Oxana had died. Pain twisted through her left ankle, and she doubled over to clasp it as panic sunk in. The door slammed shut. Her system flooded with adrenalin. "Mary, I can't be in here."

The nurse stood silently, her back to the door.

Amanda caught a smell, almost a taste, of something metallic. Was Oxana's blood still in the crevices of the stairwell? Her breathing grew ragged. "Get me out of here." She extended her hand.

"I can't," Mary said, her voice flat.

Why on earth couldn't she? What was going on?

"I know you figured it out," Mary said, her eyes focused on the floor. Her face was so pale that her reddish freckles stood out like a constellation in the night sky.

Amanda had so not figured it out! Sal had sworn that Mary wasn't capable of—what word had she used—*treachery*. So, what did Mary think Amanda had figured out?

Visceral memories machine-gunned through her head—landing on the soft warm body, the dead eyes staring into her own, her hand slipping in hot blood. She spotted something on the linoleum. My God, were those speckles of brain matter? Coldness spread through her, seeping into her fingers and toes.

She experienced a moment of numbness, a blessed second of disconnection.

Then the pieces snapped into place.

Sal had vowed Mary didn't create the threatening letter, but something far worse became clear.

Mary was the killer.

Amanda's panic skyrocketed. She needed to stall the nurse until she found a way out. "I don't know what you mean." She used the most soothing voice she could muster. "Figured out what?" Her eyes widened, and she hoped they expressed bewilderment, not fear.

"No need for games," Mary said, reaching into the pocket of her scrubs.

"Stop!" Amanda flung both hands in the air. Oh God, what would it be—a knife? A syringe?

"You know I can't stop." Mary snorted a brief, snotty laugh. "That's the problem." Tears filled her vacant eyes. "I can't stop."

Killing Oxana must have bred a hunger to kill again. Amanda scanned the bleak stairwell, letting the full irony sink in.

The nightmare began here, it would end here.

But it didn't have to.

"No!" Amanda screamed, using the force of her shout to propel her towards Mary. But her attempt was defeated by her lame ankle. She fell to the floor, whimpering at the impact. "Please, don't do this."

"But I have to," Mary's voice cracked. "It's the only thing left to do." The muscles in her forearm clenched, her hand tightening around the object in her pocket. She stepped forward.

Amanda opened her mouth to scream but her throat choked out any sound. Why hadn't Fight and Flight taught them to fight when injured?

Fast as a whip, Mary pulled the thing out, saying, "Take it!"

Amanda squeezed her eyes shut, bracing for the stab of a needle in her arm, the blade of a knife on her exposed neck.

"Take it, Amanda." Mary's words were quiet, spoken through tears.

There was no stabbing, no slicing. Amanda opened one eye, her left one. Mary was kneeling on the floor sobbing. She clutched a bottle of white pills, the same as the ones the coroner had found.

"Please Amanda. Save me from myself."

Forty

Elaine insisted Amanda get treated, in the privacy of Sal's suite. Nurse Nelly diagnosed a mild sprain of the ankle, prescribing rest, and ice to reduce the swelling. Amanda couldn't understand how a *mild sprain* could hurt so much and was grateful when Nelly gave her a pain pill.

The nurse remained calm as she wrapped the ankle with a tensor bandage, her manner starkly contrasting that of Elaine, who collapsed on Sal's sofa with a pained expression. She whimpered, "It's all my fault."

Amanda looked to Sal, who was filling glasses with water. If Elaine was involved with Oxana's death, she was doing a terrible job of feigning innocence, and Amanda was tired of sidestepping the issue. Not that she could sidestep anything right now with a throbbing ankle. "What is your fault?" Amanda asked.

"Me and Nelly." Elaine's lips barely moved as she spoke.

Nelly looked up from her bandaging duties, alarm rising on her face, even as her oversized glasses slid along her nose. "Don't, Auntie Elaine." A hand flew to her mouth and she dropped the roll of gauze, which unfurled from Amanda's ankle. Nelly grunted, sitting back on her heels then began again, keeping her head down.

"Maybe I should switch out water for something stronger," Sal said, setting the tray of glasses on the coffee table. She handed one to Amanda for her pill then slapped her hands to her hips, saying, "Alright Elaine. Spill the beans. You and Nelly what?"

"We needed a new nurse." Elaine sighed, slumping deeper into Sal's sofa.

Sal said, "What with one killed and one killing herself."

Elaine nodded in agreement. "But we couldn't get a new nurse. Nobody wanted to work in a place where nurses ended up dead or drug-addicted, and both stories had spread." Elaine sat up and took a glass of water. Her eyes still held a faraway look, but when Nurse Nelly sat beside her and draped an arm around her, Elaine's focus returned.

Nelly took over. "I was itching to leave Manitoba and live in BC, so when Auntie Elaine told me the situation, I packed up and bought a plane ticket."

"Sounds fine to me," Amanda said, raising her swaddled ankle and resting it on the coffee table. "What was the problem?"

"Documentation." Elaine seemed to choke on the word and took a long drink of water.

"Any idea how long a BC Nursing application takes to process?" Nelly asked, then pointed at Sal's window. "Mountains? Ocean? Everyone wants to be here."

"I was desperate. You can't run a retirement home without a full retinue of nurses. For gracious sakes, there are enough things to go wrong." Elaine looked at Sal and Amanda. "So, I hired her."

"Then we got caught," Nelly said and she looked scared. "Working with a pending application is a big offence."

No wonder Elaine had been such a wreck. No wonder Nelly was so nervous. "But you're still working," Amanda said.

"Technically, I'm not," Nelly said. "And that might be another problem." She smiled at Elaine. "But she's my only aunt, and I need to help her."

"The Nursing Union is filing a claim against Singing Swans and threatening Nelly's licence," Elaine said, "But I've hired a lawyer and am countering." That explained the barrister letter that Elaine had swept off her desk and out of Amanda's sight.

A dead nurse, one in rehab, cancelled move-ins and a lawsuit. "You've got a lot on your plate," Amanda said.

Elaine frowned. "It's more of a platter, really."

~ ~ ~

Toni's Jeep screeched to a halt in front of the retirement home, and she leapt out, yelling, "Mands, you okay?" She didn't look too good herself. Her face was puffy and red, her anxiety revved up.

"I'm okay," Amanda said, letting Sal help her up from the bench they shared, wincing as she hobbled across the pavement. "Toni, Sal. Sal, Toni. Sorry you're not meeting under better circumstances." The two women exchanged greetings.

"Sprained ankle," Sal told Toni. "She needs rest. And ice, to reduce her swelling and chill some scotch." She hoisted Amanda under her arms and tucked her into the front seat of the Jeep, careful with the bandaged ankle. "My Dear, you get some rest. I'll work on the investigation board." Sal turned to Toni. "Thanks for getting her home."

After quick goodbyes, Toni settled into the Jeep, and turned to Amanda. "WTF happened?" Her bejeweled eyebrows raised to an arch, and lines crossed her forehead.

Amanda let out the breath she hadn't realized she'd been holding. "I thought it was D day for me. D meaning death," she said. "The upside is that the incident triggered a detail from the crime, one I'd forgotten. It was a hail of white pills, Vicodin, showering down on me and bouncing around the floor. I remembered looking up from Oxana's body, seeing Mary turn and run out of the upper stairwell."

Toni nodded, saying, "She'd snuck into the stairwell to get her fix but got a shock instead."

"Exactly. She'd have seen me on top of Oxana, heard my screams and high-tailed it out of there." Murky images swirled in Amanda's thoughts, the pain in her ankle preventing them from coming into focus.

"So, in her mind, you knew about her addiction." Toni made no move to start the engine, Amanda noticed, as tiredness fell around her like a heavy curtain. Toni continued, as if she couldn't drive and talk at the same time. "Did she steal the pills from the Nursing Station? Or the patients?"

Amanda rolled down her window, inhaling the warm air and fragrance of roses in bloom. "Not sure. She might have skimmed a few here and there. Unfortunately, the residents probably wouldn't have realized. She'll be admitted to rehab, on The Singing Swans' dime." She felt her eyelids closing.

Toni fired up the engine and pulled out of the Lodge's driveway. "I'm glad you're okay."

"Thanks." Amanda looked in the side-view mirror, willing her focus to return, so she could stay awake. She chose a black Range Rover, concentrated on bringing it into clarity. "Enough about me." She inspected Toni, who hadn't bothered to gel, or even wash her hair. The tangled black nest gave her a sinister look. "How are you? Keira told me your news."

"Yes," Toni said, slapping the steering wheel. "I have gonorrhea! Like an 1820 sailor's wench." Her voice cracked as she continued, "Gaz swore he didn't know he had it, but he did admit to sleeping with other women. Said, he's a single man." Her voice dripped with disgust as she pulled to a stop before merging with traffic on the commuter road.

"That little shit." Amanda's head started to throb along with her ankle.

"When I said I was going to the doctor for antibiotics, he asked me to get them for him too." Toni slammed on the brakes for a red light. "Fecker has built a multi-million-dollar business but can't get himself antibiotics to cure the STD he's been spreading around to who knows how many women?" Fear spread across her face. "I assume they're women. I had to have an AIDS test."

"I'm sorry," Amanda said as they squealed away from the light. A check in the side mirror, where she noticed the Range Rover switch lanes, a few cars behind them. Her powers of concentration were winning against her fatigue.

Toni's tone switched to grief. "I never asked if he was seeing other women. I just assumed he felt the same as me." She choked back a sob. "I'm such an idiot!"

"You are not an idiot. You fell for him, and figured he fell for you. We've all done it," Amanda said. She had a terrible track record with gauging lover's motives. She patted Toni's arm. "He's a prick."

"He is, isn't he?" Toni yelled. "Or am I overreacting?" She dropped to a whisper, "I thought he was *the one*." The traffic light ahead flicked from green to amber as Toni blazed through it.

"You're not overreacting, and he wasn't the one. He's a jerk." The Range Rover made a noisy acceleration, speeding through the amber light. Amanda was tired and had just been traumatized, but fatigue and PTSD be damned, this was too much of a coincidence. "And there's a jerk on our tail, too." Amanda pointed out the car, her pulse picking up steam. "Been riding us since we left the retirement home." Her mind raced through possibilities, each one scaring her more than the last.

"Fecking men!" Toni screamed as she stuck her left hand out the window and stabbed her middle finger repeatedly in the air. Then she slammed to a stop and laid on the horn.

Cars swerved around her, then began a symphony of honking.

One guy yelled, "Don't stop in the middle of the fucking road, Lady!"

Toni's elegant comeback, "Muthafucka!" left pedestrians staring in alarm.

Amanda had pulled out her cell, slapped on the camera, swiveled in her seat, and snapped with a shaky hand. The Range Rover driver remained a mystery, hidden behind tinted glass as he dropped his speed, fell behind them then skidded onto a side street.

Amanda checked her pictures, which were out of focus. Why hadn't she steadied her hand? "Damn it." Why hadn't she zoomed in on the license plate?

Toni released the horn and pulled her hand with its offending finger back inside the Jeep. "Asshole." Her tone was jovial, as if the incident had purged her anger.

But Amanda's heart continued to thud as she had a new thought. Was that the same SUV that had squealed away from her and O'Keeffe days ago in the driveway of Singing Swans?

Or was it just the kind of coincidence that sends a shiver up your spine?

~~~

Toni pulled up in front of Amanda's house, hopped from the Jeep and eased Amanda out before helping her up the porch steps and into her flat. Amanda was woozy and so fatigued she only waved at O'Keeffe. Toni got her settled onto the sofa, then got her another painkiller, an icepack, and a blanket. "I'll take doggie for a walk. You rest." Toni gave Amanda a hug then pulled back to study her. "In case nobody told you, you're doing amazingly well handling all the shit life's been throwing in your face." She turned away before Amanda could reply.

"Thanks, nobody has told me that." Had she been strong over these past hellish weeks? To her, it just seemed like she'd been putting one foot in front of the other.

Toni clipped the leash onto the excited dog then glanced at
~~~

the sofa, saying, "Get the icepack on that ankle." She whistled for O'Keeffe to follow, her hand scratching her crotch. "I'm gonna get one too."

As Amanda plunged into slumber, an image of the black Range Rover drove into her mind. Whoever he was, she hoped like hell he didn't have her address.

Forty-One

When she woke to a blaze of morning light, Amanda wondered why she was sleeping on the sofa, in yesterday's clothes, O'Keeffe nestled against her. The pain in her ankle twigged a memory of Mary trapping her in the stairwell.

Damn, it hadn't been a dream. It was real.

She threw off the blanket and checked her ankle, which was double its normal size. An unholy shade of purple bloomed at the edge of the bandages. Slowly, she stood and eased her weight onto that foot. Not too bad, but she'd have to be careful. Ibuprofen and caffeine should help. She retrieved the room-temperature icepack from the floor then limped to the end of the hallway, into the bathroom.

Gawd, she looked like she belonged in a horror film. The bruise on her cheekbone had turned a sickly shade of mauve and darkened the circles under her eyes. She would need to trowel on makeup before facing the world. It took longer than usual to perform her morning ablutions, everything being just a bit more difficult than it had been yesterday.

When she finally got around to making coffee, she saw the familiar mound of executor paperwork on the kitchen table. Had Mount Executor grown bigger? She knew she had to get those tasks done. Damn *The Case of the Mean Nurse who Everyone Hated.* It had taken up too much time and energy.

Regret stabbed at her. Had she let her mother down?

The familiar toxic cocktail of grief churned in her gut.

"No," She yelled, stopping herself from being pulled into the vortex of pain. "Not going there." There were more pressing things to do.

O'Keeffe sauntered into the kitchen, rumpled from sleep. "Morning, Girl." The sight of the dog brought a wave of happiness and Amanda joined her on the floor for a cuddle. Then she poured a coffee and made breakfast for them both. Afterwards, with a few painkillers and a fresh icepack on her elevated ankle, she opened her computer and the email with the photos Mai had downloaded from Oxana's phone.

The photos were as Sal had described. Oxana and Twin Peaks out on the town. Snaps of local landmarks, the places that made Vancouver such a great place to live. But it was those final shots that she studied closely, the selfies Oxana had taken an hour or so before her death.

Oxana looked beautiful in her stage makeup, the red wig contrasting with the blue sky and green strip club. She wore the same chic dress that Amanda had seen when they collided outside of Elaine's office. One photo showed her offering a wave, another one blowing a kiss. They were the kind of shots taken with someone else in mind, someone you love. Who was that for Oxana?

The final selfie had a different character. Gone was the breezy attitude. Oxana's face registered alarm—something must have happened at that moment. From there on, the photos switched angles and captured the red brick industrial building, which Sal said was directly across the alley. All these shots were out of focus, as if Oxana had snapped them quickly or with a shaky hand. A couple of them held a flare of light, like the sun bouncing off a window.

She took a sip of coffee. What had triggered Oxana's alarm? She must have heard or seen something. Something that shocked or scared her. But as closely as Amanda looked, she couldn't see anything out of the ordinary.

The jangle of her cell phone startled her, and she answered with a thudding heart. It was Sal, asking what time Amanda was picking her up. It took a second for her to realize Sal's meaning. She laughed, saying, "I am not going to a stripping audition."

"You must. We need to prove that greasy barkeep Luis killed Oxana. Maybe it was jealousy, maybe it was blackmail—"

"Or because of something she caught on her cell photos." Amanda shifted the icepack to her face. It stung. "Let the police do it."

"They're useless. We're better detectives than them," Sal said in a scoffing tone.

Amanda's knuckles whitened as she clenched her coffee mug. "I am not going to strip."

"We'll be in and out in a half hour." Sal chuckled. "Probably a widely-used comment in a strip club." When she didn't get a response, she asked, "Would you rather I do it?"

An image sprang to Amanda's mind, and it wasn't pretty. "I wouldn't put it past you."

Sal's voice softened. "By the by, Elaine got the most touching email from Oxana's sister, all the way from the

Ukraine. How much Oxana's money helped the family, how much they loved her and miss her." Her tone was smooth as honey. "We owe it to that little minx of a nurse."

Amanda did not appreciate Sal's manipulative tactics. She sighed. What had she gotten herself wrapped up in?

"Oh bother, I have to go. Someone's ringing my doorbell," Sal said chuckling. "Hopefully, you'll ring a few at your audition."

Forty-Two

As soon as Amanda got off the phone with Sal, O'Keeffe's pleading looks reminded her that it was time for a walk. The fact that she had her leash in her mouth was also helpful in getting the message across.

Carefully, Amanda tested her ankle again, relieved that the combination of icepack, painkiller and coffee had reduced the pain and swelling. If she took it easy, she figured she could manage.

She let O'Keeffe out then turned to lock the door behind them, double checking that it caught. Stress had made her anxious. She shook her head at her own neuroticism. O'Keeffe snuffled her way down the steps. Amanda followed, slowly, using the handrail to help her. Not too bad, she thought.

They had just begun their trek when the door of a beaten-up Honda Civic popped open and a man in a linen suit stepped out.

It was Jeremi.

A ray of sunlight bounced off something in his hand. A gun.

Amanda started to run, pulling O'Keeffe behind her.

Stupid, stupid, stupid. How could she have missed the signs?

How Jeremi had somehow heard of Oxana's death and called it a murder long before those facts were announced. How he'd been desperate to hide something when O'Keeffe nosed into his office. Jeremi knew a lot of people, so why not Oxana? Maybe he had a relative at Singing Swans. Maybe Sal was right about him being a counterfeiter. Or maybe it was about drugs, some link to The Jewell. One thing was clear.

He was the killer.

"Amanda!" she heard him yell but didn't look back. She had no idea where she was running. Instinct fueled her. Her form and speed were terrible. This was more of a frantic hobble, one that caused her to yelp every time she landed on her bad ankle. O'Keeffe passed Amanda, running a few feet ahead, her leash taut, smiling as if this was a game of chase.

"Stop!" Jeremi's cries were winded, which was no surprise since antiquing and chit-chat were probably his only forms of exercise. "Amanda, I just want to—"

Just want to what, to shoot me? Her legs and lungs burned but adrenalin pushed her on. It was O'Keeffe who ended the game, suddenly squatting to take her morning pee. Amanda snapped to a halt with such force, she pulled her shoulder. "Damn it. O'Keeffe, come!" Amanda panted the command, but it was too late. Jeremi caught up and grabbed her arm. She screamed, hoping that a neighbour would hear her.

Jeremi pulled her close, his obnoxious cologne punctuating the air. He panted, "Why did you run?"

"Hands off! Back away!" Amanda shouted, using the first rule of Fight and Flight. For some strange reason, she snapped her hands into karate chop position just as she heard a house door open. A woman shouted, "Hey, Colonel Sanders. Get off my lawn!"

"Don't scream," Jeremi hissed to Amanda, but backed off when he saw the scolding neighbour. He took a step away from Amanda, both hands in a gesture of surrender. "Okay. It's okay." He made himself loud enough for the blessedly nosy woman to hear of his cooperation.

A glimmer of sunlight illuminated the metal object in his hand, and Amanda yelled, "He's got a gun!"

Nosy slammed her front door shut and Amanda's anger flared. She was so done with being scared. Besides, Jeremi couldn't exactly shoot her when they were outside, in plain sight.

She lunged at him, knocking him to the grass and loosening the gun from his hold.

Her ankle throbbed as she straddled him, pinning him down. She kept one hand flat on his wizened chest as the other fumbled around for the gun. He struggled beneath her, shifting their position and that brought the gun into her sight. She lunged for it. "Yow!" A fierce pain ripped through her shoulder, the same one O'Keeffe had just hurt. It felt like a muscle tearing. But pain be damned, she had the gun in her hand.

Or did she? The thing Amanda found in her hand was more of a walkie talkie than a weapon. "What the hell is this?"

"You know darned well what it is," Jeremi wheezed. "A perfect reason to turn me in to the cops."

She un-straddled him, sliding onto the grass with a surge of relief. He couldn't kill her with this thing. "Why are you chasing me with a walkie talkie?" Amanda sucked in deep breaths then called out for O'Keeffe, who emerged from the shrubbery.

"Oh, you are good, Amandear." Released from the power of Amanda's thighs, Jeremi sat up on the grass. "And you have very strong legs I might add. You must do a lot of squats." He straightened his bow tie, pulled a leaf from his goatee then grabbed the walkie-talkie. He held it up and, seeing something in her face, he said, "My God, you don't know?"

"No Jeremi, I don't bloody know, and you need to stop playing games with me. I've had enough!" To Amanda's horror, the dog joined them, tail wagging and began licking Jeremi's face. "O'Keeffe, stop it!"

"It's okay." Jeremi giggled. "It feels good. I don't mind."

"I do!" Amanda rubbed her shoulder, but that only made the pain worse. She pointed at the object he held, asking, "What the hell is that thing?"

Jeremi lowered his face, locking eyes with her, as though he still thought she was putting him on. "It's part of my HAM radio set," he said.

"What now?"

"Amanda, you caught me on it in my office! That's how I knew about the nurse's murder."

"From your HAM radio?"

"Yes." His shame shifted into excitement. "It is *the* most fun hobby. Forget the evening news, I get all the local gossip." He was downright giddy.

Amanda threw her arms in the air and yelled, "So, why the secrecy?"

"My license lapsed." He cast his eyes downward, murmuring, "And I didn't renew it."

"Illegal tapping of cop radios?"

"Some might call it that." Jeremi ran a hand through his short greying hair. "It's even more fun without a license. But it wouldn't be if I got caught. I thought you were going to report me." He shook his head, adding, "The look on your face the day you saw me with it in my office. . ."

Amanda flopped onto the lawn, exhausted now that the adrenalin had worn off. Her head spun as she tried to tune out Jeremi's droning monologue. My God he might not have a gun, but his incessant talking might kill her instead.

Forty-Three

It had taken a half hour for Jeremi to stop talking, but Amanda did get one useful tidbit out of him. His HAM radio allowed him to intercept taxi dispatches. Once he'd begun following the Oxana investigation, he remembered he'd heard a dispatch about an afternoon pickup at The Jewell. It stuck in his memory because the driver had described his fare as a "smokin' hot redhead but frantic as hell." He dropped her at The Singing Swans Lodge. The driver closed out the call saying, ". . . crying and writing notes like mad. Gave me a hella tip."

Jeremi finally drove off, confident that Amanda had not and would not report his lapsed radio license. Amanda was bone tired. She sat in the kitchen staring at the emergency bottle of scotch while eating Saltines and icing her shoulder, ankle, and cheekbone. When her cell phone rang, she ignored it. It rang a second time and she reached to flip off the ringer when she saw the call display, VPD. The police? A knot twisted in her stomach as she answered it.

"I'm in detainment camp!" It was Sal, her voice an octave higher than usual. "Remember how I reported Oxana's phone to the cops yesterday?"

"I do."

"Well, Beaston sent two goons, who stuffed me in a blacktop and brought me to his lair!"

"Beaton had you picked up?"

"Yes, it was them at my door when you and I were on the phone. You're my one call. I need you to be here when the big lug questions me." Sal was getting winded. "Or to bust me outta here." She finally took a breath. "And hurry, I don't want to miss your audition."

"You've got to be kidding me."

"You won't break me out of the slammer?"

"Of course, yes, I'll come and help you. But I won't do the other thing."

"Durn it all, the chucklehead just arrived." Sal spit out the words, then added, "Come here or don't, but you're going to that audition. The Jewell is the key, and we need access to it!"

"Don't yell at me."

"I'm not yelling!"

"You're being very loud, which is also known as yelling."

Sal's voice decelerated a few gears, into a whisper. "I'm in a fix."

"I'll be there as soon as I can."

"Hurry," Sal said, adding, "Tsk tsk. Handsome enough man. Too bad he's such a crumb."

Amanda hung up and, for who knew how long, sat contemplating the blur of kitchen table. Pain radiated from multiple points of her body. Fatigue weighed her down. *Come here or don't but you're going to that audition. The Jewell is the key.* A warm sensation of the dog licking her ankle brought her around. "Thanks for the kisses, Girl."

She got up and lumbered into the bedroom, where she opened the top dresser drawer, and pulled out her sewing box. It was an old kit of sewing basics, something she rarely used. A gift from her mother. Under the bags of assorted coloured thread, a candy tin of loose buttons, and a few tools she had never understood the use for, she found what she was looking for. She clasped her hand around the small velvet box.

When Amanda was born, her father had shown up at the maternity ward with a gift for his wife. The diamond and sapphire earrings must have been a huge splurge on his humble teacher's salary. That was only one of many stories she'd grown up hearing of her father's love and generosity. Amanda hated that she couldn't remember her early years with him. He had died far too young. Her mother had pressed the earrings into Amanda's hand the week before she died.

Amanda looped the earrings through her earlobes, letting their power course through her. Then she stepped into the closet.

Forty-Four

"What took you so long?" Sal wailed when Officer Riley admitted Amanda into Beaton's office. The place remained sparse, decorated only with an industrial wall clock, a camera hanging from the ceiling, and Riley stationed at the door.

This time, Beaton rose from the desk to greet her and comment on her clothes. "Did we take you away from an athletic activity?" he asked.

She shrugged. It wasn't his business if she wanted to wear two layers of track suits.

He took a few steps toward her. His limp had improved, but he was quick to notice hers. "Did you hurt yourself Miss Sunderson?" He pointed at her ankle, then glanced at the bruise on her cheek, a smile creeping across his chiseled face.

The tips of Amanda's ears burned at the memory of how she'd been ogling him when she collided with a concrete pillar at the hospital. She cleared her throat and nodded. "I'm fine, thank you." She turned to Sal. "Sorry for the delay. You won't believe —" She stopped herself, not wanting Beaton to know any more about the details of the past 12 hours. That she'd been cornered by a drug-addicted nurse, tailed by a black Range Rover, chased by a HAM radio wielding Jeremi. Jeez.

Sal wiggled her face at Amanda. "No need to be hush hush on anything, my Dear." She nodded towards Beaton. "We've completed the questioning and I've told Officer Beaton everything."

"You did what?" Amanda squinted. Sal had been at odds with this cop since Day One. Why would she suddenly cooperate? And why the respectful moniker rather than her usual *Beaston*? "You told him everything? Willingly?"

"Yes, of course," Sal winked. "No spinning of coloured yarn. No hiding of any jewels." She practically trilled the words.

Amanda knew Sal was lying and trying to speak in code. An image of the yarn-laden investigation board dropped into her mind, then one of The Jewell. Sal had put a *No* before both references, meaning she must have left out details from both. Amanda couldn't know if she got the mystery code right but decided to avoid those topics. "Okay," she said, patting Sal's arm. None of this was okay but she wanted Sal to know she would play along.

"She told me everything willingly," Beaton kept his face in neutral gear as he continued, "because she was unwilling to be arrested." Then he raised his brows.

Sal waved a thick hand, "Well, there was that little chestnut too."

"Arrested?"

"Withholding evidence." Beaton sat, and opened the case file folder, now two inches thick.

Sal shrugged. "I told you Sir, I plum forgot about finding Oxana's secret locker and phone." She was using a baby voice now.

Amanda said, "You'll have to forgive her Officer, she's old." And a bit of a pain in the ass.

Sal narrowed her eyes.

The last time Amanda was here, detained, Joyce had come to her rescue. She had swept in, radiating Chanel Number 5 and legal prowess, and filling Amanda with confidence. Damn it, why hadn't she called Joyce to help? The run-in with Jeremi had derailed any clear thinking. She scratched her head, horrified to find a few hairs come out in her hand. Great, now her hair was falling out.

It was too late to call for help. Amanda had to step up to bat. She recalled Joyce's first question to Beaton and followed suit. "Are you filing charges against Ms. Falconetti?"

Beaton shrugged. "She has cooperated fully." His voice held a note of surprise. "So, for the time being, no charges."

"All right, so she's not under arrest. This is merely a detainment?" Amanda mentally wiped her brow in relief. She remembered Joyce explaining, *cops can detain someone if they have reasonable grounds to suspect a connection to their investigation. Answer their questions.*

A faint smile spread on Beaton's face, as if he guessed that she was copying Joyce. "Yes, a detainment." He added, "And this time it was fully explained to the detainee." He kept his eyes on her. Was he waiting for her to trip up? In her peripheral vision, Amanda could see Sal contorting her face as if trying to communicate something.

This was all bullshit. She wagged a finger at Sal then at Beaton. "Just tell me what's going on and stop with the shenanigans!"

They both started nattering at once, like toddlers fighting over a toy. *Ms. Falconetti should have told us— He treated me like a common criminal—. Blah blah blah.*

Amanda raised both hands like a crossing guard, one in front of each face. "Stop, both of you!" Once they quieted, she silently counted five Mississippi's, before asking, "Officer Beaton, do you have any new information you're willing to share with us?"

"No Miss Sunderson, because you're not on this case." Beaton said then turned back to his notes. "We have everything we need. You're both free to go." He looked at the clock then scribbled on the file.

He didn't add the disclaimer he'd once given Amanda, *Just don't go far.* She recalled her chat with his partner Officer McIver, the real Officer McIver, who had assured her that Oxana's body couldn't be collected by her family until the coroner released it. She knew that Beaton's ticking time bomb had been a fake and she deliberated telling him that she knew, but when Sal tugged at her arm, whispering for them to go, she knew there were more pressing issues.

"Fine. Call me if you need anything more, Officer Beaton," Amanda said, adding, "Or, of course, watch the replay from your recording." She pointed to the camera.

"That thing?" Beaton said, "Hasn't worked in years. They refuse to replace it." He shrugged. "Budget cuts."

~~~

The lobby of the police station was quiet, so Amanda and Sal sat
~~~

in the waiting area to debrief.

"Please explain," Amanda said, waving a hand in the air.

"First let me say that your makeup looks very professional," Sal said, her gaze sweeping over Amanda's clothes. "But that's not much of a stripping costume. You look like a Russian shot-putter."

"I figured, the more layers the better." A nylon track jacket and tear-away pants covered Lycra track jacket and tights, which covered a t-shirt and shorts, which covered a bikini.

"We should change your stage name to Russian Doll." Sal pointed to her own clothes, a floral housedress. "Luis told you to leave Big Daddy at home, so you're bringing Big Mama instead." She perched her mighty hands on her purse. "Unfortunately, I didn't have the presence of mind to grab the fedora as the goons frog-marched me out of my home."

"I'll use this." Amanda pointed to the bandana around her neck, which she'd added as one more prop. Anything to keep from getting naked.

"Ok. Here are the beans." Sal described what she deduced from Beaton's line of questions. "There were areas of bruising on Oxana's body, from a large signet-type ring."

"We already knew that from what the coroner said."

"But what we didn't know is that this ring was worn on the left hand. They believe the mark was left when the killer pushed her down the stairs." Sal continued, "Beaton suggested my size fit the bill, plus I had opportunity and motive, that being our nurse's mean disposition." Her jowls quivered as she shook her head. "I disappointed him when he threw a pen and I caught it with my right hand." The memory left a delicious grin on her frosted lips. "Oh, the look on his Dudley Do-Right face."

"The killer is a leftie," Amanda said, filing the clue among the others they'd gathered. "Ok. Here's my update." She recounted the story of the black Range Rover chase. "I got a photo of it, but not a good one." Amanda remembered how much her hands had trembled as she tried to snap a picture during the high-speed chase. She pulled out her phone and found the photo, which was so blurry that the license plate was impossible to distinguish.

"Did he see you take this?" Sal scrutinized the picture.

A lump caught in Amanda's throat. "I imagine he did, but I couldn't see through his tinted glass." She then debriefed about Jeremi, their Keystone Cops chase sequence and the secret he'd been hiding."

Sal listened as she fixed a fresh star tattoo to Amanda's cheekbone. "So, he's a nutter but not a killer."

"Except for the killer cologne." Amanda winced at the sting of Sal's touch.

Sal untied the bandana and experimented with different styles on Amanda's head, before settling on one. "Hip hop it is." She sat back, looking pleased with herself. "We have both had a big day."

"That's an understatement." Amanda slumped. "I'm so tired." The day had been endless, and it was nowhere near over.

"Pish. Don't worry," Sal cooed. "Just a quick strip while I solve the murder and you'll be back to the bottle of rye you've been tippling." She waved a hand in front of her nose.

"It was scotch."

"Much better." Sal stood, asking, "Did you off-load Oxana's

photos onto your phone?" At Amanda's confirmation, Sal said, "Good. We'll start there. Let's visit the back of The Jewell, try to figure out what our girl might have seen or heard." Sal clutched her purse and extended a hand to Amanda. "My Dear, time to go."

Amanda didn't move.

"Come on, I'll buy you a drink."

That sounded like just about the only thing that would make their plan bearable. Amanda nodded and stood. "Thanks."

Sal swatted a paw, saying, "It's the least I can do considering you'll be getting your kit off."

Forty-Five

The Jewell was a two-block walk, its emerald-green walls shimmering in the sun. Sal sent Amanda around to the back before saying, "I'll sweep the perimeter."

Amanda found the small parking lot empty. The red brick industrial building featured in Oxana's final photos, stood across the alley. Amanda shielded her eyes and scanned the windows, which were barred on the first floor. A loading bay held a sign, *RR Trucking*. A gaping dumpster spewed a rank stench.

Sal returned. Her face was beaded with sweat. "Nothing suspicious. Anything here?"

Amanda shrugged, calculating the spot where Oxana had taken her final photos and planting herself there. "Oxana was taking selfies here. Something made her turn around." Her eyes scanned the area. "Something tossed in the dumpster?"

"Something in one of those windows?" Sal pointed at the red brick industrial building, raising a hand against the sun's glare. "Remind me to pack sunglasses next time."

Something tickled Amanda's brain. "The sun is in our eyes," she said then looked in one direction then the other. "What was the timestamp on Oxana's last photos?"

"3 pm." Sal said as she patted her face with a tissue.

"It's 2:30 now, so the sun is in roughly the same place." Amanda raised a hand and mimicked Oxana's selfies poses. "Oxana had turned this way, so the sun lit her face. She was a showgirl, knew how to work the light." She noticed Sal's quizzical look. "The sun is angled toward The Jewell," she explained, pointing at the other building. "That place is heading into shadow, so the flares of light in Oxana's photos weren't sunlight."

"Mamacita!" A voice pierced the air, sending a stab of fear into Amanda. Luis stood on the small concrete landing at The Jewell's back door. "You ladies lookin' for somethin'?" He grabbed hold of the rusty railing, rocking it back and forth before leaning toward them, as if trying to make his small frame seem bigger. "Come here." Sal shot Amanda an affirming nod and they crept towards the steps, Luis reigning at the top. He scrutinized Amanda then Sal. "What the fuck?" He wheezed a laugh, his gold teeth glinting. "You're like a white version of Madea!"

"I prefer Big Mama," Sal said, winking. Cool as a gin and tonic.

They all joined in a laugh. Just a couple friends having a yuk.

"Come in. Have a drink." Luis narrowed his dark eyes. "I insist."

A twitch began in Amanda's cheek.

The women walked up the concrete steps, squeezing past Luis on the landing before stepping into the cool dim club. Pop music throbbed. It took a minute for Amanda's eyes to adjust and identify Twin Peaks dancing on the raised and brightly lit stage. Maybe five guys were littered around the audience.

Luis nodded to the bar stools and the ladies sat, Sal ordering two bottles of beer. "Harder to Roofie bottles than glasses," she whispered. When she pulled a twenty from her bosom, Luis cackled. "Big Mama, what else you got in there?"

"Oh, you know." Sal swatted at him, winking. "A bit of this, a bit of that."

Amanda hated beer but was desperate for any pain killing measures. Her shoulder and ankle throbbed, and her stomach roiled at the idea of how the afternoon would unfold. Would Luis realize they were onto him? What would he do? Drag them to the depths of the building? She grimaced at the thought of what was behind the door marked 'Private.' She was thick in images of torture chambers when Sal elbowed her.

Luis was leaning over the bar, close. Too close.

"Mamacita, I don't know what kinda 'recs you're on, but you ain't listening." He snapped his fingers. "Gimme your dance music. I'll take it to the DJ."

Damn it. She'd completely forgotten.

"You got no music?" Luis paused, shaking his head. "You get hired and you pull that, I'm gonna kill you."

Amanda started to shake.

Luis slammed his hand on the bar, saying, "I'm kidding!" He bent over in a laugh, his greasy hair falling against the bar. "The look on your face!" He straightened, then pointed two fingers and thumbs at them, shaping them into guns, pulling the triggers. "I like you two!" His snickering led to a coughing spell. Once it was over, he said, "DJ will have something. Whadya want?"

Amanda looked at the stage. Twin Peaks' perfectly sculpted figure was poised upside down on the pole, not an inch of fat on the body she maneuvered with gymnastic precision. Amanda couldn't compete with that if her life depended on it. She took a slug of beer, choking on the bitter bubbles.

Maybe she could just lean against the pole and sway? Yes, men loved that sultry barely moving kind of sexy. What did it matter anyway? It wasn't as if she wanted to land a stripping job! This was about creating a distraction, while Sal got to the bottom of things. "Something slow," she told Luis, who pulled another gunshot gesture then headed to the DJ booth.

Amanda leaned into Sal. "Every part of my b-body and b-b-brain are telling me to hobble the hell out of here."

"You'll be brilliant!" Sal waved her hands. "If I had your figure and mobility, I'd love to be a stripper for a day." She must have seen the fear in Amanda's eyes. Her attitude softened. "Just shimmy to the music, give me a chance to snoop on Slick Luis." She pointed to Amanda's track suits. "Peel off a few layers. That'll use up a couple of songs."

Twin Peaks' set finished to a smattering of applause. "Give it up for Twin Peaks!" The DJ continued, "I'd hike up those mountains any day." Twinnie smiled, clapping for herself with those garish nails, before gathering up a few scattered bills and slipping on her shoes. She swept up her clothes, folded her long legs over the edge of the stage, then strolled buck naked past the DJ booth and through the 'Private' door.

Luis returned. "You're up Mama—" he snapped his fingers, asking, "What's the name again?"

Amanda blinked, unable to recall her stripper name. Or her

given name, date of birth, or current location. She clutched the brass rail that edged the bar, sure she was about to throw up. Sal stood from her barstool and tapped a finger to her cheekbone. Right, the star tattoo. Amanda said, "A-am-Star."

"Right, like the train. Choo choo!" Luis returned to the DJ booth.

"Giddy up," Sal said then gripped Amanda's elbow and steered her to the stage, Amanda limping along her version of the Green Mile.

When they got to the stage, Amanda realized it was too high to mount with a bum ankle. Ah, too bad, she thought turning back to the bar. Sal blocked her and Amanda fought the urge to faint as Sal folded her to a sitting position, hoisted her legs and slid her onto the stage like a beached whale.

"Ladies and Germiacs," The DJ boomed, "A warm welcome to a very warmly-dressed Am-Star!" A few customers clapped. Sal offered one final shove and an A-okay gesture, then headed back to the bar. A grizzled hippie coughed, banging his beer bottle. "Luis, one more here!" Otherwise, all seemed deadly quiet.

Other than the roar of Amanda's pulse.

Riffs of a synthesized guitar began, a hallmark of the Dire Straits ballad, *So Far Away from Me.* Amanda rolled onto her stomach, hoisted herself to her knees and crawled toward the spotlight, trying to keep time with the beat. She recoiled when her hands met with a sticky spot on the floor. It took ages to reach the brass pole that stretched to the ceiling. Sultry lyrics began as she clutched the pole with both hands and clawed her way up. About as graceful as an elephant seal.

She stood and realized, to her relief, that the spotlight obliterated her view. The chorus kicked in and she tried to find her rhythm. Letting go of the pole, she joined her arms in the dance, unzipped her nylon track jacket then peeled it off. Sexy—until she got trapped in the stretchy sleeves and had to jerk her arms about like a marionette in seizure to free herself. She put some action into her hips, trying to make up for the blunder.

It was a good song. This really wasn't such a bad gig, she thought, until she raised her arms and a fiery pain tore through her injured shoulder, making her howl. Some guy mistook it for a moan of pleasure and shouted, "Take it all off!"

Dear God.

At the next verse, she ripped off her tear-away pants to a few whistles, until the crowd saw the tights beneath. Angry murmurs echoed and the DJ rumbled, "Babe, you gotta actually *strip* to get the job."

Amanda attempted a sultry laugh, toying with the zipper of her second track jacket, until the back door opened with a loud *clang*. Light spilled into the club, creating a halo around the massive form that filled the doorway. Recognition scratched at her brain. Big guy, spikey hair, coveralls. She tried to keep time to the music as he made a show of pushing his sunglasses onto his head. It was the trucker from their visit when Sal was disguised as Big Daddy. The one who'd bragged that nobody messed with him. He scanned the room, saw Sal, and froze.

Weird. He couldn't recognize her—Sal as Sal looked very different than Sal as Big Daddy. Amanda lost the beat of the music, her fingers fumbling to peel off jacket number two. At the reveal of another layer of clothing, a t-shirt, someone shouted, "You're killing us!"

The trucker was yelling at Luis, who threw his hands up in a stop gesture. What was going on? And why was the trucker marching straight towards Sal?

Another command from the audience, "Take off the pants!" set Amanda's hands on autopilot, pulling off the tights while her brain tried to make sense of what was happening. When she revealed the pair of shorts underneath, the DJ tapped the microphone and muttered, "Might wanna keep your day job, Hun."

Her feet nearly left the stage when she felt something brush against her bare leg. She found a grinning guy, with a few missing teeth, rubbing a bill against her. "Fiver for the shorts, Doll." He dropped the bill on the stage. She'd just started on her t-shirt but came to a dead stop when she heard the back door slam.

She turned to find everyone gone. Trucker. Luis. Sal.

So Far Away from Me.

Flashes of insight lit up her brain. Trucker pushing up his sunglasses—with his *left hand.* His recognition of Sal—he'd *been to the Singing Swans.* Oxana's truck drawing on the bar coaster—pointing to *a trucking company.* Trucker had done something and Oxana had seen it, got a photo. Luis wasn't the killer. Sal must have figured it out too and that got her dragged into the alley.

"The shorts, Doll!"

Still on autopilot, Amanda unbuttoned her shorts. A blast of cool air hit her stomach at the same time as she heard a fleshy *thud* against the back door. The bridge of the song unfurled—Good God, did it never end?

What the hell was she doing? A killer had Sal in the back alley and Amanda was waiting for a song to end?

Fuck that.

Amid boos and hisses, she reverse-engineered her way off the stage then speed-limped to the back door, the half-off t-shirt thwapping against her bare spine. She charged the door, hearing a distinct *thud*, clang of metal and yelps of pain, but the scorching light made it impossible to see the people she'd sent skittering like pool balls after a perfect break shot. She raised an arm to shield her eyes.

Cries of pain from Luis, as he tumbled down the concrete steps. "Mamacita—what the hell?"

Sal was pinned against the metal railing, surprise painted on her face, the trucker atop her.

His eyes bulged at the sight of Amanda. "You!"

If the guy had been scary at a distance, he was terrifying up close: his weathered face a map of past traumas, purple veins wending across a bulbous nose, thin hair spiked to daggers, bloodshot eyes.

He winched himself off Sal and lunged for Amanda, his hands locking onto her shoulders. She roared in pain. Startled, he released his grip, stumbling backwards into the metal railing and shoving Amanda against the door. It slammed shut with an echo of finality and enough force to send a ripple of pain up Amanda's spine and into her teeth.

He rebounded off the railing and swept a beefy hand across his sweaty face. A fat insignia ring glinted in the sun.

"You two bitches," he said, speaking in low tones, "Been a pain in my ass." He clubbed each consonant like they were baby seals. "Warned you once." A bizarre smile glazed his features. "It's too late now." His chest swelled, revealing *RR Trucking* with the logo of a Road Runner below.

Sal jumped him from behind, wrapping her substantial arms and legs around him. He twisted in jerky circles, a dog chasing his tail, trying to grab her. "Get off me, you fuckin' weird old drag queen."

Her wig was askew, but her face was tranquil as she clung to him, reprimanding, "Young man, that was simply uncalled for."

"Bobby!" Luis climbed the steps on hands and knees.

Trucker spotted him and shouted, "Grab the bitch!"

Luis stuttered, "I got nothin' to do with this Bobby!"

Bobby roared, bucking Sal from his back, sending her flying. Amanda watched Sal as a flash of her mother flickered in her mind. Those final days. So helpless.

Fresh anger flared in her.

Sal landed on Luis and the two of them tumbled to the base of the steps, in a tangled, moaning heap. A voice squeaked, "My Dear, get the prick."

Amanda stepped toward Bobby, spitting her words, "What did Volga have on you?"

Bobby's face twisted into a fresh smirk. "So that's how you wanna play it—you want details?" He tilted his head to one side, his neck cracking in a sound that sent a shudder through Amanda, along with an image of Oxana's lifeless eyes. "Goddamn gun wasn't supposed to be loaded."

A loaded gun? Gunfire—that was the flash of light in

Oxana's final photos.

Bobby cracked his knuckles, saying, "Why'd the dumb stripper have to take selfies in fronta my office?" He stepped toward Amanda, a crooked grin spreading over his face.

When the club door flew open, it startled all of them. It was the toothless guy from the stage. He pointed at Amanda, saying, "You didn't take yer shorts off. Gimme my fiver back." He swayed, too drunk to notice he walked into the middle of a showdown.

Bobby took a step towards the guy, saying calmly, "Here man, take five from me." He punched him square in the face, maybe costing the guy another tooth and knocking him onto the floor of the bar. The door slammed behind him.

"Who'd you shoot Bobby?" Amanda said, surprising herself at her boldness.

His eyes glazed over, as if seeing something in his mind's eye. "Can't come here from Alberta, tell me how to run my business. . ." Bobby's focus returned, and he stepped forward.

An eerie calm flooded Amanda as she took a step back, landing her against the door, with nowhere to go. She might be trapped, but she had one thing, and she was going to use it.

"No!" she screamed.

Bobby laughed, tilting his head skyward. When he righted it, Amanda was ready. She rammed the flat of her hand into his nose, recoiling at the force that rippled up her arm and penetrated her shoulder. She waited for him to collapse with a bloody nose like Daniel had when she'd pulled the stunt at Fight or Flight.

But this guy didn't go down.

Oh, shit.

His upper body contracted, like he was winding up a punch, when Luis yelled from the steps, "Bobby, man you gotta stop!" Anger puckered Bobby's face and he swung towards Luis, his momentum costing him his balance.

Now.

Amanda tapped Bobby on the shoulder.

He grunted in surprise, instinctively turning to her. It must have been her grin that triggered his puzzled look. He paused, allowing her to get close enough to see his pupils dilate.

She took one step, coiling all her force into her other leg and snapping her knee into his groin.

Hard.

He collapsed in moans of agony as Amanda threw herself on him. "Looks like *we two bitches* got you, Bobby."

"I ruined my best fucking cookbook on you nosy hags!" Bobby thundered as Amanda whipped off her t-shirt and hog-tied him. She said, "Don't worry. Where you're going, you won't need a cookbook."

A police siren swelled, and a cruiser skidded into the parking lot, lights flashing. Riley and Beaton jumped from the car, guns drawn, yelling, "Everyone down!"

"We've got this under control officers," Amanda called from her perch atop Bobby. She turned to Sal, still on the pavement, and offered a salute. Sal returned the gesture. Riley strode up the steps and snapped a set of handcuffs onto Bobby, while Beaton held back. Amanda stood and looked at him, wondering why he was smirking. Then she remembered she wore only a pair of unbuttoned shorts and bikini top.

She struck a pose, like a Miss World contestant, aiming it directly at Beaton, who quickly averted his gaze and got busy studying the pavement.

It was official. Today was the worst day of her life.

And one of the best, too.

Forty-Six

"Don't worry," Sal said when Amanda pointed at her conservative grey dress. "Nobody else died." She ushered Amanda and O'Keeffe into her suite. "A week of R & R worked wonders," Sal said, hugging her friend. "You look better than ever." She greeted the dog, unclipping her leash.

"Thanks." Amanda's bruises had healed, her appetite had returned and she'd caught up on her sleep. Best of all, she'd completed nearly all executor tasks, reducing Mount Executor to one slim file folder. She noticed that the investigation board remained on the wall: a mishmash of sketches, numbered sticky notes and webs of coloured yarn. The sideboard was still laden with snacks, packs of tea and a kettle. Sal grinned broadly.

"No." Amanda shook her head. "No more sleuthing—" but she was cut off by the sound of shattering pottery. *Bam!* O'Keeffe snuffled what was once Sal's gift cactus from 'her favourite person.' Amanda rushed over, saying, "Naughty!" but stopped at the sight of a glint in the dirt. She raised a finger to her lips as Sal joined them with a broom and dustpan. The miniature gnome had smashed open, revealing a tiny microphone.

Sal wrapped it in a rag, saying, "How the smelly bully kept

tabs on us." She laughed. "Joke's on him, probably only heard me muttering to myself. Grocery lists, railing against the evening news, sorting laundry." She petted the dog, adding, "O'Keefe, you finally found a clue. That deserves a treat." She pulled a dog bone from the depths of her sock-stuffed bosom. The dog joyously accepted it, dragging it under the dining table for some private gnawing.

Sal returned to the investigation station. "So, Nurse Oxana caught Bobby's crime. He saw her, and she saw him seeing her."

"Twin Peaks said that Oxana was upset, grabbed her purse and some bar coasters then fled out Jewell's front door," Amanda said, pacing. "Jeremi heard a report on his HAM radio—a cabbie describing a hysterical fare from the strip club to the retirement home."

Sal pointed at the coaster. "Oxana knew she was doomed, so drew a truck and number one to indicate Bobby. Don't know why she didn't write it out—"

"Panic," Amanda said, "Or maybe she forgot the English words." She wagged a finger in the air. "She willed her phone to you knowing you'd been a trucker and would be able to figure it out."

Sal dusted imaginary dirt off her shoulders before the satisfaction on her face slid into another question. "Riddle me this. Why go to the Singing Swans Lodge for her shift? Why not go directly to the cops?"

"Mistrust, maybe fear of Bobby's retribution." Amanda had long-since worked out the string of events. "Bobby caught up and confronted her in the stairwell." She raised her chin, feeling a strange sense of pride in Oxana. "But Oxana was no pushover, she stood up to him. He searched for the phone, but she'd already stashed it in the secret locker."

"He demanded she hand over the phone, but she wouldn't. Nasty thug exploded, snapped her neck, Sal said, tapping her sketch of Oxana's body.

"She slid to the bottom of the stairwell, bleeding out from her head. O'Keeffe and I entered the lower-level stairwell, and —"

"You went off your nut and O'Keeffe ate brain matter." Sal snickered.

Amanda fought a wave of nausea, then continued, "Nurse Mary snuck into the stairwell to pop some Vicodin, got a birds-eye view of the body and sloshed her pills everywhere. She snuck out, probably to make up an excuse for being there, then came back and screamed blue murder. All that cost valuable time, in which Bobby fled."

"Told you we were ace detectives," Sal said, checking her watch. "Aha." She marched to the living room and grabbed a small suitcase. "Time to go." She clipped on O'Keeffe's leash, handed Amanda her backpack then corralled them out of the suite. "You must have known there would be consequences."

Perplexed, Amanda stumbled to keep up with Sal and the jouncing dog. At the elevator, Sal stabbed the call button, smoothed her dress, saying, "I look much better in grey than orange, but it might suit you." Her expression was inscrutable.

What in hell was going on?

Sal avoided eye contact, shooing them into the elevator, as she continued, "Withholding evidence, tampering with evidence, lying to the police. . ."

Sal was turning them in?

Coldness sunk into Amanda. "B-but—" The elevator belched them into the lobby and Sal steered them past Reception. Mai didn't look up.

Amanda's heart galloped. "Listen, Sal. . ."

"You had to know there'd be a price for all we've done." Sal stopped, pub on one side, dining room on the other, dreaded stairwell beyond.

A pit opened in Amanda's stomach. Through it all, she had never once questioned Sal.

"Snooping, hacking a phone. So many infractions," Sal said then she flung open the door to the Long Neck Pub, shoving her friend into darkness.

Amanda struggled to get a breath.

The lights snapped on. A crush of people yelled, "Surprise!"

Amanda threw a hand to her chest. Sal was laughing so hard that there were tears in her eyes. "I was messing with you." She wiped her cheeks, smearing her pancake foundation. "Oh, the look on your face. My Dear, I didn't know your eyes could get that big."

Amanda was swept into a mosh pit of affection. She crumpled into tears, turning the pub's buffed oak paneling, crown moldings and mirrored bar into an exquisite blur.

The guests of honour!" Elaine welcomed them, looking like the happy woman Amanda had met a month ago.

Bartender Tom appeared with a tray of icy champagne flutes, saying, "Your friend Joyce is away on lawyer business, but she sent her best regards, and a few bottles too."

Toni and Keira mashed Amanda in a hug. She raised a

shaky hand to wipe her eyes, then took a gulp of champagne, saying, "Alright, Toni, let's see a picture of your new guy." Since the STD episode, Toni had dumped the gazillionaire and shifted her focus away from men. Thank God.

"I'll do you one better," Toni said, opening a few snaps of her denim jacket. A furry head poked out. "Finally have a guy to keep me warm at night."

O'Keeffe reared up on her hind legs to snuffle the tabby kitten. Amanda grinned, saying, "I'm glad you're over Gaz."

Toni's expression hardened. "Oh, I'm not quite finished with him yet." Revenge sparkled in her eyes.

Sal opened her suitcase, revealing a pile of feather boas. She draped a red one over Amanda with a kiss on her cheek, wound a smaller one around O'Keeffe's neck, then made her way around the room.

Nurse Nelly skittered into the pub, holding up an envelope. "My BC Nursing Accreditation arrived!" That set off a round of cheers as Elaine updated Amanda. "The Nursing Union dropped their claim, due to our extenuating circumstances. Offered us a small fine, which I paid happily and immediately." She slumped with relief. "Both Nelly and the lodge have been cleared. New residents are moving in, and the budget cuts are over!"

Amanda let her happiness settle in, just as the air shifted. The exuberant mood took a turn as the next guest walked in.

Beaton.

Amanda's heart caught the rhythm of conga drums in a salsa band.

Elaine raised a hand, shouting, "Everyone take a seat. I asked Officer Beaton to explain what happened to Oxana, so we can have closure." She nodded to him then sat down and propped her feet on a chair. She turned to Amanda, saying, "I'm off the clock. Tomorrow, I'll be on a plane to Hawaii."

Beaton had bulked up since Amanda last saw him. His muscles strained against his uniform, but she didn't mind. Toni whispered, "Beefcake is hot!" Amanda shrugged in response then busied herself getting O'Keeffe settled under the table.

"Ms. Wetcomb informed me that you all heard the basics, through the grapevine," Beaton said, aiming his gaze at Sal.

"Our nurse was a stripper!" Mrs. Hyde-Bowles yelled, and the room erupted in laughter. Pendy leaned across their table and patted her friend on the arm.

"Correct," Beaton said. He recapped the events that Amanda and Sal already knew but added one twist. "Bobby snapped Oxana's neck, but that only incapacitated her."

Murmurs filled the pub. Tom took the opportunity to top up everyone's champagne as the officer continued, "It was the shove down the stairs that did it, launching her to the base of the stairwell, where she hit her head and bled out." The room fell quiet.

"Creepers Jeepers," Sal said, "Would she have survived the broken neck?"

"Doubtful." Beaton shook his head. "But that detail meant there might have been two killers. A brute, who snapped her neck. A second person who pushed her down the stairs." He addressed Amanda. "You could barely unscrew a bottle of water, but Ms. Falconetti did possess the strength. That, and her incessant questioning of the residents shone a light on her."

"Is he suggesting I'm a brute?" Sal's voice was indignant.

"A chatty brute." Between the details, the view and the banter, Amanda was thoroughly enjoying herself.

Mai appeared at the doorway with a massive bouquet of flowers. She stopped at the sight of Beaton and leaned against the doorjamb while he continued.

"Moments later, Amanda entered the bottom stairwell and fell on the body," Beaton said. "She used her right hand to push off, resulting in a bloody handprint and bruise on the nurse's left shoulder. Along with her DNA and residents' testimonies, we had enough to detain her."

Amanda muttered about how fun that all had been as Beaton went on. "Bruising arose on the body and the coroner found a unique imprint on the sternum, one suggesting a left-hander." He held up a photo of an insignia ring, the one Amanda had seen up close on Bobby's fat fist. "After snapping Oxana's neck he spun her around to face him, grabbed the front of her scrubs then used that momentum to shove her down the stairs. That's when his ring slammed into her sternum." Beaton added, "Then he slipped out of the building—"

Mai shouted, "He did not sign out." A roar of laughter filled the pub.

Amanda added more details, "The letter threatening to turn us into vegetables, the Range Rover that chased Toni's Jeep, how Bobby recognized Sal." She smiled. "He had returned to the scene of the crime."

"A few times," Beaton confirmed. "Even signed a sloppy 'Road Runner' into the register. Mai later made a positive ID." He turned to the doorway and acknowledged her with a tip of his cap. "Criminals often get involved in their own case, to relive their victory, or to control the investigation."

"I'd like to control his mouth," Sal murmured.

More details unfurled in Amanda's mind. The day that Mai had returned her earring, loudly announcing that Amanda had been the one to find Oxana. The man at the reception desk—it had been Bobby. She recalled the illegible scribble in the Visitor Log the day he'd delivered the eavesdropping cactus. Mai had been away from her desk, so he had only pretended to sign in.

"Bobby even called Police HQ, posing as a resident's son," Beaton said, "Filed a complaint about Sal and Amanda's questioning."

"It wasn't the residents who complained about us!" Sal slapped a meaty hand to her forehead, leaving a mark in her foundation. She added, "They were thrilled with the scandal." Even now, Pendy and Mrs. Hyde-Bowles were glued to the cop's report.

Beaton gave Sal a sidelong glance. "When our amateur detectives snooped at The Jewell, Bobby recognized them and followed them back here. Later, he tailed Toni's Jeep, probably seeking Amanda's place of residence."

"Frickin' jerk," Toni said, plunking the kitten beside O'Keeffe who gave him a maternal licking. "But how did you know about the showdown at the strip club?"

"Ms. Falconetti's telephone voice is rather loud," Beaton scoffed. "When Amanda arrived at HQ dressed in multiple layers and more makeup than a streetwalker, it was easy to put the clues together."

She liked the way he said her name, but one question still burned. Despite Amanda's research, she wanted confirmation on her deductions. "Who did Bobby shoot, and why?"

Beaton shifted his muscular weight just enough to generate a fresh thrill in Amanda when the room filled with the *thump thump* of a walker. "That mutt again?" Scowly Orthotics pointed a gnarled finger at O'Keeffe. "What on earth?" The kitten snoozed on top of the dog, who wore one of Sal's feather boas. Amanda swore that those blue curls tightened in shock. "A dog, a cat and a bird? Health code violations!" Scowly angled her walker back towards the door and the thumping resumed. "I'm calling the police." She passed Beaton, in full uniform, exiting The Long Neck Pub with all the speed of a garden slug.

Once the guests released their stifled guffaws, Beaton cleared his throat and got to the heart of the story. "Robert Riznowski, Bobby, aka Road Runner, owner of RR Trucking. His problems started with increased competition and sky-rocketing fuel prices, which hurt his bottom line. He got the brainiac idea to increase profits by scamming the employees. False freight claims, underpaying for mileage, refusing to pay their waiting time. A lot of his guys quit, but—"

"The new guy confronted him," Amanda interrupted, rapping her knuckles on the table and recalling the disgruntled truckers she'd overheard at The Jewell. "Didn't know enough to be scared of Bobby."

Beaton nodded. "He'd come to Vancouver seeking work. Went missing. Lots of news coverage, wife pleading his return." Sadness echoed through the bar. "Both men were desperate, Bobby to keep his business profitable and this guy to support his family after losing his job in Alberta oil when the sector tanked." He raised a hand, adding, "No pun intended."

Sal snorted, "As if we'd ever suspect Beaston of making a funny."

"The altercation happened in Bobby's office," Beaton said. "At one point, he pulled out his Smith and Wesson. Swears he wasn't planning on using it, didn't even keep it loaded, just wanted to scare the guy. But there was a tussle. Bobby fired, shocked when the gun exploded. Victim died on the spot." Beaton accepted a glass of water from Tom. "But things got a lot worse for Riznowski when he realized he had a witness." He took a long drink of water, before saying, "The irony is that Oxana's photos of the shooting are just hazy flashes in Bobby's window. Nothing clear enough to prove he shot someone. Useless as evidence. But he never saw those photos, so he didn't know. Hard to say if Oxana would have kept quiet."

"Bonkers," Keira said. "What'd he do with the body?"

"Rolled it in a rubber mat, tipped it out the window and into the open dumpster. Homeless guy found it. Victim's body has been returned to his family. Bobby is in jail, awaiting trial." Beaton looked at Elaine, whose eyes were dreamy, either at thoughts of Hawaii or in appreciation of Beaton's physique. She cleared her throat then thanked him. He tapped a finger to his cap and turned to leave. Amanda stood, making her way to him when Mai loaded the bouquet of gerberas, roses, and sweet peas into her arms.

The card was addressed to her and Sal. Amanda opened it, saying, "From Oxana's sister, Anya." She'd already received an email from Anya, saying that the family was arranging the paperwork and logistics to repatriate the body. Amanda looked at Beaton, a cluster of women surrounding him, and wondered if he'd known that Oxana's family had decided against coming to Vancouver to collect the body—the threat he'd used against her. Would she ever be able to trust him? But when he locked eyes with her and aimed a salute, she wasn't sure it mattered.

"Read the note my Dear," Sal said, scooping the dog and kitten into her generous lap, where they snuggled among the folds of her dress.

"Yekaterina Oxana was devoted sister and daughter, but her life was hard." As Amanda read, she felt a familiar ache clench her heart. "The moneys she sent to home made family ends meet."

"I think her stripping made a few other ends meet too," Sal said.

"Easy now." Amanda continued reading, "We give Yekaterina a proper funeral, grateful to have her on homeland. *Spasiba.* PS: If you come near Odesa, visit please." Amanda welled up, dropping to her chair. The pain of losing her mother might have softened, but she knew it would always be part of her. As it would for Oxana's family.

Sal put a glass of champagne in Amanda's hand and raised her own. "Here's to solving the case."

Amanda hoisted her glass. Toni, Keira, and Elaine joined in her toast, "Here's to friends."

~~~

They arrived home late, but happy. O'Keeffe headed straight to bed while Amanda padded into the kitchen, opening the file folder that held the few remnants of Mount Executor. She had
~~~

already safely tucked her mother's passport and driver's license in her sewing kit. Now, she paged through sketches and watercolours, studies for paintings that her mother had been planning. She pulled one out. It was a gestural drawing, made with speed and wildness. Splashes of blues, white and red depicting a lighthouse on a craggy shore. A golden halo served as a beacon, a saviour for any ship that might find itself lost in the rugged swells.

Amanda walked to the living room, held the unfinished piece up to the familiar blank wall, and smiled.

It would be the perfect spot.

Acknowledgements

This book never would have crossed the finish line without my core team, The Substantives. These stunning novelists and writing architects have given wise critiques and loving support. I'm grateful to Lara Sleath for inviting me into a writing group ten years ago and for indulging my obsession with plot points. Beth Boyd has the heart of a poet and the grammar of an English professor; thank you for the help with grammar, syntax, tense, and backstory. The lyrical Laurel Mae Hislop of Manna Mark Books offered invaluable insights throughout and was instrumental in my first foray into self-publishing. Substantives —I love you!

My beta readers offered fresh, unexpected insights, and a birds-eye view that I was too close to see. Becky Burchert, Margarita Hobbes, Mari Kane, and Melanie Lytle have my huge thanks for the time and care they gave to my final draft, which turned out to be nowhere near final!

For the friends who cheered me on along the way, even when there was no evidence that I was really writing a novel—thank you.

With gratitude for Mum, the inspiration and fuel for this story.

About the Author

Nancy Baye lives in Vancouver, BC, with Dixie, the wonder-dog. A recovered actor, she embraced the gig economy long before it was trendy and continues to freelance as a writer and editor.

She has written, performed, and toured short plays and monologues with her company Cancer Crusader. Nancy story-edited the animated tv movie *Hal and Holly Moose* (ABC Family Channel), co-wrote the tv sitcom *Permanent Residents* (Happy Fish Productions) and wrote the short film *Rose 1.0.* Fiction includes ghost-writing three YA novellas about a sassy cheerleader with an all-star heart. *Solo Sunderson* is her first mystery, and book one of the *Solo* series.

Manufactured by Amazon.ca
Bolton, ON

29669184R00178